CROWNE JEWEL
THE CROWNE BROTHERS

CD REISS

CROWNE JEWEL

CROWNE JEWEL

by CD Reiss

© 2023 Flip City Media Inc.

If you think anyone in this story resembles you or someone you know so much that you can take me to court for it, I'll buy you a drink, toast the hot coolness of you and your friends, then give you my lawyer's number.

Pirating this book, either as uploader or downloader, will trigger a malware virus designed to silently infect every device you own for six years, after which time your fucking around is going to have a big find out phase.
Try me.

I ALSO WROTE THESE

MORE CROWNES

<u>Iron Crowne</u> ~ Enemies to Lovers

<u>Crowne of Lies</u> ~ Marriage of Convenience

<u>Crowne Rules</u> ~ Forced Close Proximity

Fake Crowne ~ Fake Relationship

Crowne Jewel ~ Enemies to Lovers, Bodyguard

CONTEMPORARY ROMANCES

Romances for the sweet and sexy romantic.

Star-Crossed | Hardball | Bombshell | Bodyguard | Only Ever You | Lead Me Back

CHAPTER 1

LYRIC

Hey my Luxies, I'm doing a table-for-five thing at the exclusive, members-only Noho Room with my besties. Check out this salad! It looks like a pastry LOL. What are you doing tonight? I hope you love your life as much as I love mine! Crowne out!

#luxies   #luxelife   #lifestylesofInstagram   #lyriccrowne #Lyricsluxies

"I'LL GIVE you a thousand dollars to put that phone down." Anton taps the table with three fingers. He's wearing a silver bracelet. The top of his hand has a Ukrainian trident tattooed on it.

He didn't have that in New York.

"I'm working," I say, tapping out an Instagram post and then speeding it off into the cloud. Now I have no excuse to look at my screen, but I'm not taking orders from Anton, so I scroll around for funsies and pretend to ignore him.

"Is that what you call it?"

The muscles under Anton's Issey Miyake black turtleneck have filled out in the last three years. They're smacking Kelly silent. Once we're out of here, the pent-up verbiage is going to come spilling out of her like a pot of rice that's been on the burner too long.

Dinner's been torture. I'm supposed to be talking to Laing about boosting his content, but before my drink even arrived, my worst-ex-ever decided to accept an invitation shouted at a traffic light. It's been tense ever since.

"How about," I say, still not looking up, "I'll give you two thousand to tell us what you've been doing for a living."

"Put it away and I'll accept your two grand."

That's an offer I won't refuse, and it's not even the money. I put the phone, glass-down, onto the table and fold my hands over it. Jake's trying to get the check. Colleen looks as if she wants to crawl under a rock. Liang and Kelly watch, rapt, as Anton takes a pause, appearing to chew on the inside of his mouth before wiping his lips with his pristine napkin.

The scruffy half-beard is new. The brown hair's a little shorter and better cared-for. His voice is deeper and his skin's lost that dewy, still-officially-in-his-twenties texture. He still pauses before he answers a question. Still as cocky as a man whose momma never told him no. Still the best-looking guy in a restaurant full of good-looking guys.

"Tell us, Anton, about your exciting life. In detail."

"I've been working for the government." He places the napkin on the table. That's the answer. Six words that account for something like fourteen percent of the entire US population.

"So you've been... a garbage man?" I get a burst of laughter from Liang.

Anton and I are locked in a battle of stares. His eyes are a darker brown, but mine are prettier. He breaks first.

"I take Venmo," he says.

Every girl in this room wants him. I've already seen two get sneaky selfies with him focused in the frame. He's only paying attention to me because we had a thing years ago and I've spent the entire meal ignoring him.

"I'd have to pick up my phone to Venmo you a thousand dollars."

"It was two thousand." He holds up two fingers.

"You gave me half an answer."

"Oh, shit…" Liang laughs so hard his face is red and tears smudge his mascara, but he's not making a sound. This is how he gets when he's tired.

Tucking each hand into the opposite elbow, Anton leans on the table, talking low as if there's a secret he's willing to tell in the Noho Room.

He leans into me, tapping the table. "If you didn't have all your little accounts to tell you how to think and feel, who would you be?"

I mirror his posture. We're locked in a stare that could drill a hole in a cinderblock wall.

"First off, I don't have any little accounts. Second off, I'd think and feel like Lyric Crowne, thank you, so I'd be the same badass bitch you see right in front of you. Who would you be, Anton? If we weren't stuck at the same light this afternoon? If Liang hadn't recognized you in the car next to us? If he hadn't invited you here, would you even exist? Or would you be just another LA asshole with lots of money and no job?"

That tight mouth loosens then tightens the other way when the control of his smirk goes out the window. I'm not satisfied though—frown defenestration notwithstanding—because I have his attention. The fact that I even want it is breaking my brain.

"You're giving me the choice between invisibility and dinner?" he asks.

"Don't be invisible," Kelly says from the universe outside our stare. "That would be a crime."

"Invisible would be an improvement," Jake mutters, patting down the front of his pressed blue shirt.

Fuck this shit.

I take my gaze away and pick up my phone. Notifications. Comments on a week-old post from Cheetah Club, because Meta has no sense of time. Liang's back-of-the limo shot, posted the day after, comes across my feed. I helped him filter the color so his lipstick matched his jacket.

"You're getting love!" I show him my screen.

Liang's makeup tips for men deserve a better following, and I'll be damned if I'm not going to help him get it. He gave up on acting. I won't let him give this up.

"That was all you," he says.

"Not even." I heart some of the comments.

"Well, they finally boosted it. Oh, look at—"

Anton takes my phone.

"Hey!" I try to grab it back. He holds it out of reach. I tamp down a raging fury that's too big and hot for the Noho Room.

"What would happen if you didn't have this?"

"I'd be as boring as you," I say with my hand out. "Give. It."

He holds it out on his palm, and when I take it, his thumb twitches and runs along the length of my pinkie. Besides the explosive line of sparking nerve endings, I don't feel anything. Nothing at all. Not a shot of arousal to my core or a warm melting inside my thighs. I am a cold rock of resentment.

This is what I tell myself.

The check gets placed in front of Jake, who asked for it, and now stares at it as if it's going to fly up his nose and suffocate him.

Anton picks it up before I can get it.

Fine. He can have this one. He owes me.

CHAPTER 2

LYRIC

I'm sorry.
This is unbearable.
I am weak without you.
I am useless with you.

THAT WAS HIS NOTE. Four lines, like a broken, postmodern five-line poem he didn't finish because he couldn't find anything that rhymed with *unbearable.* I stood at the kitchen table of my SoHo apartment with the paper tilted toward the sunlight, trying to see the impression of what came next.

Was he choosing frailty or futility?

He wasn't useless. Not to me. He had to know that.

I would have told him as much. Reassured him. Explained that once I didn't feel cornered, I'd be able to think about everything with a clear head. But I got sent to voicemail over, and over, and over. That was his answer. He didn't want reassurance or explanation. He wanted out.

I never forgave him for choosing weakness.

After he left, I came back to Los Angeles with Liang—

who starred in the movie I'd made after college—swearing I'd start something new.

I never speak of those two years. It's as if it never happened, which is how I like it.

"Your brother's opening a new club?" Liang snaps me out of it, holding up his phone to a post from Club Amea.

We're at the valet. Anton stands a little aside from us, talking to Colleen.

"Yeah," I scoff. "Dante thinks he's hot shit."

"Yeah," Jake agrees with a shrug, tucking his fall of hair behind his ear.

I wish we hadn't run into Anton at that stoplight because frankly, it hurts to look at him.

"I'm sorry I invited him," Liang says. "I thought you'd be happy."

"I am. It's fine. He's the reason I leave men alone."

Well, he's part of the reason. The other reason is that the men have sucked, and I'm unfortunately not into women.

"I thought it was Neville," Jake says.

He asked me out a bunch of times the first month I knew him, but finally got the hint when I wrote the word NO on a piece of paper and told him to look at it the next time he imagined me saying yes. He apologized and hasn't brought it up in, like, four months—but some days, it seems as if he wants to give it one more shot. He's a good-looking guy. Doable—if you like hapless and socially awkward—but it's still a no.

"Neville was the experiment that proved the hypothesis."

"It's masked cowboy theme!" Kelly holds her phone up to show us. "Partnership with Ozzie Dots on costumes." She looks back down to read the text. "Invitations go out on the 15th. They're saying it's going to be really hard to get into."

"Manufactured desire. Dante is such a dork," I mutter, waving to Colleen as she gets into her Tesla.

Kelly's car is right behind. The valet asks Liang if he has the Honda, which means he's next. The herd is thinning.

Where's my freaking car?

Where's Anton's car?

Where are the aliens to tractor beam me up to space?

There's a weight on my shoulder. Anton's hand. My whole body turns into the camphor he used to rub into the back of my neck. Thick. Gelatinous. Hot and cold at the same time.

"What?" I snap.

"Are you all right?"

Am I? Why is he asking? Why does he even care? I move away from Jake, pulling Anton to the side.

"What the fuck is your deal?" I demand.

"Why do I have to have a deal?"

"You disappeared three and a half years ago. Now you show up two and a half thousand miles away and want a thousand dollars for half an answer."

He dips his head a little, coming close enough for me to get a breath of his cologne, which is nice. Really nice. Thick like bread that melts on your tongue with spice on the roof of the mouth.

Also, hard. Unyielding. Musky. It's like burned things.

In New York, he wore something sweeter.

"I answered your questions," he says. "You're just not hearing me."

I'm still not hearing him. I can't hear anything over the rush in my head. All the thoughts I've avoided push against the wall I've built to keep them away. I should just walk away from this conversation, but I can't move.

"You owe me an explanation."

"You have all the information you need." He says it slowly, as if he's tasting the words. "There's nothing more to say."

"You see, Anton." I put my hand on his chest and pinch a crease of wool between two fingers. Speaking as slowly and seductively as he did. "That's why you are, and have always been, a fucking bore."

"There's no one more boring than the bored."

"That explains why you hung around me for how long?"

"You were different then. You didn't do so much talking without saying a single thing."

I push away from him and stand back to look at my Insta. I never claimed to be deep. At least, not since New York, and I'm happier this way. I'm annoyed that he's insinuating it's a bad thing.

No, I'm annoyed that I'm thinking about this at all. It's like squeezing the bottom of a half-filled balloon. The rubber in the hand gets loose and thick while the taut bubble on top is membrane-thin. Everything was even and cool, but now there's an imbalance. The bottom is starved, and the top is ready to burst.

"You never paid me the thousand dollars you owe me." Anton's suddenly right there. I didn't even see him coming.

I jump and look up from the phone. His eyes seem blacker, and his lips are definitely more relaxed.

"You never gave me your Venmo."

"It's in your contacts."

"No, it's not."

"Check."

With a sigh, I check, and there it fucking is. A for Anton, right at the top. With a few swipes of my thumb, I send him a thousand dollars. "Happy?"

He nods and stands shoulder to shoulder with me. Jake shifts over to stand by us.

"I'll send it back if you look up from that phone for five minutes."

"Keep it."

"Are you afraid of me?"

He still knows where my buttons are, and he's still pushing them. Asshole.

"Whatever. Listen. How about you go tell your 4Chan buddies what a stuck-up bitch I am, Mr. I-Work-For-The-Government, and leave me alone."

He takes a deep, calming breath. I'm glad I'm getting to him. That's what I was trying to do, but the win is naggingly unsatisfying.

"Just be more careful," he says. "That's all."

"Are you all right?" Jake asks me, looking more boyish than ever. Jesus, I must look like some damsel in distress.

"Yes," I say through a clenched jaw.

"Come. Let's talk." Anton pulls me farther away from Jake, who seems to be wondering if he should intervene.

I don't need these two guys whipping out their piss-makers over me. I have to take control of this. I wave Jake off with my phone-hand, and once we're a distance away, I jab Anton in the chest with the other.

"I'm not a puppy."

"I know that, Lyric."

"I don't come when you say." My cheeks fizzle like a drop of water on a hot pan, because I used to.

"Not anymore." A twitch of his mouth tells me he's thinking about shit I've spent years not thinking about.

"Fuck you."

"Listen, in all seriousness."

"From the bottom of my heart. Fuck you."

"I've only been here three weeks." He's going to keep talking no matter how many times I say fuck you. "We'll probably see each other again."

"Los Angeles is huge. There are at least a million stoplights. Do the math."

"Were you always this exhausting?"

I scoff, shaking my head and turning down to my phone for some little shot of dopamine, but I face him before the app has a chance to open. I'm getting more annoyed with him by the minute.

"Thanks for the advice, you walking, fucking turtleneck. And thanks for sitting at dinner like you owned the joint without once saying, 'hey sorry about fucking off,' or like, 'I wrote you a note but forgot the explanation part.' I really felt like I was going nuts, so good job on really committing to the gaslighting."

"I wanted to talk to you before I left."

"And?" I can't let him finish telling me what he wanted, because I don't care. "You didn't."

"There were reasons."

"Cowardice?"

He lets out a short laugh.

"You gave up everything you said was important to you and ran back home like a child."

Talking to him is like throwing a rock against a brick wall. The rock bounces, which is against its nature, and the wall is still a wall.

Yet, the rock persists.

"Apparently, I was the worst. Glad you bailed on me?"

"Is everything okay over here?" Jake asks again. This time, his fists are balled up and ready as he looks at

Anton's face as if he's trying to figure out if his arms will reach it.

"Yeah," I say, a little deflated. "It's fine. Stand the fuck down."

The valet pulls up in a white Range Rover. Butterbomb, my pastel yellow Mini Cooper, stops right behind.

"This is me," Anton says, giving Jake a short wave before turning back to me. "It was good to see you again."

"Sure."

He walks to his car. Even from behind, he has the swagger of a man who bought the world on the cheap, fixed it, and has the upsides humming along nicely, which is intimidating enough to be sexy. If he hadn't already abandoned me years ago, I'd enjoy peeling off his turtleneck.

Jake rushes to the Mini Cooper and opens the driver-side door as if he's wearing a shining suit of armor instead of pressed jeans.

"Your car's coming. You don't have to open my door."

"I like to."

"Okay. Bye." I catch Anton before he disappears into the Range Rover. "Where have you been?" I call to him.

"Maybe I'll tell you next time." He gets in his car while my body floods with anticipation and my mind says, *fat chance, fucker.*

When I put the car into drive, my hand is shaking.

Fat chance.

CHAPTER 3

LYRIC

WHEN I WAS in the fifth grade, I started socking away half of my allowance. When I graduated high school, I didn't take it to my father's finance guy like four previous Crowne kids. That guy eats turkey sandwiches on Wonder bread and smells like a humidor. No. I went to the lackey junior analyst, Reggie. The guy in the striped tie with his hair parted on the side who—every time I saw him—was grating his teeth as though his jawbone was at war with whatever the top part of your skull is called.

I said, "You're gonna wear your molars down."

He said, "You try spending eighty hours a week buying at a five percent dip and selling at the five-year mean. Your dentist's gonna love you too."

"Anyone can buy on the cheap," I said. "Maybe you don't know when to sell."

His reply was a soup of shit I didn't understand—percentage positions and target ranges and short hedges. What he said wasn't as important as what I heard—confirmation of my assessment. Reggie wouldn't ever be a slick player, but he was a predator, and he was always hungry.

"Keep your fangs sharp." I gave his grindy ass a check with very clear instructions. "You make the calls. Double it in four years and you double your percentage."

If he did what I asked, he could buy a house in the Valley. I was going to use that money to make a feature film right out of NYU. Back then, I didn't know what the movie would be, but it was going to be raw, edgy, shocking. A monumental debut from a visionary young director.

I wrote *Standard Deviation* during my fourth year, finishing the ninth draft the night before commencement.

Anton was on campus for his half-brother Mike's graduation. Apparently, a degree in cyber security is a real thing. He told me they were eventually going to start a business together. He told me he was originally from Los Angeles and came to New York to work on a startup.

Anton didn't tell me he was personally funding the startup or that his father was a literal Russian oligarch. I found that out myself. But by then, he'd charmed me. Or broken me. Trying to figure out which is too painful.

I made my movie, and Anton and I were inseparable until the day he left me that note.

I like to think that poem on a scrap of paper he left on the kitchen table was a complete shock, but the first thing I thought was, *you should have seen this coming.*

My five brothers never ask me for anything if they can avoid it. I'm the baby in the family, and a girl, and not a controlling ass like most of them, so what could I possibly help with?

Colton's the only one who's not a domineering capitalist, so he had no problem asking me to boost his girlfriend Skye's performance on my Insta. Cool backstage video intercut with the stage act. Twenty-nine seconds. Post at seven forty-five a.m. for max engagement.

The video is what I should be thinking about as I drive up the 15, into the Mojave Desert, where the Shooting Star Music Showcase is happening.

But it's not. I'm looking forward to helping Skye, but seeing Anton over dinner three days ago was like getting knocked into while walking a narrow ledge on the side of a really tall building. I thought there was more room, and now I'm teetering between being normal-whatever and falling into I-can't-think-about-this-right-now. So I've gone out more, talked more, posted more, hung out with friends more.

And now, here I am, alone with my thoughts because Liang needed to be early to do Skye's makeup—which is on me because I set that up—running the *My Life with Anton* slideshow.

I sing with the radio so loud I can't hear my own neurons firing.

It doesn't drown out the visuals.

Winter. Location scouting on an empty New Jersey beach. Anton's top two shirt buttons are undone. The collar flips over in the wind, laying itself against his jaw as he estimates the distance between the abandoned lifeguard stand and the boardwalk.

My forehead on my desk. He puts my hair in a ponytail. Smell of camphor as he rubs my neck.

Midnight on my birthday. In bed. Eyes closed. Anton slides my phone into my hands. Says, "open it." There's a new square on the home page. Gold with a black L in the center. I tap it as if I'm opening a box in bright paper. He'd created a production scheduling app, just for me, with just the things I needed. It must have taken a hundred hours to make and was utterly perfect.

Two in the morning. Running lines with Liang. Anton gets home from work and brings us warmed bagels and cream cheese.

Anton telling me not to feel bad about promising Liang a career and not delivering. It's life.

Anton fucking me until I cry.

Carrying me to bed when I'm too tired to fuck.

And then.

Poof.

No. Not poof.

There were things—events and choices—but in the end?

Poof.

Fuck poof.

If there's one skill I've mastered in my twenty-seven years on this planet, it's mental hygiene. I think about things that need some thought. I don't waste time getting emotional about things I can't control, and I especially don't bring myself down when there's enough shit outside myself to get down about.

So I don't think about *Standard Deviation* or moon around about its failure. It's done. Lesson learned. Nothing to talk about.

If I start thinking about Anton, and it makes me pissed, or misty, and there's no point to feeling either of those things, I stop thinking about him. It's all good.

I don't make movies anymore and I've dated once since him. It was an utter man-fail. I don't put myself in a position to fall in love and I'm not going to court disaster again. That's all, folks. Problem solved.

Sometimes, I think of new movies.

Sometimes, I even start to write them.

Most of the time, I second-guess myself twenty pages in.

Is it commercial enough? Too derivative? Too experimental?

The rest of the time, I don't even start, because... what am I trying to prove already?

Traffic on the 15 is light enough to zone out, and from the slideshow of past events, I create a scenario where I'm shooting in this desert, with a filter that intensifies the late afternoon glow and accentuates the blue cast of the long shadows. But there's no story to put here. Just a tone. I have no more stories.

There's not much alternate to this alternate reality.

This is not mental hygiene. This is stewing in shit, and I don't need to feel like this.

I focus on my plans for Skye's backstage video, because I may not be good at shooting and cutting an entire feature film, but once I got back from New York, I realized I was good at something—getting people to like my stuff. The dopamine rushes broke my wall of self-reproach. I needed it, then I made a career out of it, and now I can help Colton and his girlfriend.

The showcase starts an hour after sundown. Once the sun sets, the red lights will come on. They're set up where people walk so no one with a lawyer on speed dial falls on their face, but they all point down so that when you look up, there's nothing but stars.

I came last year with friends. There's always someone around. Colleen with her workout routines and stories of dating. Liang with his lipstick and incisive emotional intelligence. Jake with a sadness that makes a lie of his superpowered gaming persona.

Without them, the mental dust bunnies roll out from under the furniture.

Just one more festival.

Aren't we getting married anyway?

What if I recut it?

Cars are parked in a long, curving asphalt oval. Food trucks line up on one side of the lot, blue port-a-potties on the other. I pass all that to the lot behind the security line, with the trailers and equipment racks. I park next to Liang's dust-covered Honda, check my face, and get out.

How can you do this, Anton?

How can you think I'm doing something wrong?

When I take a selfie against the desert backdrop, I realize there's no signal. I switch to Starlink, which is never great, but the Musknet's better than nothing.

I am a social media influencer. I was never successful at anything else.

It's not a calling card! I didn't just make a two-hour sample!

My agent let me go. Anton held me so hard that night.

Instagram's pretty slow. My notifications barely load. DeliaDeal put up a funny story about yesterday's post. *Tap-tap.* I check out her profile. Her life's supposedly a mess, but her grid's clean AF. *Flick.* Yesterday's post was also funny. *Tap-tap.* She tries to put on fake lashes. Hilarity ensues, and I bump into some person IRL. Apologize. They grunt. *Pull down.* Notifications load.

Poof.

Events. Choices. It came down to poof.

I wander around the equipment trailers, hearting mentions, glancing up for Colton or Skye.

The Hornet Records trailer is right at the end. From afar, I see Colton come around the corner with a guy in a tech hoodie, turn to someone on the other side of the trailer, answer a question I can't hear, and walk in my direction.

My loser fuckup of a brother is acting as if he's neither a loser nor a fuckup. I'm still not used to it.

Hawaiian sunset from Moira. *Tap-tap. Flick.* Hermione's puppy. *Cute. Tap-tap. Flick.* An ad for leggings. *Flick.* A Chris Evans reel. No time to watch now. Poof. *Tap-tap.* Poof. *Flick.* Poof.

"Lyric!" Colton tears me away from a meme about the weather in Florida to wave me over. Tech guy strolls into the shadows. "Thanks for coming." He kisses my cheek and keeps his hand on my shoulder as if I'm going to run away. "You know what you have to do?"

"Skye and I made a plan. Two videos. One slick thing of her singing." I pull back my thumb, then my forefinger. "Another authenticity piece about the anxiety. You're going to love it. Hundred K views minimum or we'll keep doing it until virality strikes."

"I really appreciate it. She's in the trailer if…"

He says more words all strung together, but what's the actual difference? From behind that trailer walk two men wearing yellow lanyards with tags on the end. One's in a T-shirt and tattoo sleeves. I don't know him. It's the one wearing the black turtleneck and sports jacket in the middle of the desert that turns my brain into a beehive.

"Lyric." Colton snaps his fingers in front of my eyes. "Did you—?"

"What the fuck is he doing here?"

He turns toward the men. Tattoo sleeves has peeled off. There's only Anton now.

"On loan from Dad, why?"

I give zero energy to what goes on with the family business. My oldest brothers can fight over running it, but I'm no Shiv Roy. That job sounds like a huge drag.

Now I'm thinking, going forward, maybe I should pay better attention.

"Anton," Colton calls him over. "This is my sist—"

"We know each other," I cut him off.

"Cool, cool." Colton says from somewhere on the moon.

Knowing Anton doesn't mean I'm cool with him once, much less twice, but I can't stop looking at him. He's eye-magnet north to my stare's magnetic south.

"I have your pass." Anton pulls a blue lanyard from his jacket pocket.

The tag has my name and says PRESS in big black letters. I take it, making a huge effort to not touch him.

"He does digital security consulting for Dad." Colton flips off the info as if it's nothing, but I'm pretty sure it's everything. "You good?" he asks Anton.

"Squared away."

"Thanks for the help. I gotta jet, yeah?" Colton backs up toward the clamshell stage and addresses Anton. "You can stay for the show if you want."

"I might," my worst-ever-ex says.

Colton disappears from my attention, leaving Anton and me alone in the desert. I'd rather die of sunburn than be here, but I can't leave when there's an unanswered question jabbing my brain.

"I thought you were a garbage man," I say.

"Maybe I was." He shrugs. "Maybe I still am."

"Why is a garbage man wearing a blazer to a concert?"

And why is he not sweating at all? He's probably been here for hours, and he looks as fresh as a guy who dressed for the weather.

"You think garbage men don't wear jackets?"

"Not Jonathan Behr bespoke jackets, no. But maybe you blew all Daddy's money and got a rich wife."

"There's no wife. And you know I was never a garbage man. Not, of course, that there would be anything wrong with that."

Defending my entitlements would take both energy and time. For Anton Markov, I have one but not the other. Or the other, and not the one.

Neither.

Both.

"How did you get a job with my father?"

"It's consulting, and I have experience he needs."

"This is why you wanted us to be okay."

"Yes."

"Did you tell Dad we knew each other in New York, or did you skip that part?"

Lips tight, eyes narrowed a little, he shakes his head. And that's when I realize that though the same number of years have passed for both of us, he's somehow much older.

"It seems you're the one who skipped that part," he says.

"So you didn't disclose it?"

"I disclosed what I had to. I knew you. We were close friends. But since you didn't seem to think the real nature of our relationship was worth mentioning, I kept your confidence."

"A lot of fancy words for avoiding full disclosure."

Why am I acting mad? I don't want full disclosure. If I

wanted to go into detail with my family about my string of humiliations after graduation, I would have.

"I can tell him," Anton says. "Or you can."

"I'll let you know." I start away, but it's not that easy.

"Did I mean so little to you?" he asks.

The answer is caught between the wall of anger and the sea of regret.

It's yes.

It's no.

Poof.

"You guys okay?" Skye, wide-eyed, in a robe with her hair in a bag. She holds a Pez dispenser in her fist so tightly she looks as if she's choking Garfield.

"Yes," Anton says, looking at me hard—as if he expects me to go along with him just because she's here.

"Fantastic!" I say.

Agreeing to his expectation is sensible... this time. If Skye's clutching her Pez dispenser, that means she's anxious already. There's no reason to upset her right before her show.

"Nice to see you again." I give him a short nod and loop my arm in Skye's to walk her to the trailer. I hold my head high and don't look back at him even though I really, really want to.

"You know him?" she asks in a whisper, and I'm too stunned to answer.

"Who told you?"

"It's kind of obvious."

"We're old friends." We turn the corner to the trailer. I decide to stick to what Anton told Dad. "We hung out in New York, back in the day. Whatever." This is not a conversation I want to be having. "Hey, I'm thinking, on the authenticity reel, can we get one of your friends in? They can talk about how to not make an anxious person more anxious?"

"Sure, I'll ask Halley. And... so..." She leans in to whisper to me. "Was he that hot when you met him?"

"Skye! I'm going to tell Colton."

She laughs. "Colton's too much of a man to get jealous."

"I'm going to be ill."

A security guy with the left sleeve of his jacket tucked inside opens the trailer door. He's missing that arm.

"Thanks Mike," Skye says.

"Hold up!" I stop short and look at him. I only met Anton's half-brother a few times, so it takes a minute. "Mikhail?"

"I go by Mike. It's easier." He smiles. "Good to see you again."

"I... how have..." I can't help but look at the place his arm used to be, and I hate myself for it. I'm certainly not going to ask about it. "... you been?"

"At war. Otherwise, fine."

"Ah." I realize he's explaining the loss of his limb, and now isn't a good time for a bunch of questions. "Well, I'm glad you're here."

"Me too." He tilts his head toward the inside of the trailer.

I thank him and go in.

CHAPTER 4

LYRIC

THE TRAILER IS MUCH SMALLER than the ones movie stars get on-set. It's more of a camper.

Liang is already there, laying out his little pots of creams and colorful makeup. Next to him, a woman with bright pink braids plugs in a blow dryer. Another sits in the breakfast nook, flipping through a fitness magazine as if she wants to tear it apart.

"Liang." It's too crowded to kiss, so we wave. "You look amazing. The lashes."

"The shoes." He bats his fakes then flicks his hand at my chunky, strappy yellow platforms.

"Hey, Lyric," Pink Hair says. Becca. That's her name, and the magazine girl is Fátima.

I greet and kiss everyone I can reach, then lean on a counter because there's nowhere to sit. While Skye gets her makeup and hair done, I get a pre-show picture of us and post about how excited I am to be at Shooting Star with my brother's girl. Hashtag, excited. Hashtag, new music. Hashtag, go girl.

"You know the hot new security guy?" Skye asks Becca.

"Uh, hello, yes," she replies.

"Hey," Fátima says with a sharp look at her girlfriend. "I'm right here."

"And I love you, baby, but…"

"We knew him in New York," Liang says, rubbing toner over Skye's face. "Lyric and him—"

"We were in the same friend group." I separate Anton from the second half of that sentence the way a guillotine separates a neck from a head. "After NYU, I hung around. He was… there. So was Lena Dunham. Do you want to hear about the time she was so drunk she peed in the bathroom sink at The Electric?"

"Ew!" Becca exclaims.

"Yeah, and it was one of those fountain, basin, things in the middle of the room so… you're welcome."

I get the chorus of *ughs* and *grosses* I was hoping for, reducing the possibility of discussing Anton again.

Flick. Flick. Tap-tap. Load, you fucking shitbag. *Scroll-flick.*

Fátima slaps her magazine shut. "They should have let Bex do my hair. Then I'd be in the print."

"Show Lyric the online spread, honey," Becca says, then turns to me. "She looks amazing."

Fátima sighs. "I can't get signal, but it's a fail. I shouldn't have bothered."

"You can determine what failure means for yourself," Liang says, then whispers to Skye, "Look up," before adding, "Like, you can say acting didn't work out, but I love doing stage makeup—"

"You were an actor?" Skye asks, blinking her new false lashes.

Liang glances at me. He can say what he wants. It's his

life. But he's always respected how little explaining I like to do.

"It's a bitch of a business," he says.

"I bet you looked beautiful on film." Skye blinks hard. Only one eye is done. She looks like *A Clockwork Orange*. "These lashes aren't that distracting."

"He damn well did." I'm too vehement and my phone isn't loading.

There's a hard rap at the door. Through the frosted glass, I see a man in black, and for a split second, my heart leaps, thinking Anton didn't leave like he said he would.

That reaction isn't going to work. I remind myself that I hate him and open the door because I'm closest, ready with a comment that'll cut right to the bone.

But no. It's the stage manager with Skye's schedule. It's time for everyone to hurry up and wait. I can do that by myself, without the questions.

"I have to go check the view from the pit."

There's plenty of time to take a walk around the place and find the best angles to shoot from.

Skye's going on after Soap Scum, so I have to be backstage by then to do the anxiety video. Then I'll have to position myself in the press box, which is already filling up with music journos.

I should have brought my good camera, but I didn't want to make a big deal about this and get Skye anxious. It would all look really good with the big lens though. And if it's too dark, I'll be wishing for a tripod.

It's fine. My phone has the best lenses Apple ever made. I

get to be low maintenance. Pretend I know nothing about nothing.

Pacing, I run the thing over in my mind. We're going to show the Pez dispenser my brother gave her to focus on whenever she gets anxious. Then her buddy Halley joins in. Then I ask questions. Then, mentally, Anton gets in the shot and I have to shoo him away.

He keeps jumping into the movie screen in my head. It's like a reverse-poof.

With over an hour to kill, I get a Mexican Coke from the taco truck. Scroll the feeds. Find a folding chair. Scroll as the sun sets. Work, work, work. Ari and Belle are at a low rider show in Echo Park. Xav is out with friends I've never seen before. Or maybe I have. The questions disappear soon after the double-tap, and I'm looking at Jake and his mother, staging a home in Calabasas. Unbelievable how popular a real estate account can get.

"Miss," a woman says, flashlight shining red on my hands. "You'll have to dim that completely or put it away. It's too bright for outside." She flashes the light on my press badge. "You can use it backstage or in the press booth."

She's being nice, but she's also ready for a confrontation. I put the phone away. She can fight with someone else.

"Okay."

I pace around the outer edge of the event. It's gotten really crowded and there are already people milling around the stage, organizing cables and whatnot.

Even in the dark, through all these people, I recognize Anton by the steady gait, walking the perimeter clockwise to my counterclockwise. Then I catch his scent. The new one. Bread and fucking. But he knows it's me already, of course, and stops, hands in the pockets of his bomber jacket, waiting for me to close the gap.

Power play. I can avoid him or go right to him. Either way, I lose the upper hand.

So, fuck it. It is what it is. I go right up to him. "Don't you have a job to do?"

"Not at the moment."

The allowed lights tinge the edge of his face red, but it's not enough to see him clearly. I can't tell if he wants to talk or if I'm in his way.

"What kind of security do you do? I'm, like, genuinely curious."

Is he smiling? Does his head move just that slightly because he's looking at my body? Or is the heat from the rising music and cheering crowd?

"I thought you knew what I did."

"Right out of Columbia you spent your father's money on a business you abandoned. You got a really expensive education to wind up in sanitation."

"Garbage needs security too."

Is that supposed to be a joke? He says it as if he's telling one, and I smile.

It's not even funny.

"Mike and I do mostly digital. Some personal when we have the extra staff."

"Uh-huh. Like bodyguarding?"

"We did that back home. We're going to do it all eventually. Grow it into something huge. World-class." He shrugs. "For now, it is what it is."

"Anton and Mike's World Class Security Services Inc?"

"The Markov Group."

"That's actually much better."

"I'm glad you approve."

"And what are you doing for my father?"

"It's small." He shrugs. "Contract jobs when his staff's overloaded, which they are right now. Family when necessary. We're flexible."

"Like you were for 'the government?'"

"You're not going to let me live that down."

"I am not. Did you lie to impress me?"

"I told the truth. I didn't say *which* government."

Never mind the servers and shit—in the dark, outside, with crooning background music to the right, the desert to the left, and a canopy of stars above—I am at my most vulnerable. My anger and my attraction can't hide behind the mental chatter. They argue amongst themselves, and it's a fucking riot in my head.

Fuck him. Fight him. Fuck him. Fight him.

"I think"—I put my hand on his chest. The touch seems to surprise him, but it surprises me even more—"if you're going to be around like this, we should ignore each other better."

"Good. Then we never have to talk about anything that happened."

I pat his chest. "Glad we figured that out." I start to shift past him, but he's not done.

"I'll give you a thousand dollars to stop walking away."

Poof.

Fuck this guy. I'm not even going to get on his case about accusing me of walking away when he's the king of it. It's too easy.

"Do I look hard up for money?"

"I'm giving you an excuse to clear the air with me."

I should just give him a finger he won't see in the dark

and continue on my way, but of course I don't. "Why do I need one?"

"Because it's been years and the excuses change."

"Shit happened, Anton. It's not going to go away for a thousand dollars or an excuse."

"Shit happened, and you never mentioned it to your family?"

My hands punch my hips and stick, which is good because they want to punch him. "That a problem?"

He shakes his head, looks away, swings an arm, gives every gesture of surrender I could hope for. "You're right. Never mind."

Before he can walk, I go right up to him. I'm here for Skye. I didn't come here prepped for this. It's not fair. I won't let him get away with it.

"You can't dredge up the swamp then 'never mind' the mess. So you start. Clear the air. Go."

"I didn't want to hurt you."

"Noted. Thanks."

"You didn't want me," he says.

"That's not what I said."

"You gave me back the ring."

"Because I wasn't having your baby, Anton. Isn't that why you gave it to me? Not because you loved me but out of some old-world sense of duty?"

"You think that was all it was?"

"I'm not your obligation!"

"You get a woman pregnant, you ask for her hand. That's how it's done. I was raised the way I was raised. It's not an obligation."

"Anton, you literally just described an obligation."

I've cornered him, which was my exact intention. Hold

up a mirror. Force him to look at it. Show him what he sees. It took fewer words than I ever dreamed I'd have to use... and I did a lot of dreaming.

"Yes." He laughs to himself. "I guess I did."

I won. I don't have to see his face to know I've won. It's in his posture. He's caught. He didn't care about me, just the pregnancy I never had any intention of finishing.

I don't feel like a winner. I feel like absolute shit.

Winning the battle I've dreamed of winning for years doesn't change anything.

He still disappeared.

"I wanted you to know," he says finally, "that if you went through with it, I'd take responsibility. Maybe that's an obligation. I wanted to drive you to the clinic or the pharmacy or... I don't know how it was done."

He isn't entitled to an answer but keeping it from him isn't worth the energy expenditure.

"Miffy."

"What?"

"The pills." My anger's been sucked out of me. I'm a brittle shell without it. I breathe, then exhale in a big huff. "I didn't need a procedure. It was a prescription and too much time in the bathroom."

"Good, good." He laughs to himself again, but this time it's with relief. If thirty pounds of anger just got sucked out of me, a few tons of defensiveness fall off him. "I always wondered that."

"I was so stressed with everything going on... or not going on... my periods were all messed up..."

"I remember."

Him remembering the timing of my cycle is just too much. Too fucking much.

"I can't do this. I have to do Skye's thing. She's counting on me and now I'm all… fuck!"

He puts his hands on my shoulders and it's as if I'm back on Thompson Street, exhausted, sobbing, held together with spit and chewing gum, and he's the one thing keeping me sane.

"None of this matters," he says. "We're just filling in gaps for each other. Okay. I left because you didn't want me. I accepted that. It worked out. You let me go so I could take care of business. There were things I had to do back home. It's done. We're both better off."

Nothing he's saying sinks in. It's all *blah-blah-blah*. Words, words, words.

I'd puked on the Cannes rejection letter they couldn't just email. Amy joked that Cannes was boomer shit and I was probably just knocked up.

I'm on the pill, I said. And I don't miss.

Sundance is GenX shit. They used email to tell me *Standard Deviation* was a no.

Toronto. *Non*. Berlin. *Nein*. Venice. *No*. Nashville. *Naw*. Brussels. *Neen*.

A world map of rejection. He saw me. He saw how I was.

Then I peed on Amy's extra test from a two pack.

Then I had a ring I wasn't ready for, and he was gone.

And still—the rejections came. He didn't come back.

My insides are empty, and his armor seems to have disappeared. I put my hand on his chest, half-expecting to touch vulnerable skin and bone. But it's just hard muscle under a jacket.

He puts his hand over mine. I expect him to take it off him. He should. I may even want him to because I shouldn't be touching him at all.

I push him away.

"Whatever." I say it out loud so he can hear it, but I'm really talking to myself. I can shake this all off. I've done that for years already. Not a problem.

The squeal doesn't rise as much as explodes. The mic feedback from the soundcheck stops as suddenly as it started. It jolts my brain. A crowbar in the crack between my outer life and my inner.

"I need to get out of here for a minute," I say. "Nothing personal."

That's a lie. All of this is very personal to me, but not to him.

I look around for a place to go.

"Have you been to the VIP section?" he asks, flicking on a little red flashlight.

"There is no VIP section. Believe me, I'd know."

He makes a huffing sound that's part laugh, part scoff, but mostly scoff.

Without asking if I want to walk into the dark with him, he disappears into the night behind a red oval bobbing on the ground.

Am I supposed to follow him like a puppy? Or is he running away like a dog?

He uses my curiosity as a leash, and before I know it, I'm chasing him and his little red light into the deep wilderness.

CHAPTER 5

LYRIC

HE WALKS into the darkness slowly, checking behind for me.

I'm here. Of course. Curiosity might have killed the cat, but it hasn't hurt me yet.

Carefully, because though I can walk fine in my strappy platforms, I'm not about to break an ankle tonight, I follow Anton to a set of split-wood log steps in the side of an incline. Below us, the musicians finish the sound check.

"You're still here?" he says from above me, a silhouette outlined with stars.

"What did you expect?" I demand, catching up to him.

"I didn't think you'd actually follow me. You should, I just didn't think you would." The red light shines on every step as we climb side by side.

"You thought I'd be afraid? Intimidated? Have you met me?"

"Intimidated? No. Not you. Watch your step here. Annoyed, maybe."

"Yeah, well, you are annoying."

He could be insulted. He could argue. He could do an I-know-you-are-but-what-am-I and say I'm the annoying one. All he does is make a left along a narrow trail and stop at a far, dark point.

Here I am in a situation I'm usually pretty good at avoiding—alone with a man I knew once, but who could have changed into any kind of monster in the last few years, with no one near enough to hear me scream.

"Just through this brush," he says, pulling back a branch and flashing his red light into the leafy gap between two shrubs as tall as trees. "Be careful. There are thorns."

Anton goes first, pushing away prickly branches and dropping them when I'm through. This leaves him with his arm over me for a split second each time. I step forward and he reaches ahead to clear the way, but something tugs at my skirt. I gasp as if a spider crawled up my leg. He shines the red light down.

A thorn's caught my skirt. Before I can free myself, he leans down and carefully does it.

"You should have worn jeans," he says.

"If I'd known I was going to breach a thorn bush tonight, I would have worn steel pants."

"That would suit you."

He says it so matter-of-factly that I'm not sure if it's a compliment or what, and he's already on the other side, holding out his hand. I refuse it. This isn't a first-floor window. It's not even a curb. It's a couple of shrubby trees.

He steps into the center of a flat crest with a picnic table and a fire pit in the center. Music starts to rise from the clamshell below. I can see it by the red lights bathing the stage and the dotted ones along the pathways. To the left, the mountains border the spray of stars in the shape of an engagement rate line chart. We're alone in a dark so pure it shimmers with light.

"Wow."

We're washed in starlight. The strip of Milky Way breaks for the black mountains. The sky is the table at a kindergartener's birthday party—pressed with splashes of glitter, sequins, confetti.

"There's still too much light down there to really see." He points toward the gradient of light at the horizon. "Once the moon sets—"

"There!" I point at a string of light that's gone before the word is finished.

Another falling star appears and I don't bother pointing it out. We look up at burning rocks falling through the atmosphere until the moon sets, then—just as the sky goes dark enough to shine and the scattered meteors turn into a full-blown fireworks show—he decides to open his mouth.

"Do you like what you do?"

"What do you mean?"

"For a living."

"You mean the social media stuff?" I ask.

"You didn't have a plan B. It was directing movies or nothing. This is nothing, I guess?"

"You're insulting me?"

"No, no." His denial is too fast. It's complete bullshit, and it's followed by a shrug. "You used to talk about being heard. So, you're heard now."

"I'm going to do a post." I take out my phone to record this starshow. All it needs is a me-face looking awed and wowed. "You want to get in? Or are you being the International Man of Mystery tonight?"

He doesn't answer but doesn't get in the frame either. I

angle for the selfie, trying to get the lighting right. When the sky's lit, my face is dark and when I can get my face in, the sky's blown out.

"Here." I take his hand and put the red flashlight near my face. I'm lit like a horror movie, but at least I'm lit. "Red light tricks the exposure." I change the angle until it's right. "One, two…" I hold up my fingers, and on the third, I drop my voice to a whisper. "Three… Hey, you guys. I'm in the Mojave desert at the Shooting Star show. Up in the VIP section, we have a perfect view of the meteor shower. Check this out." I tilt the camera to the sky and leave only a sliver of red face. "Amazing. Crowne out."

I cut the recording and put down the phone. He drops the light.

"Thanks." I save it, then look up. No one told the meteors the video was over. They just keep falling. "It's hard to look at when it's not in a frame. The enormity of it."

"Yet you told everyone this was the VIP section," Anton says, sitting at the picnic table, facing out.

"That was your idea."

"I was joking."

"You? Joke? Nice try. Better luck next time."

"It was a joke when I said it. When you say it like that, it's a lie." He looks at the meteors streaking down like a curtain of light as if he's not accusing me of much… just stating facts.

"Is it a lie if it doesn't really matter? The friction in the air —the literal *air*—is burning ancient space rocks to ash, and that ancient, burned-up space rock ash is falling on us right now. Does it matter if VIP means very important person if everyone is a VIP to someone? They're just rocks. And that was the trajectory. All the little fires in the sky are chance encounters."

He nods in understanding, then turns his gaze in my direction. The night is cold, but his attention is as hot as a meteor burning through the sky.

"Why are you up here with me?" he asks. "When you hate me?"

We have ancient space-rock history that I forgot for a minute. But here it is.

"Don't mix up me being here with forgiveness."

"Don't confuse looking at the stars with having a thought in your head."

Back in New York, Anton and I said a lot of things to each other. We argued like a normal couple, but he never, ever, even slightly implied I was stupid or hollow.

"Where have you been, Anton? It's been what? Three years and change? What blocks have you been around?"

"Every block in the city, twice a week."

He reverts to a garbage man joke. Of course. It's not even funny.

"To think, you wanted two grand for that answer. I can listen to you be a coward for free."

He doesn't shoot back a witty retort or make some dismissively breathy sound. I have to stare to discern his features, my pupils opening as far as they'll go. In the moonlight, his eyes seem darker and his jaw seems squarer. His hands fold together between his knees, thumb pads pressed together. My dumb quip was an accidental bullseye. This is the first unguarded moment I've seen him have since he's been back, and that makes him more of a man than any of the hard muscle under his turtleneck.

"You're right," he says, finally.

Being right is supposed to be satisfying and cool, but

when he admits guilt to the same deflection I'm guilty of, it's like getting pulled into the mud.

"I was scared," I say, apropos of nothing and everything. "I didn't want to be a mother yet and you came with that ring and I wasn't ready for that either. It was too much adulthood in the space of a week."

He nods. This may be enough explanation for him, or it may be that he suspected this already or it may be that carrying around all that muscle is giving him a backache. I can't spend my last sparks of energy caring only to find he morphed into a scrap of paper with four stupid excuses on it.

"Look, Anton." My feet are apart and my voice crackles with resolve. "Let's never, ever talk about this stuff again. It's just not smart. Let's leave the sludge at the bottom of the swamp. Let the water at the top stay clean. Let the fish do their fishy shit and we just… be cordial. We don't have to like each other. I'm happy. You're happy. But we're not friends. Okay?"

In the starlit darkness, he nods. My phone buzzes in the familiar rhythm of a reminder notification. From the stage, the music changes. It seems as if it's changed a couple of times already.

"A ceasefire," he says. "Not a treaty."

"Yes. A truce."

"I accept."

"I do too." I'm distracted now, digging out my buzzing phone. "Shit! I'm going to be late."

CHAPTER 6

ANTON

SHE IS LUMINOUS. She is powerful. She is a lava stone sharpened to a microscopic edge. Every rich brat has social media presence. Every one of them has more empty shells following them and tracking their every decision than is healthy for them, or the shells, or society. But Lyric doesn't have an M at the end of her follower account because she's just like the rest of them. She's nothing like them. She pierces the camera. She *connects*.

Blindingly radiant. Safe. Unbroken. In the exact place she belongs with the exact people she belongs with. The best, most beautiful square in a monochrome quilt.

I was the one who was confused. The persona isn't the person. She may still be radiant, but she's no longer whole. I mishandled her, and those cracks are shaped like my betrayal.

The cease-fire is justified and necessary. It will protect her from me.

Lyric's phone illuminates her face. I can see her distress in all its glory.

"Shit!" When she puts away the light the clarity of the vision diminishes, but I hear it in her voice. "I'm going to be late."

Something like "let's go," or "come on," comes out of my mouth, but she's already running in the general direction of shrub we came through—at the wrong angle. There won't be an opening where she's going.

I catch up to her as she's trying to get through brambles that will have to be cleared away with a chainsaw.

"Over here." I push aside a bough and shine my red light at the empty space.

"Thank you."

"This one." I reach forward to pull a branch away.

She pushes ahead and won't let me help. I'm too slow. All I can do is give her the light and let her figure it out.

"Jesus," she says as a bough almost slaps her in the face. "I promised I'd be on time." She finds the right path through. Her platform sandals make the downhill impossible to balance. She's more likely to fall ass over teakettle than make it back in one piece. "And this is the only thing…" I follow her through to the open space that slopes down to the steps. "…that I've really wanted to do since forever. The only not bullshitty thing and now… whoa!" She slides on the gravel.

I overreact, choking back a scream, and grab her. "Be careful. This slope is treacherous on the way down."

I sound too serious. She's not going to die out here right in front of me, and I'm reminded that I work for her father. If I had to, how would I explain to him that I was out here with her?

She shakes me off. "Thanks. I got it."

The second time she slides, she rights herself without help, but she's going too fast. It's too dark. I have the light and she seems to be gauging her speed on how much she can out-hurry me. I catch her at the top of the steps, blocking her way before she falls down them.

"Stop," I demand. "For one second."

"Anton."

"Take off those shoes."

"There could be glass, and also… move."

"It's not worth it if you break your ankle."

"Yes, it is." She tries to go around me. I don't let her. "It takes too long to get these on and off."

"Then just slow down."

"No one ever asks me to do anything for them and the one time someone does, I'm late? I'd rather break my face."

She's not going to break her face on my watch, but she tries, stepping sideways and launching forward. I catch her before she lands in a shrub, wrapping my arm around her waist.

"You are a huge pain in my ass."

"Let me go," she growls, turning to bite my head off.

"No." I duck and pull her into me, standing so her waist is over my shoulder.

"Put me down, Anton," she says without struggle or shriek. Her deadly shoes are in front of my face, but she doesn't kick.

"I will." I aim the red flashlight down the steps, noticing how they curve and dip. There's no way anyone could run down them in hiking boots, much less platforms.

"Anton!"

Turning sideways so that she's behind me, I take the steps as fast as I can. "A few more."

"God, I hate you. This is not how a truce works! Put. Me. Down!"

At the bottom, I take one more step to where it's flat and get her to her feet. There are no obstacles between here and the lit pathways.

"Go!"

"Fuck you."

She tells me to fuck myself with the tone of a thank you and dashes to the concert. The shoes make her run with short, fast steps. When she gets to the lit area, I take my eyes off her.

Avoiding her on social media was easy until it wasn't. I deleted social media to get into Crimea. By the time I loaded Instagram again, she was perched at the top of my feed, reminding me of what I'd loved and lost.

She looked fine. Happy. Unencumbered by what I'd done and how I'd done it. I used that as an excuse to forgive myself, because I'm a coward, like she said, and I watched her over and over for the same reason.

Taking out my phone with one hand, I touch my ear with the other, looking for the bud her voice used to come through, but that comfort is long gone. I don't need it anymore. There's no shelling in America, and I've heard her voice in real space.

I check the path she ran to and catch sight of her at the end of it, showing her press badge to security. She disappears behind the curtain to the backstage.

The trailer is a few minutes' walk. I'll check on Mikhail. If I told my brother about my conversations with Lyric, he wouldn't be surprised they went nowhere. When he caught me drowning out the gunfire with her videos, I told him it was nothing as if he'd believe me. The videos and posts are meaningless trash. It takes a decently intelligent human one viewing to see right to the bottom of them, though I watched far more times than that.

All that time, all I wanted was for her to see me back. Mike said she'd never live up to how big I'd built her in my heart. He was right. She's an empty version of what she was. He said I was obsessed. He was right about that too. I knew it, but I needed her videos to get me through the war.

Lyric was very real to me in New York. After I left, she was just a voice and a glowing face I could consume when we had signal. She became flat. Meaningless. A useful habit. An addiction. The drug exists. It doesn't care who swallows or snorts it. Doesn't need to be loved. It just needs to be needed. She wasn't comforting me. She was just comforting.

Coming back to Los Angeles broke my addiction. We lived in the same city for so many years but met across the country, so I didn't think I'd run into her so soon in California.

I don't need her anymore, and she never needed me. We've made peace.

Everything is as it should be. I don't need her to see me anymore.

So why does everything seem untethered?

A dark form stands beside the Crowne trailer with an orange dot next to it, swinging up and down. My half-brother's smoking. He's a secret child of my father and one of his many mistresses. Didn't get a dime when the old man died. I didn't think I could hate my father more until I found that out.

"Hey," he says on the exhale.

"*Pryvit*."

He came back to the US a few months before I did, but instead of moving home to Pennsylvania with his mother, he came to California to be near my mine. She treats him as if she gave birth to him, which she didn't. "You're in America, fucker. Say, 'hey, whassup' like you never worried about anything."

"Fuck hey." Except I say it in Ukrainian, just to be an asshole. We've both spent most of our lives in the US, but his Ukrainian is better. "You're security. You have one hand for defense and you're using it to kill yourself."

I shouldn't be self-righteous. I smoked in Ukraine because we were all going to die anyway. When I landed in America, I stopped, but Mike couldn't.

"Digital defense." He drops the last of the cigarette on the ground and stamps it out. "I need one finger for that."

He was sent home when he lost the arm. I followed when we got the Crowne account, which had nothing to do with Lyric. We were pitching something completely different. Logan gave what we found to the internal corporate teams and Ted Crowne, his semi-retired father, offered us a contract to do digital security at the margins of what their teams could be stretched to do. The personal stuff. The family. Threat prevention. I've managed to consult for Lyric's family for almost a month without seeing her.

"Where were you?" Mike asks. "You smell like you rubbed a woman all over you. Did you forget to shower this morning?"

Mike gets laid so often his entire apartment smells like sex, and he's bitching about me smelling like her perfume.

"Lyric," I say.

"And?"

"And nothing. No surprises."

"Is she going to make this job difficult?" he asks.

"No."

"How do you know?"

"We agreed to a truce."

"And she'll honor it?"

"Yes!" I'm getting annoyed with him. Mike needs to hear me say the woman I left behind is a disappointment. That she was a three-dimensional human in my imagination while, in reality, she spent three years flattening herself into a two-dimensional cartoon. But I can't because it doesn't matter. "We're staying away from each other. The end."

"Is she better or worse outside a little square? Now that you're not watching her talk in three-minute increments, over and over—"

"Okay, okay. Enough. Stop making nothing into something."

"She got fucking cute though. Those shoes." He whips his hand back and forth as if he touched something hot. "I'd like them bouncing over my shoulders."

"Keep your head in your commitments." I sound tightly wound because I am.

"I am." He slaps my arm. Sometimes, when he does that, I wonder if he's trying to remind me that it's my fault he didn't come back from Ukraine whole. "At the very least, I'm committed to smoking and making The Markov Group a real company."

"That it?"

"No. Just, please. Don't fuck this."

He's worried, and that deserves my respect. I can't fail him.

"I won't."

"Why don't you go check on the principals? Me and Roscoe will keep eyes on the trailer."

"Sure. Fine."

I'm about to walk away, but Mike shouts out a suggestion.

"Maybe fuck her once. Get her out of your system."

"No." I walk backward and put my fist to my chest. "Nothing." I open the fist as if I'm showing him that my heart is empty.

She irritates the fuck out of me. I must be addicted to being annoyed.

Flicking on my red flashlight, I head to the backstage area. The music coming out of the bandshell is thick and heavy. Soap Scum suits the band as a name.

Did Lyric get there in time to do her video?

I shouldn't look for her. I should stay with the clients. Put away my empty bag of fucks and do my job.

It takes a second for my eyes to adjust to the light backstage, which is probably normal, but the sudden wattage blows into wide-open pupils like a bomb going off.

The first person I see is Lyric, of course. I may have convinced myself that I don't need her videos anymore, but her living presence still has a pull on me.

"Someone got through," Colton says, jutting his arm back and pointing at his sister.

She's looking at her phone. Tapping. Swiping. Shaking. Doing all the things a person does to a phone when it's not functioning.

"What happened?" I need him to start from the beginning —what he observed before he came to his conclusions.

"Someone got to my sister's phone and locked all her accounts."

"Let me take a look." I approach Lyric with my hand out.

She looks up at me like a lost lamb and hands me the phone as if I'm the one shepherd who can get her home. That level of trust takes my breath away.

"It logged me out," she says. "And now I can't post."

"The satellite may be down."

"It's not. Look." She puts in her code. I navigate to the settings app, and everything seems to be right. "The website loads." I'm agitated. I want to kiss away her panic and I can't. "Anton, if you can't help, just—"

"I have it." I'm being snippy, because yes, she can pick up a web page easily on Starlink and there's no signal otherwise and I should call Mike and get him over here, because she's distracting me with the image of those shoes over my shoulder. "Just calm down."

"I am calm. I'm really fucking calm."

There's not a relaxed cell in her body. Is she lying to herself or me? Does she expect either one of us to believe it? Her brother and Skye are at the stage entrance with their backs to us, and I realize Lyric needs everyone else to believe it.

"Try a different kind of calm," I say. "Is *anything* working?"

"I can do everything else. I have email. I have texts and I can call you right now if I want to, which I don't. But the social accounts are flat-out fucked. Halley signed into my account from her phone, and I can get in, but it's still locked."

I hold up Lyric's phone. "Can I take this?"

"It's the accounts, not the phone," she says from low in her throat as if I'm acting stupid on purpose.

"You were supposed to be protecting all the devices," Colton says. "So I don't know what happened here, but something did."

"What happened here is that Lyric isn't under my purview. Had she been, she wouldn't have a seven-letter password without a 2FA app."

"What's the point of the phone authenticating the phone?" she sneers.

"The point"—and now I'm a little snippier because I can tolerate anyone doubting me but her, apparently—"is for when someone's accessing *your* account from *their* phone."

I wait for her to nod, and I see past the impatience and rage. She's breaking my fucking heart. I mean it. Lyric Crowne has never seemed so out of her depth.

"How do you know I'm hacked?"

"I don't. It's going to be all right." I say it with all the professionalism of a man who knows what he's doing and she looks at me as if I just told her my balls itch.

"How do you know?"

"This is what I do." I put the phone in my breast pocket. "Let me just take this—"

"Quit it!" Colton hisses. "Skye's going on and she needs peace, okay? Lyric, let him check it out. Dad would say to."

"Dad's not paying my cellular or my Elon-fi bill. So, no." She shoots me this look of disdain I never thought she'd direct at me again. "No." She reaches into my jacket and snaps out her phone.

She doesn't move that fast. I let her invade that space. I allowed it as a primal reaction to her being a woman invited to touch me. I button the jacket.

She pauses, phone in both hands, looking up at me with big brown eyes as if she realizes what she did and as if she also needs to downplay the shock of what just happened.

"First," she says firmly, "we need to rule out bad signal."

I can't even tell her she's right before she storms out.

This is the Lyric who wrote and directed a two-hour movie right out of college. Headstrong. Uncompromising. Intransigent.

The charming, affable Lyric who produced *Standard Deviation* also made the silly videos that Mike mocks me over.

They were a lifeline, and she needs to make more.

I peel off to find Mike. We can figure this out.

CHAPTER 7

LYRIC

REACHING into Anton's pocket is so intimate, in a way, that I stand there in shock that he doesn't grab the phone back. I stand there for a beat, waiting for his reaction.

"We need to rule out bad signal," I say, pretty sure that makes no sense whatsoever, but he doesn't disagree before I run out to shoot Skye's stage video.

It looks fine. This lens is ninety percent digital fakery, but it's fakery I understand, opening up the aperture until she glows in the red light.

Then she's done, and I'm trapped.

That's how I feel, staring at my phone, which used to be connected to my life but now somehow isn't. I can't comment, like, or upload anything. All I want to do is get out of the desert and check my accounts on regular cellular—even wifi once I can get it.

Back at the trailer, I congratulate Skye and shrug off my digital exile as a glitch. Anton's talking to Mike as if the bomb's ticking and they don't know whether to cut the red wire or the blue. I want to know if they're talking about me, but I also don't want his help.

All I need to do is get in range and that's one thing staying here isn't going to get me.

Outside, it's dark the way the wilderness gets, and since the show's still going on, there's no one on the roads in or out. It's just me in Butterbomb, the headlights revealing ten feet of shrubs on either side of the road.

I'm sure it's nothing.

Maybe it's something. If I can't get into my accounts with regular signal, I'm going to lose all my shit. This is my life. The analytics. The data. All the knowledge I've gained about how this world works is going to be worthless. Then what am I supposed to do?

Do you like what you do? For a living?

And losing all that in front of Anton? The guy who'd known me when I was a different girl with different dreams? Who doesn't respect what I've done since he blew me off?

For a minute, I wonder if he did it.

He could have. He wasn't spiteful when I knew him, but what's happened since then? If I've changed this much, what's to say he hasn't?

It was directing movies or nothing.

This is nothing, I guess?

That walking turtleneck yanked my deepest regret out of my head, threw stonewashed jeans and a Gap T-shirt on it, and spoke it out loud. And yeah, I'm mad, because I was holding on to that idea. I don't know why. It was deep where I didn't have to explain it.

The idea was—it's time to quit this job.

No. I'm too good at it.

You wanted to direct movies.

I have too much to lose.

You did direct one.

And Anton knows it. He was there for every second of it —from getting Liang for the lead, to getting into that one little festival in Vermont. From up-all-night-working-on-act-three, to up-all-night-crying-over-the-reviews.

Reminiscent of Naked Lunch, *without the originality of the most banal adaptation or the nourishment of an actual sandwich.* ~ Screengrab

A one-woman circle jerk ~ Filmdude

Aptly titled, Standard Deviation *is at once quite standard and also cartoonishly deviant* ~ Insider

Crowne strives to be a female Boots Riley and fails spectacularly ~ Collider

"No one's going to see it," I tell myself. "It's gone. Poof."

Poof.

If Anton could disappear, so could *Standard Deviation.* Instead of buying myself a splashy public showing at a rented theatre, I read the room. I refused a low-rent, direct-to-stream deal just so no one in the world would see it ever again. I told my family it went fine but I lost interest. I'm just another flighty heiress who blew a wad of money on her vanity.

"Fuck this shit!"

Fuck this shit with a fist full of fuck. I hate time. Space is worse. How far away is the fucking freeway? Why didn't I ask Liang to wait for me? How did I end up on a dark, winding road in the desert? I got more crunch under my wheels than a granola factory and I can't even see a sign for the 15.

No, wait.

I should be on the 15 already.

I tap the center console screen. The map's just a gray-on-beige grid.

"Fuck."

I pull off the road, slamming on the brakes at a prickly pear plant that could rip the grill right off. Half a tank. How far will that get me when I don't even know how far out—or in—I am?

I get out and hold my phone up to the sky, hoping to catch the wind blowing the GPS the right way, or maybe one of those shooting stars is a satellite.

Nothing. Not a lick of signal. The Musknet's spotty as fuck.

Headlights appear on the horizon.

If I'm as lost as I think I am, I could hail this person down, risk getting raped and cut up into pieces, just to get help I may not need. With a minute to spare before I have company, I put the phone up again.

The Range Rover arrives as I'm thinking maybe I should get my ass back in the car and lock the doors. Anton gets out.

He won't rape me and cut me up into little pieces, so why do I feel screwed?

CHAPTER 8

ANTON

She's got a fourteen-minute head start. That's a lot.

I told Mike what happened. He went back to check the logs, but didn't expect to find anything, since Lyric's not on their network. He doesn't rib me for detouring past the backstage area where my ex would be, and he doesn't break my balls over the fact that I'm chasing her across the desert to the 15 freeway.

The road through the desert is in pretty good shape, but it's dark and there's no railing between the pavement and bare earth. Just two inches of raised asphalt.

It's a clear night, so the brake lights are visible from a mile away. Someone's stuck. I'll call for a tow once I can get a connection, but I'm not picking up whoever this is. I don't have the time. I have to catch up to Lyric, and it's not just my job. It's personal. She needs to know, even after everything that happened between us, that she's going to be all right, but she shouldn't do anything with that phone until we check it.

At a thousand feet, I recognize the stopped car as a Mini

Cooper, and the girl holding her phone to the sky is Lyric Crowne.

I pull over and get out. She puts down her phone.

"You followed me." My headlights make her eyes translucent.

"Did I?"

I did, but I'm not going to admit it.

"Why else would you be in the capitol of Nowhere?" She holds the phone to the sky as if she's photographing the North Star.

"What are you doing?"

"Trying to see if it's a satellite problem before I get into cellular range."

"That was the right choice." I step close enough to see her lower lip tremble.

"No." Her jaw tightens as if she doesn't want to say the rest. "Actually, I'm lost, okay? I don't know how to get GPS on the Musknet and I'm incompetent and now I'm lost."

"You're not lost. I know where we are."

"I don't know where *I* am. That's lost."

Pity isn't the word I'd use for the swell inside my chest. Not compassion or empathy. The swell is from her dropping the girlboss act for one second and reminding me of who she is.

"You're going the right way. You're just impatient."

She turns to the darkness of the road ahead, then the road behind. I resist the urge to touch her face and guide it back to me.

"Are you sure?"

"Yes."

After a long exhale, she faces me. "I'm sorry."

"For?"

"For… I don't know. Lying about why I'm on the side of the road? Being a bitch when you told me I wasn't lost? Or like, in general." She looks away from me at her phone, swipes uselessly, and drops her hand. "But not anything from before."

I remember something about the two of us standing on the side of the road by two separate cars on the way back from the Hamptons. The road had been empty and dark then too. We told each other a running story with no end.

"I'm going to have to write you up, Mrs. Longbottom."

Lyric bursts into a laugh I haven't heard in years. Not the way she does on hours and hours of video or the way she has in the few moments we've spoken since I got back. It's an old laugh from a younger woman. I didn't think she had it in her anymore.

"But, Officer Everhard," she says with a smile, "my husband would be so mad if I got another ticket. Is there anything I can do?'"

"Well, ma'am—"

"Brenda. Please call me Brenda."

"And you may call me Officer," I say sternly. She tries to look coy and almost gets it. "Brenda, if I helped you out for nothing in return, that wouldn't be fair."

"I'll pay anything you want." She fights the smirk and nearly wins but makes no signal about how far she's willing to go tonight. I don't even know how far I'm willing to go.

This is the point in the role play where I'd tell her the exact price of the ticket in the filthiest, most degrading terms, and she'd clutch her imaginary pearls and beg to pay in money. I'd give her a choice. On the car or in it. I'd take her from behind or the front. A spanking with my hand or the belt. I never knew which she'd choose, but she only timed out once to tell me her options were inadequate.

"I'll give you a choice," I say, getting my face closer to hers. I loved her the last time we played this game. I don't now. Not at all. But not loving her doesn't mean I want to hurt her.

"Anything, Officer Everhard."

Poor Mrs. Brenda Longbottom. The things I did to her were utterly depraved, but it's the laughter afterward that makes me lean into her. I don't have a short list of choices for the prude housewife with the lead foot. I can taste Lyric's breath on my lips. Feel her chest against me when she inhales and feel its absence on the exhale.

"Your choice…" I take her by the back of the head and pull her to me, gripping her hair as if a tightened fist is the only way to consolidate my willpower.

"What was it she used to say?" Her eyelids flutter. "Would you mind kissing me first, Officer?"

"Are you playing with me?" I ask, but I don't care about the answer. Before she's done saying "yes," I'm already pulling her face to mine.

I kiss her hard, the way a man who doesn't give a shit would. Like an animal, I grab her mouth with mine, and she bends under me, fists against my chest, letting my tongue wedge itself between her lips. A sound escapes her throat, vibrating down into my ribs, and she pushes me away.

"I shouldn't—" I start.

"Officer Everhard was always a lousy kisser."

I can't help but smile. He was, but on purpose. Now I want to kiss her again, but the right way, and that's not going to happen.

"Just keep going." I take two steps away from her. She

needs space, and she's been clear about what she wants to do with the next few hours. "I'll be right behind you. When you get to the turn, hit your blinker. If it's the wrong direction, I'll flash my brights."

"I'm still mad at you," she says as she backs toward her car door.

"I'm aware."

"And Mrs. Longbottom is too."

"She's the most stunning picture of misery and destitution I've ever seen."

Smiling, she brandishes her middle finger and starts getting into her car.

"Lyric," I call. She stops halfway in. "I need your phone."

"I'll shove it up my own ass first."

She gets in. The desert absorbs the sound of her door slamming shut. I rush to follow before I lose her again.

CHAPTER 9

LYRIC

I GET into my car and lock the doors. He's in the rearview, and he's going to stay there until we hit the 15.

His kiss wasn't lousy. It was a meteor entering my atmosphere, burning hot as it streaked across my lips, only to disappear into stardust. I can still feel it. Even when he's pretending to be someone else, Anton knows how to kiss. At least that didn't change.

"You better not be on my ass the whole way, Officer Everhard," I say to myself.

I don't mean it. He'll stay behind me as long as he wants to. Maybe as long as he can taste me on his lips the way I can taste him.

And then what?

"Nothing." I put the car into drive. "That's what."

In the rearview, the dots of his headlights remain at a safe distance, no matter how slowly I go. I imagine the pace pissing him off so badly he rushes ahead, cuts me off, stops. Then he gets out, erect as a flagpole, pulls me out of my car and says, "Your taillight's busted, Mrs. Longbottom, and now you have a choice… I deliver this ticket into your mouth or your cunt."

No. Too soon.

He says, "Five on the ass or three inside your thighs." And I say, "My husband will see the marks," while knowing he won't because Larry Longbottom hasn't fucked his poor, horny wife in a year. Then Officer Everhard pulls Brenda's hair and says, "Ass it is." while sticking his hand up my skirt.

I sort out the story in my head, reworking it over and over and choosing the perfect shot sequence until, over the top of a hill, I see the 15 stretching out into nothing. By the time I hit the on-ramp, I'm so fucking aroused I wish Anton would stop me, but he just speeds up, and with a wave, he passes me on the way back to Los Angeles.

The morning after Skye's act, I still haven't gotten up her anxiety video.

It was never the Musknet. The Wi-Fi at my house is working fine, and I'm still locked out. Phone and laptop— nothing. I tried last night when I got home, but I was so tired I couldn't think. I went to bed, and when I woke up, it was still fucked.

It's fucked with VPN. Fucked when I turn off the VPN. Fucked when I steal the neighbor's wifi, and fucked on cellular.

Editing the two videos keeps my mind off the fact that I won't be able to upload them.

My phone rings. At least that works.

Unknown number. I pick it up anyway.

"Hi, Lyric?"

"Yes."

"This is Kevin P. from Meta."

Kevin P. is a VIP rep. All he does all day is stroke accounts with an M in their follower count. I have a lady like that at TikTok, but I'm dogshit there. Fifty thousand follows and hit-or-miss on virality—mostly miss. If she ever returns my email with more than a form letter, I'll throw a party.

"Hey, Kev."

He spends—and I time this—forty-five seconds explaining that the call is being recorded for customer service and ass-covering purposes.

"I understand and agree."

For the four hundredth time.

"So," he says, "I got your message, and I have a few questions."

He proceeds to ask me everything that would have been answered if he'd just taken the message at face value. I'm so patient with him I should petition for sainthood. I wonder how that's done while I pull weeds out of my little garden, water the tomato plants, knock down black widow webs, and kick the pebbles that escaped onto the pavement back onto the driveway. I'll probably have to let a priest or a cardinal or something know how awesome I was not to drive over to the Meta office in Silicon Beach to murder Kevin P.

Be a saint. Be a saint.

"So?" I ask when he's done, as Liang pulls up in his Kia and I get out of the way so he can park in the driveway.

"So," Kevin replies, all man-in-charge, "I have everything I need. We're going to look into this."

I punch the button to close the gate behind Liang.

Saint Lyric. Saint Lyric. Saint Lyric.

"Fine! Great! Thanks, Kevin!" I hang up before Kevin asks me if I need anything else.

Liang's in teal bellbottoms and strappy pink platforms.

"How's Kevey?" He hands me a little shopping bag as we kiss hello.

"Useless." I peek in the bag. It's exactly what I need to beat Kevin to the punch.

"Have you seen last night's reel? It's on *fire!*" He taps his feet faster than a jazz drum.

"Skye's makeup? From the trailer?"

"Yes!" He takes out his phone and flicks the screen. "I got a message about a *job*." His last word is barely contained. "I have to stay calm. Could be bullshit. But if it's not…"

He holds the phone out to the video of Skye getting her makeup done. He's cut her transformation together with shots of him winking with a little *tink* sound or a star-shaped flash in his teeth. It's charming as hell, but also shows off his skill with makeup.

"Liang. For real." I scroll while he holds up the phone. "Those are great numbers."

"Aren't they?!" He holds his hands to his chest, hugging his Instagram. "I have you to thank. I owe you."

"God, no. Don't be stupid." I head for the house. "Do you want something to drink?"

"I forgot to bring Fresca."

"I have some."

Once inside, he gets a can from the fridge while I kneel on the living room floor and tear open the box he brought me.

"I had no idea what to ask for," Liang says, cracking open the can. He'll have it on ice, with a straw, even though it's as cold as it can get without turning into a solid cylinder. "So I said give me the most expensive Android you have, with everything."

"Perfect." The two-foot-long receipt is among the packaging. I don't care what the number on the bottom is. "I'll Venmo you."

"So, the guy who messaged me? I checked him out on LinkedIn." Liang sits on the couch with his grapefruit soda, staring at his phone. "Assistant head of marketing for Starlight. The makeup brand? He wants me to meet his boss, but she can't take a meeting until like... after Christmas?"

"Sheesh." Wedging away another layer of packaging, I get to the Android itself and pluck the black rectangle from its tight plastic nest.

"But they're both going to be at the Amea Club's Cowboy Masqued Ball."

"Oh, he's sneaky. I like it."

I turn on the Android. Swapping devices negates the possibility that the problem is with the phone. Making it a different manufacturer just moves the similarities one step further apart. Or not. I'm throwing darts at the wall here because I don't want to storm into the Meta offices like Karen-on-fire so they can show me how I'm the one with the problem.

"I have to stop watching these numbers." Liang puts his phone on the coffee table. "Before I turn into a zombie."

I lay the Android on my upturned hand. "This thing's huge."

"Do you even know how to use it?" Liang squints at it as

if it was stolen from a secret military project his uncle at Lockheed-Martin can neither confirm nor deny exists.

"How hard can it be?" I slide the new SIM card into the slot. "Smash cut to Lyric sobbing as she throws her brand-new phone into the toilet."

Liang laughs. "So," he says, extending the o, "you're going to the Amea Club thing?"

I shrug, turning on the phone. "Dante never invites me to any of his club things."

"You don't ask?"

"No. I love him, but he's a dork. If the party was actually cool, it would shatter my image of him. So I never go, and he stopped inviting me." The phone runs through its welcomes and loads itself like a person woken from a long nap. I flip through the instruction manual. "This is fine. It's like a man —complex inner workings controlled with under five buttons—just less haptic feedback."

Having picked up his phone again, Liang leans back on the couch.

"Anton's been working out." He says it casually, without looking up.

"Mm-hm."

No truer words were ever spoken, but I'm not going to get all up in my head talking about him. I don't want to rehash the past or build sandcastles on Future Beach.

"What are you doing?" Liang asks.

"I'm just setting it up."

"You could be a Samsung commercial with that smile on your face."

I shrug.

"You want to tell me something?" He puts down the phone.

I shrug again. I'm going to throw out my shoulder at this rate. "App downloads are pretty fast."

"You disappeared between the trailer and Soap Scum."

Pretty fast is suddenly not fast enough. Shaking the phone doesn't make it come any quicker—same as an iPhone or a man.

"Okay, Instagram's loaded. Let's see."

"Well?" He slides down to the floor with me as I enter my apparently inadequate seven-digit password, hold my breath for a spinning icon, then watch my account open like a flower in springtime.

"I'm in."

"Awesome."

"I was in last night. I just couldn't do anything." I tap out a quick, empty update with a selfie from last night, then hit *Share*.

"Did you post it?" Liang asks. "I don't see it."

"No." I hit the blue button again. It doesn't post. "Shit." Share. Share. Share. Nothing happens. If I do it one more insanity-defining time, I'm going to—*Share*. "I can't post." Going back to my timeline, I try to comment. Nothing happens. I hit a heart. Fuckall. "It's like the account is locked, but I've never seen a lock like this before. There's no dialog box. No warnings. I'm screaming into a fucking void and the void's throwing it all back."

"Should I tell your followers what happened?"

"No. God, no."

"One more day and they're gonna start getting sleuthy."

He's right. I'm going to become a conspiracy theory.

"Okay. Tell them I'm..." Tired? That means depressed. Taking a break? They'll think I'm having a breakdown. Hacked? Closest to the truth, but only people with racist trash in their archive seem to get hacked, and only after the racist trash was discovered. "Tell them I'm planning something big."

"Such as?"

"Big and secret."

"Do you really think that's going to go well?"

"I'm creating a vacuum of desire."

But I'm the one with the vacuum, and it's not going to get filled with an Instagram post.

"A bot-army could have reported you for some shit," Liang says.

"Kevin would have called me. Like the last time."

"True."

I toss the Android on the couch. It rings.

Liang and I stare at it.

"You sure you made a new number?" I ask.

"I did. Based in Saskatchewan."

"Maybe it's the Mounties."

Maybe Anton is at the door. He says he's from the Canadian Mounties and he's here to question me, but what he's actually going to do is fuck me senseless and call me a dirty criminal.

"It's not the Mounties." I crawl to the couch and grab the phone. Unknown number. Shocking. "Someone's playing a game with me."

I haven't even picked the phone off the cushions and I'd bet the house my disappearing, turtleneck-wearing, me-abandoning ex is the one calling me.

I shouldn't answer it. That would be the smart thing. But if I'm being honest with myself—and I guess honesty is today's policy—I feel like playing. I want to be led around on a wild goose chase that ends at this new, mysterious version of my personal, terrible, long-missing note-leaving lover.

"Hello, Anton" I say, and wait for him to explain how he got this number.

There's a click, then a robotic recorded voice. "Home roof, solar, energy saving estimates available to—"

I hang up and put the phone back on the table.

"Spam." I'm disappointed. Like a kid in a sea of wrapping paper on Christmas morning, looking for that one thing she missed that'll fill the hole where joy should be.

"Damn." Liang gets up. "You can't have a number five minutes anymore."

"Yeah." I stare at the Android, waiting for something to happen. My heart's still pounding from the thought of hearing Anton's voice on a new phone, from a number he shouldn't even have. I expected him to wield that kind of power. I want him to. I'm playing a mind game with myself.

"I can't waste my entire day watching my follower count," Liang says. "I'm going to the gym. You wanna join? Get in some short-shorts and a little tank? Maybe meet the hot trainer of your dreams?"

"I don't dream about working out, okay? We're all going to get old and die. It's a sucker's game. The house always wins."

"All right, sunshine. Thanks for the reminder."

"Get out," I say cheerfully, searching for my iPhone. I find it under the receipt for the Android. "I'll Venmo you."

You never gave me your Venmo.

"You need anything, you call me."

How did Anton get on my Venmo?

"Hey, so…" Liang says at the door. "The thing at Amea

Club? They invited a bunch of influencers, but I don't have enough of a following so… I'm wondering…"

"I'll take care of it."

"Thank you!" He throws his arms around me.

Calling my brother is the least I can do. But Liang never wants to hear about how shitty I feel about promising him the moon and stars for starring in *Standard Deviation*, only so it could tank so badly his acting career went down with it.

"It's nothing. Go. Shoo. Before you mess up your face."

The door closes. Liang's gone. I Venmo him the cost of the phone.

It's in your contacts.

Anton might know how to do this hack.

Did he do this?

He was there last night. Backstage, he handled my phone, and now he wants it? Why? Just because the lock is on both phones doesn't mean the iPhone doesn't have some kind of evidence of his hack.

Is what I'm thinking possible or sensible? Crowne Industries wouldn't hire a security guy without a background check. Right?

Can you background check a man's intentions?

A text comes in on my iPhone. It's from a number I haven't seen since I was young enough to get excited about it. Anton and I both need to go through our contacts and do some deleting, obviously.

**—Did you get home ok last night
or am I calling search and rescue?—**

This guy. He can't just ask me if I got home all right because that would imply he doesn't already know… and

God forbid he's not the all-seeing eye on top of the pyramid. What a waste of a beautiful face and a hot body.

Maybe not a total loss. That kiss was a mistake and a worthwhile addition to his repertoire of confusing features.

> *—just because I pretended I wanted to fuck you while pretending you were someone else doesn't make you responsible for checking on me—*

He doesn't answer. The three-dot signal appears and disappears, which makes it seem as though he's typing and deleting, but it doesn't tell you shit.

I know that like I know my favorite filters, but it still bothers me.

—Glad to hear you're fine.
I need your phone—

He needs my phone so he can remove his little digital fingerprints or whatever. I don't pretend to know the details, but he did this. I know that. I should give him the Android just to fuck with him.

> *—Come and get it—*

Logan's in charge of the company now. Maybe he was the one responsible for hiring Anton. Was he paying attention to who I dated in New York? It's not like I was ready to tell anyone in the family and subject myself to the presence or absence of Mom's prescient "tingle" that told her the future of a relationship. I need to talk to Dad about it. I loved Anton once, but if he did this hack, that's not cool.

—Where are you?—

—Find me—

I put down the phone, near giddy with delight at my challenge, because I won't be here. I'll be at my parents' place in Bel-Air, pulling the rug out from under his dirty tricks.

CHAPTER 10

LYRIC

CROWNEHOME IS MY PARENTS' massive place in Bel-Air. My oldest brother, Byron, built this house on the best hill he could raze. It was supposed to have five pools and a discotheque. Then he fell in love with an environmentalist and stopped building massive houses to prove how big his dick was.

I have no idea how big his dick is. That's gross.

Byron scaled down his ambitions and the house's footprint. Now it has two pools instead of five and only ten thousand square feet of patio overlooking the canyon. Mom and Dad bought it, which was ridic, because it's still too big for two people. If you don't know how to get around, you can get lost, and even if you do know how to get around, you really only know how to get where you're going. One wrong turn and you're in some extra kitchen or billiards room or whatever.

Dumb as the purchase seemed when it happened, they had a plan. Four of the six of us are partnered off. Colton and I are the only ones not pumping out babies, and I'd bet a million followers he and Skye are going to drop me a niece or nephew soon. There's always someone else around the house, which was exactly their plan. The house is a progeny magnet.

Chalk one up for strategic parents.

After putting the code into the gate, I take my car up the driveway and park in the underground lot.

Here's what I figure. Assuming Anton did this, he's got some kind of plan. He's trying to get something out of me. It's probably not money. His father was a legit Russian oligarch. Nobody has more money than those people. This has to be personal. Is he looking to humiliate me? Hurt me? Is he out for revenge?

The house has a seemingly infinite number of patios, but the only one you'll see the Crowne kids on has a normal, rectangular pool and a view of the canyon. That's where I find my sister-in-law, Mandy with her new squishy baby, sipping from a bottle of Fiji water. It's late October—a little too cold for a swim, unless you can heat your pool to eighty-five degrees, which Mom insists on. Steam comes off the water's surface, where someone's doing laps. Probably Mandy's husband and my favorite dork brother, Dante.

That's fine. I can tell him to invite Liang to his party.

"Hey, Lyric." Mandy and I cheek-kiss and I take Teddy, who's still young enough to bounce on my knee.

"How's the Teddah-monstah?" I gnaw on his fat little neck and he giggles. Cool Aunt Lyric has arrived.

The swimmer stops swimming. It's Logan. We wave to each other, and he starts the next lap. Show-off.

"Where's Dante?" I ask Mandy before zerbitting on my nephew's neck. "Where Daddy?"

"London."

"Another club?"

"Yep. He loves it now that he can do it on his own." She flips her sunglasses down over her eyes and looks over the canyon. "Byron finds the properties. Dante does what he wants with them."

"So, the one in Echo Park? Amea, is it? Everyone's talking about the opening."

"The one you're too cool to come to?"

"That one. Can he invite someone...?" I stop when she turns to me, looking over the tops of her sunglasses. "Not that kind of someone." I cut off her questions. "A friend."

"Send their social over to Vanessa."

"Okay, but they don't have the follower count Dante's looking for. It's not even close. And I think, personally, that he's using a really weird benchmark for who's cool enough to show up at his little shindig."

Teddy fusses. I bounce him. He quiets a little, but the fuss is just beneath the surface.

Mandy reaches for her son. "It's about who can promote it, not who's cool or whatever you call it." Sitting up, she shifts her neckline to the side and puts Teddy on her breast.

"It's about not being able to personally tell the difference between what's trending today and what was cool back when Millennials mattered."

She sighs. "Send the socials and I'll see what I can do?"

"I need something more definite."

"Okay, so the last time we did this—"

"That was different."

"The private rooms are not supposed to be leaked."

"They're not classified documents."

Teddy drops off her breast, sleeping like a baby should.

Mandy tucks back in and dabs the milk off the corners of his open mouth.

"Guests need to come in knowing they're not going to get caught in the background of a selfie."

"Then why is he inviting follower counts?"

She sighs. We went through this when it happened. I know all the reasons. Yes to promoting but only from certain areas. Outside the club. Public spaces. Taking phones away at the door is a disaster. Guests sign an agreement to abide by the rules, and they do, except for the one time Colleen—who has a personal Insta with three hundred followers—bragged to her friends that she was in the same room as Brad and Cara Sinclair.

That went over like a pile of bricks.

Hellie, the nanny, comes over and takes the sleeping baby.

"I heard what happened to you." Mandy leans back in her chair. "Any idea who did it?"

"Just an idea."

"How are you surviving?"

"Meta's working on it. I'll get it back soon." I pick up my phone and put it down. I'm using my old iPhone, but even if it was the Android, there wouldn't be anything there. "I can still email, I guess? Texting works."

My phone buzzes. Anton again.

—Correct. Texting works—

"What?" I say.

"I confirmed, 'texting works.'" He's right behind me, putting his phone in his pocket with that smirk I used to like so much—black clad from chin to foot, sleeves pushed above his forearms. Eyes dark and bright. Behind him, the vivid blue sky makes him look like a falling crow feather.

I'd set the light meter for the railing and shoot him with a tight aperture to really hit the contrast. Pan down on entry to give that dark-angel-falling-from-the-sky feeling.

"What are you doing here?"

"Anton had some things to review with me," my dad says, coming from an entirely different direction as if they want to ambush me on two fronts. All I need now is Mom—

"Lyric!" Mom says, clearly surprised to see me. She holds out her skinny arms for me. I get up to kiss her. She's frail and Parkinson's makes her unstable. It's not right to ask her to bend down. "You didn't say you were coming."

"Yeah. Just to… uh, I wanted to talk to Dad about something."

"I'm intrigued," Dad says.

"Later." I try really hard not to look at Anton when I say it.

"You changed something." Mom looks me up and down, then right in the face. She tips up my chin. "Not the hair. Makeup the same."

"I didn't change anything."

"Ah, I know." She wags her finger at me. "You're not looking at your phone."

I'm old enough to be emancipated from my mother's care, but not too old to roll my eyes.

"She detached it from the end of her arm," my brother Logan says, having appeared from nowhere like everyone else in this house, drying off with a bleach-white towel. "Alert the media."

"Not willingly, in case you care." I throw myself back onto the chair. "I was hacked." I give up on not looking at Anton and shoot him a look that would burn holes in his turtleneck if there was any justice in the world, which there isn't.

"Oh dear." Mom sits in a chair beside me and puts her hand over mine. "Did they take anything?"

"Not the bank accounts or anything like that. Just the social."

"Did they ask for a ransom yet?" Anton asks as if he isn't the most likely suspect.

Mom rubs her arms, glancing from me to him and I don't like it. I don't want to hear the word tingle or lifemate or anything about her having a feeling about me and this man.

"No." I shoot him a dirty look. He did this and I may not know why, but I'm not letting him get away with it.

"Anton," Mom moves her attention his way, "is this something you can help with?"

"Hell, no," I interject.

"Lyric and I already spoke about it," he says before I can say *hell no* a hundred more times.

"And?" Dad asks him.

"She's not interested in my help."

"Lyric. This is serious," Dad says.

"Meta's working on it. If they don't have it fixed by tomorrow, you can call Mark."

"Today, it's your social media," Dad says in that patient dad-tone. "Tomorrow it could be something else."

"Your financials," Logan says, putting on his shirt. Thank God. No one needs to look at that. "Your passwords. Your camera roll." When everyone's heads snap toward Logan, he holds his hands out as if his suggestion was purely innocent. "None of you have ever taken a picture of a document to send to your accountant?"

"Your identity," Anton adds.

"Dad," I say, standing as if the chair just caught fire, "we need to talk."

"Let's eat first," Mom says, reaching for Dad. "I need a hand getting to the table."

He gently helps her up. I want to marry someone that devoted, but I also don't want to stall.

"Anton," Dad says as he helps Mom up, "come eat with us."

Anton looks at his watch and my eyes are shooting him with so many *don't you dare even* bullets, but all he does is drop his arm and say, "I have some time."

"Excellent." Dad claps Anton on the back as though he's the sixth boy Dad never had but really wanted and walks him to the dining patio.

"Why do you look like someone took your housekeys too?" Logan asks. His hair is wet and his T-shirt sticks to him in the places he didn't dry enough. It's always weird when he doesn't wear a suit.

"You came all the way here to swim? Don't you have your own pool?"

"You came here to eat? Don't you have DoorDash?"

"Whatever." I snap a look at my phone. Nothing's changed. I'm locked out of the office. Might as well get a flip-phone from Best Buy. And Anton's still here, talking to Dad by the long table as if they have things in common.

"She has a right to be mad." Mandy and Logan were friends before she married our brother, so she gets to defend me. "And frightened. Getting hacked is terrible."

"Thank you," I say to her before addressing Logan. "And fuck you."

Mom is now chatting with Anton and Dad. Aren't they all so very cozy?

They're aware I know him from New York, and they never even asked if I can bear the sight of him. Not that it's the sight of him that's the problem. I can't *stop* looking at him.

On the way to the table, Mandy pulls me aside. "You knew him, I hear?"

"In New York. It was nothing."

"Are you okay with him?"

I'm not, but she's not asking me if I *like* everyone at the table. She's asking me if I feel threatened or unsafe. That's a lie I won't tell. "It's fine. Why?"

"I just have this feeling."

"What feeling? Not like Mom?"

"No," she says definitively. "Wait. You mean Mom's tingle? Right?"

My mother says she gets a tingly feeling whenever she sees a couple that's going to get married. It's horseshit, obviously, but she had it with my brothers and their current partners.

"Yes."

"Why would you ask?"

"I don't know. She was rubbing her arms. And since Dante and Ella aren't here to make a tingle for you or Logan, I got a little freaked out. So..." I keep talking and talking. "... I'm just confirming Mom didn't tell you she tingled and you're not having the personal equivalent of a 'feeling.' Right?"

"It just seems like you're not happy he's here."

"Whatever. Happy is relative. Fleeting. Who's ever really happy?"

"Okay, Lyric." She laughs. "I'll take your word for it."

We get to the table. When we were kids, Mom cooked a lot of our meals, but that's not possible anymore, so they hired a whole staff to feed them and anyone else who happens to be around.

"Hey, Nellie," I say to the kitchen staffer who's bringing out a jug of jasmine iced tea. She's been with us a long time. "How are you?"

"Very good, and you? You haven't posted today."

Nothing goes unnoticed. Nothing.

"I'll get to it. How's Marcus?"

"Big. Almost as tall as Byron." She shakes her head.

"Hopefully he won't be half the dick."

She laughs as if my crudeness is in any way unusual. "Go sit. We're serving in a minute."

I'm annoyed that Anton's here, but my family and everyone around us is really cool, and that throws water on the fire of hate I have for him. I figure I can wait to talk to Dad until after lunch.

CHAPTER 11

LYRIC

LOGAN HOLDS out chairs for Mandy and me, one in each hand. He pushes his friend's in first, so I do my own. He sits on the other side of the table, next to Anton, who's planted himself right across from me. Dad's at the head. Mom's at the foot.

"So," Dad starts, "you two knew each other in New York, then?"

Anton watches me as if I'm Twitter and he's doomscrolling.

"Yeah." I pick up my phone and look at nothing. Not even an email. I open the news as if I care. "We were friends. Then he left."

"When was this?" Mom asks. We're served layered salads and iced tea with jasmine.

"Three years," Anton answers.

I scroll through the *New York Times* and I still don't care about Congress, but it gives my brain and fingers something to do besides stare at the guy sitting across from me.

"Did you see the movie she made?" Mom asks. "What was it called?"

"*Standard Deviation*," Dad answers.

And no. Just no. This is not a conversation I'm having right now. My family knows I made the movie, and they know it didn't go anywhere. I told them the truth—that's just what happens to movies. No big. I found the whole process more boring than I expected and moved on. The lie was that I got bored of directing. They don't know about the string of humiliations or the fact that I quit trying, and I'm not going to sit here and let Anton tell them.

"Why'd you leave again, Anton?" I put down the phone and pick up my fork. "I forgot."

He flicks his lettuce around. I hope he's lost his appetite. "I had to go home to take care of some business."

"Russia, home?" I ask.

"Ukraine." He takes a mouthful of lettuce. "The money my father put aside for me before he died was in a Crimean bank. Since my mother's Ukrainian and my father was Russian, I wasn't trusted. I had seven days to arrive anywhere in Russia and stay for two years to establish full residency. Otherwise, they'd seize it and I'd have nothing."

I can't imagine him insolvent, but the way he swipes his hands across his chest and makes a *zzzt* sound means broke.

"They gave you seven days?" I say.

"I got the notice with ninety days."

"Wait. You knew you were leaving for three months and didn't tell anyone?"

He shrugs. "There were personal reasons."

"We would have thrown you a party." Nellie picks up my three-quarters-eaten salad and lays a chicken sandwich before me. "You could have just said—"

"He said it was personal, Lyric," Logan reprimands me like a big brother.

Instead of being mad, I'm grateful, because he's right. A girl Anton knew casually in New York wouldn't be asking.

"It was a woman," Anton says as if it doesn't matter, which it wouldn't if we were who we're pretending to be.

"Oh, yeah. I remember her. Brenda Longbottom."

He smirks. "She needed me."

"Did she? She didn't seem like the needy type."

"She was the type who'd never admit she needed anyone, but I knew her, inside and out. She didn't have to tell me what she needed, and I didn't have to ask."

"Wow." For no reason other than free-floating discomfort, I pick up my phone, but put it right down when I remember there's absolutely nothing to see there. "I never took you for such an egomaniac."

"Lyric." Dad, in the corner of my peripheral vision, pushes away his salad plate. "That's a little—"

"It's not a little anything." My attention stays on Anton and the clench of his jaw. Neither of us wants to air our laundry over a Crowne lunch, but I'm not averse to airing out some imaginary person's. "I was tight with Brenda. We were close. And your assumption that she would have broken without you is bullshit."

"That's not what—"

"She would have missed you, but she would have waited."

"Maybe I didn't want her to." He looks at me coldly, as if he's looking at Brenda and separating himself from his feelings so he can make a hard decision. That icy stare is for me. I have never wanted to punch him more.

"I'll give you a thousand dollars to tell me the real reason."

"This is getting weird," Mandy murmurs.

But Anton acts as if he doesn't hear or care. "She was very loyal. Stubbornly so. She would have insisted on coming with me."

"So what if she did?"

"Give up her own life? Her career? No. I wasn't letting her run away."

Brenda had been getting hammered with rejection and might have followed him. The idea would have been so appealing, if only the choice had been offered. Spend two years far away so I didn't have to admit to a massive lack of talent? Sold.

But if I did go with him, that wouldn't have been why.

"What if she loved you?" A burning sensation rises in my eyes, but I keep them locked on his.

He folds his forearms together, right on top of left so I can see the trident tattoo on top of his hand, and leans toward me. "I was going to Russian-occupied Crimea, Lyric. I consider myself Ukrainian, and that wasn't going to go over well. It wasn't safe for her for two years or two minutes. I either went alone and got everything or stayed with her and lost everything."

"So, you chose to go."

"I would have stayed, but she chose to let me go."

"You're right." Tearing my gaze away, I pick up my phone. "She did."

What am I scrolling through? What's on this screen? I try to focus on it so I don't cry. I will not shed a single fucking tear in front of everyone and I won't get up and leave so Mandy can follow me and ask what's wrong.

"That sounds really complicated," Mandy offers.

"Did you get your money?" Logan asks.

Typical. The seized assets were the only part of the story Logan heard. I don't think I'll be so lucky with Mom.

"I did."

"A happy ending then," Logan says before biting into his sandwich. "And Lyric owes you a grand."

"I'll Venmo it right over," I say. Finding out where he's been all this time and why he left is worth at least a thousand dollars.

A text comes in.

—You think ur better than me?—

Wait. What?

It's from an unknown number. I look over at Anton. His hand isn't anywhere near his phone. This text doesn't sound like him anyway.

I send one back.

—Who is this?—

I navigate over to Venmo, but another message banner drops in.

—U like my exploit?—

"I think I have him," I say softly.

"Me?" Anton asks. "I'm in your contacts."

"No."

I know I should hand over the phone, but I'm fearless and suddenly extremely angry.

—That all you got?—

*—Once you see what I can make you
do, you'll respect me—*

"I don't really want your money, Lyric," Anton says.

Fuck Venmo right now.

*—I can't respect someone who
texts from an unknown number—*

Three dots and then bang. Dick pic.

"Ugh!" I drop the phone on the table.

"What?" Dad asks at the same time as Mom and Mandy.

"Lyric?" Anton turns my name into a question.

The phone buzzes again. Logan grabs it.

"It's just a gross dick pic," I say.

"Excuse me?" Anton's expression darkens.

"It's like a regular weekday when you're internet famous. I get this trash on my Insta all the time. Just not on my personal phone."

"This is not a regular day." Logan scrolls.

"Thanks for telling me what it's like to be a woman in America, asshole."

"She's right," Mandy adds. "If you seem even *slightly* available, you get them."

"See?" I say, glancing at Anton's darkened expression. I don't know what's setting him off—the dick pic or my ostensible availability… and I don't even care.

"My God." Mom's practically clutching her pearls.

Instead of handing the phone to the actual owner, Logan passes it to Anton.

"What is it?" Dad asks.

"You don't want to see it," Logan says. "But, Anton, what do you think?"

"No," he says, jaw set in a hard line. "No."

"Why are you asking him?" I reach over to swipe away the phone, and I'm surprised at my success. "It's mine."

"How do you know this isn't your hacker, Lyric?" Dad asks. Before I can get in a word edgewise, he turns to Anton. "I need this taken care of."

"It will be."

"I'm deleting this." I stand.

"Wait," Anton says, reaching for phone.

I step back. He misses. Attempting to delete the pic, I get one last look at the text that came in after it.

—If it were u and me in the
blue sea of august, I'd fuck you while
you still looked good—

I cover my mouth with both hands, dropping the phone. I never want to touch it again.

CHAPTER 12

LYRIC

Swept Away By An Unusual Destiny In The Blue Sea of August -
Italy, 1974. Directed by Lina Wertmüler.

A CALLOUS SOCIALITE and a working-class brute are trapped on an island. He starts to rape her, bellowing, "Shut up and let me fuck you while you still look good!" But he only goes through with the beating, leaving penetration for the day she begs for it.

I shouldn't have explained the reference to everyone. I should have let them think it was just some weird half-poem, half-joke.

Dad's on the warpath now, and I can't say I blame him. Some vague, could-have-happened-to-anyone hack is one thing. The hack followed by a direct threat of sexual violence is an escalation he's going to address whether I like it or not.

But not now. Right now, I need to sit on the toilet in my parents' house with my head between my knees, rubbing Tiger Balm into the back of my neck.

Anton used to do this for me. He always seemed to have a

hair tie around his wrist. He'd twist up my hair and rub the ointment where I was tight. Then he'd kiss the place where my neck met my shoulders and let my hair down. When I thanked him, his lips would have a hint of cool-burning camphor.

Now I know where he went and why. There's no satisfaction in the knowledge. It's worse. I was having that relationship by myself. While I was trying to make a career I didn't have the talent for, dragging Liang into it, and feeling sorry for myself, Anton had a whole other list of deadlines he had to hit.

He's not my hacker. He didn't send that text. Blaming him for it won't sidetrack me from what happened and what didn't anymore. I'll hang onto the guilt until I figure out where to put it.

Since he left, I've taken care of my stiff neck myself, but I never seem to have the right hair tie, and even when I do, the knot isn't tight enough to stay up. I get sticky, stinky goop in my hair and I don't massage it in enough because I'm impatient where he was thorough and capricious where he was reverent.

There's a rap at the door just as I'm deciding between leaving the bathroom or spending the night in it.

"Are you all right?" It's Mandy.

"Yeah."

"Your father's waiting for you."

Of course he is. Taking up residence in bathroom number eleven was never really an option. I'm going to have to deal with this. I just hope Anton took my phone and went home already.

Mandy walks with me to the office, where my father's not actually waiting. Daddy's office doesn't match the ultramodern house. He took his old Scandinavian stuff from the Crownestead place in Santa Barbara and put it in a room that overlooks the garden with the saltwater pond. The office is like a little cubby of warm wood in this palace of gray and white. Despite the fact that an office implies business, it's where he decided to put the big family painting.

It's a traditional oil. Square like an Instagram post. Eight people, each with their own prop, sitting on a blanket for a picnic among the California poppies. And me? I'm the toddler with a tear-streaked face in my mother's arms and seven-year-old Dante's hand on my little shoulder. I am a shock of pink in the land of super-WASP neutrals.

The interior wall is folded like an accordion, leaving a wide open space to the rest of the house.

I see my parents coming—slowly but surely. Mom giggles at something Dad says. He smiles, says something that makes her laugh harder, and shrugs as if he had nothing to do with it.

Perfect couple. They were always too much to live up to, frankly. Until my three oldest brothers got married—then they all became too perfect. Now Colton and Skye, who aren't and may never be married, are just finding a fifth way to be perfect.

"Sit, sweetheart," Dad says to me when they reach the avocado-green rug.

"I'm good."

He helps Mom to one of the two seats in front of his desk. He's going to sit behind it as if I work for him. If I did, he'd have a different digital security consultant, that's for fuck sure.

"Come on." Mom pats the chair next to her. "You're pacing behind me. It's making me nervous."

Dad goes behind his desk, hitching his pants before sitting.

Drooping like an underwatered houseplant, I surrender to the seating arrangement.

"All right, Lyric," Dad starts. "Is what happened at lunch what you came here to talk to me about?"

"Yes and no."

I came here to tell him Anton couldn't be trusted. The circumstances pointed toward the guy Dad had hired for security being the one who had hacked me. But Anton wouldn't have sent that text. He wouldn't have admitted to the hack like a show-off, demanded respect like a child, or threatened rape like a psycho.

"Describe the yes or the no," Dad says. "But describe one or the other or I'm going to start talking."

That's enough of an incentive to start. I choose the no.

"I thought I had an idea who locked me out, but now—after that really bad lunch—I don't think it's them. A handful of people know I'm locked out, and missing a day of posting won't send any signals. Tomorrow, there will be questions. Not today. So the guy with the dick pic is the guy who did it."

"And do you know who it is?"

"No. But I don't want you to worry. I'll figure it out."

"And in the meantime?"

My dad says so much with so few words. He's asking me if I've thought this through, which I haven't. He's telling me he's not done telling me what he wants, which I won't like. And last, he's letting me in on the expectation that I have some kind of plan.

"In the meantime, I'll just lay low. Catch up on my Netflix binges. Order in."

"And hope this person just goes away?"

"I have an Android and a new number out of Saskatchewan. I can file forms with the LAPD, but you know what they're going to say. 'There hasn't been a crime so we can't do anything,' *blah-blah*."

"I'm putting my security team on you. I'll free up Earl."

"No, Dad. For real."

"Why not?" Mom asks. "He watched you all through school."

"Exactly the point."

"How is that a point?" Dad asks, annoyed.

"One. I'm a grown woman now and I can take care of myself."

"Can you?"

"What's that supposed to mean?"

"He didn't mean it like that." Mom gives Dad a stern look that he ignores.

"Didn't he, though? I've been paying my own bills since I got out of school without asking you for a dime."

Dad holds up his hand to stop me right there, and I know what he's going to say before he opens his mouth. "You've had plenty of resources. They didn't come from nowhere."

"Fine. I admit to a ton of privilege and a life very few humans on planet earth will ever even get their heads around. I've been exposed to literal royalty and walked the halls of power. I'm a spoiled brat—"

"I never said that."

"—who's never had to wait for anything, clean anything, or fix anything. I've never wondered where my next meal was coming from and I've had all the emotional support I've ever needed whether I wanted it or not, but I never asked for my One Big Thing, and I could have."

Each Crowne kid gets to ask for one big thing… the OBT.

Colton partied his away. Byron paid for this house. Dante opened his first club.

"We thought you would," Mom says. "For that movie. We wondered why."

Reasons. I wanted to prove I could do it on my own. But if I'm being honest with myself, I knew there was a chance it wouldn't work, and I didn't think I could bear explaining what had happened to their money. Spectacular success happens in the light. But spectacular failure stays in the shadows. It's the curse of indifference. If a movie fails where no one can hear the crash, does it make a sound?

"I didn't. I financed it by reinvesting a big chunk of my allowance, so I'm capable and I don't need or want a hundred-year-old bodyguard chasing me all over town."

"He's barely fifty," Dad says. "And in good enough shape to chase you from the Palisades to the river."

He's about to go on, but Mom cuts him off. "Ted."

He exhales. "I'm very concerned."

"I know you are. But she can make her own decisions about her safety."

"No, Doreen, she cannot."

He speaks to Mom like that so rarely I just sit silently until I figure out where I fit.

"In this case," Mom says carefully, "I think she can."

"Even if she had twice the situational awareness she exhibits now, I'd insist. But twice nothing is still nothing."

"What the actual fuck is going on?" I feel as if I'm interrupting a conversation they've had before.

"It means I'm not confident you—"

"Lyric," Mom interrupts Dad gently, "you have to admit you're not very good at paying attention. You're always looking at the screen."

"Jesus, I'll stop coming around if you can't stand the sight of me."

Mom and Dad lock in a gaze. I don't know what they're saying, but they don't need words to speak, and I've lived with them long enough to know there's a whole conversation happening.

I'm going to lose this part of the fight, and it's not even why I came all the way here in the first place.

Acceptance is freedom, or so they say. But I don't have to feel great about being followed around by my childhood minder.

"Fine," I say. "Maybe you're right. Maybe I've got a weirdo stalker. Maybe I'm not going to be living fully if I'm always looking behind my back. So, fine. Great. Send Earl over. I'll make sure I have enough grapefruit and cottage cheese in the fridge."

Dad leans back in his chair, arms folded, blue eyes narrowed. If the desk clock ticked this loud in the last house, it was never quiet enough in Dad's office to hear. He looks over my shoulder. "Logan."

My brother's dressed in trousers and a jacket. He and Anton are walking toward us from the bigger space behind me. Shoulder to shoulder, they look like a poster for a movie about assassins.

"Dad." Logan stands beside our father's chair. "Anton had a quick look at the phone."

CHAPTER 13

LYRIC

ANTON'S STANDING between and behind Mom and me, slapping my device against the heel of his hand. That bread-and-burned-things cologne is still novel in my brain, and there's an added musk of something more manly. More hormonal. If testosterone has a smell, this has to be it.

I reach for my phone, then remember the last thing I saw on it and withdraw.

"And?" Dad says, looking at Anton.

"The device hasn't been breached."

"And our network?"

"Secure. He just had her number and got bold, but I'd like to take it back with me. We can get a closer look if we clone it. Then"—he looks down at me—"you can have it back."

"Keep it. Burn it. I don't care."

"Is there anything you need to delete?"

"I have nothing to hide from you, Anton Markov."

"We'll find him." He puts it in his pocket with an annoyingly paternalistic look on his face.

All my anger is focused on him, not the real enemy. I

don't think of myself as someone who runs away from things, but I don't want to find dick pic man. I want to disappear so far into the floor he'll never find me.

"Is this the same organization you warned me about in Kiev?" Logan asks.

"I don't know."

"I'm sorry, what?" I sit on the edge of my chair. "It's an *organization?*"

"No," Dad and Logan answer at the same time, but only Dad picks up the explanation. Logan would never bother.

"The Markov Group found out I pissed off the wrong people in Russia. I have to say I admired the hustle it took to get Logan and me to the table."

"You pissed off the right people," Anton adds.

"I plugged some oil fields in 2014 and pulled our people out." Dad shrugs it off. What's a few billion in losses? "The reaction was enough to tell us we made the right choice."

"Anger and shock make a good glue for spite and action," Anton says.

"Is that a Ukrainian saying?"

"I made it up."

Dad chuckles. Great. He and Anton seem to actually like each other. I'm never getting rid of him now.

"So," Logan interrupts this meeting of the Mutual Admiration Society, "this isn't a Crowne Industries issue?"

"Probably not," Anton says.

"Then it's family." Logan holds out his hands as if there's not a damn thing he can do… which is fine because no one asked him. "Dad? All you."

Dad nods, accepting the baton, which is me. I'm just a girl without any agency here. I could be dunking in the heated pool right now for all it matters.

"I don't know who Earl is," Anton says, "but it needs to be me. It's not obvious what I'm doing there. I'm not security. We're friends."

"We are not," I mumble, dropping back into my seat.

"Anton," Dad says, "I'm not sure a digital security specialist is the best bodyguard for my daughter."

"Under normal circumstances, I'd agree. But this person knows her. Whoever you hire won't be able to get close enough to him to recognize him… or stop him."

"Dad, look, when I bought my house, I told the agent I only wanted it if it had a security system. It's been four months. It's not obsolete yet."

My realtor was the best in the city, with a huge Insta following I was willing to bet reflected extraordinary marketing skills. Her being Jake's mother added a little extra icing of trust.

"You're not safe." Dad stares into the middle distance, calculating his decision, which will be final. No matter how old or independent I get, Daddy always has to have the final word. He's going to hire me a personal nursemaid.

"I can protect her," Anton says.

"It was just a text." I can't even believe what's coming out of my mouth.

Dad draws himself out of the middle distance to look right at me. "It wasn't upsetting enough?"

"Like we said, it's a regular day in the life of a woman in America."

He and Mom do more of that thing where they have a conversation without using words and I'm too cowed to do anything but watch how they look at each other. One day, I'll find someone I can talk to like that, and who can read me without a syllable spoken between us. One day he and I will both nod the way Mom and Dad do before Dad looks at Anton.

"Stay with her," my father says.

"Dad!" I jump out of my seat. "I can handle it. You don't get to lord control over me. None of you get to say what I do or who I do it with or who's going to watch me while I do it. I'm not some football you're handing off to get over the finish line or end zone or whatever. This is my life."

Mom takes the hand that's not jabbing a finger at each of the men in the room. That's when I realize I'm so mad I'm shaking.

"Sweetheart," she says in a whisper, "I'll sleep better at night."

Even my own mother is in on it. This is some ambush sabotage bullshit.

"Great. I'm glad you all made a decision."

CHAPTER 14

ANTON

TALKING to Ted Crowne is always intimidating. He's everything my father never was. Ethical, for one. Thoughtful, for another. Ruthless without being cruel.

Then I smell camphor.

The minute I come near her, it fills my entire brain. It reminds me of stress, and comfort, and the illusion that I was ever useful to her. I touch my wrist, looking for the elastic to tie her hair up with, but it's been gone for a long time. Another time I failed someone.

That was the last lesson I needed on the consequences of losing control.

"Let me," I say when her brother starts after Lyric.

"Go ahead. See if you can get her to grow up."

"She is grown up." I shouldn't contradict a man who's writing checks to my company, but I'm not going to apologize.

I nod to Logan, then Ted, and take off after her, following the *clop-clop* of her heels echoing in the hard spaces. I catch her walking through a room lined in white couches with a fish tank that takes up an entire wall.

"Buttons," I call her by the nickname I gave her on our third date, when she wore a shirt with thirty looped buttons in the back. We laughed as I went through the gauntlet of getting them all undone without killing the moment.

"Don't call me that," she scolds, but she stops to face me. She's hurt by what just happened. She's lost control over her life, and she never could tolerate that.

"Okay. Lyric. Listen. I understand, but you—"

"You didn't write me those texts and that sure as hell isn't your dick."

Expecting her to fight over being overruled about her own safety, I'm taken aback by the suggestion that anything she was sent today would be from me. "Of course not."

"I'm going to ask you this once." She holds up a finger. "How did you end up on my Venmo?"

"Lucky guess."

"Bullshit."

"Fine. Two lucky guesses. First, that you never deleted or blocked my number. Second, that you imported your contacts into the app."

She blinks, unclenches her fist, drops her shoulders, then covers her mouth with her fingertips and laughs.

"Fuck." Her curse is just a breath. "That makes sense."

"Did you think it was me?"

"Yeah."

"Why would I do that?"

"Because I said no. You gave me a ring and I…" She looks away, profiled against the soft light of the fish tank. "I never said no to you before. I didn't know how you'd react. Maybe you got so mad you up and left. It's not vanity to think that.

You didn't disappear because you loved me that much, but because you couldn't hear no."

"But I did love you that much."

"Not enough though."

Why do I want to defend myself by claiming my love had been adequate? Why should I have to? And what the fuck does she expect out of me? Heartfelt declarations about things that don't exist anymore? Look upon this beautiful dead thing! Note the size and scope of it, the sheer depth of feeling it evoked. There was enough love there to feed a nation.

"Nothing was ever enough for you. Not enough praise. Not enough reviews. Not enough money or control or appreciation. The truth, Lyric? You were always this exhausting."

She grinds her jaw, chin high, eyes hard and unflinching. They'll dry to raisins before she blinks the welling tears out of them.

Fuck. Why didn't I just shut up?

"You're my new babysitter," she says with a sneer. "Whether I like it or not. So good luck with it. I live in West Hollywood. Finding a parking spot's going to be tough. Have fun staking me out without a permit. PVB cops are going to know you by name... because you're not invited in."

"I didn't come here to do this."

"Why did you come here? To work for my father? When were you going to call me and say, 'hey, don't be shocked if I show up'? Or do you get a kick out of ambushing me?"

"I didn't come back for this!" I hear myself shout, as if volume will push the questions back. I don't want to frighten her. I've never raised my voice in front of her before.

She crosses her arms and leans on one hip. She's not scared. I'm the only one who's scared of me.

I take a deep breath. One more second to think. "It's what's best, but it's not what I want."

"It doesn't matter what you want, Anton. It doesn't matter what any of us want. Either you can or you can't, and if you can, you choose."

"You and I misunderstand each other. This. Is. Business." The lie sticks in my throat. Earl would have done a fine job. Mike and I have men to shadow her. I could have kept out of it.

Another lie. I can't keep out of it. I need to be the one watching her.

If you can, you choose.

Yet once I came back into her life, I never had a choice.

"Business," she says as if business means pleasure, and pain, and tears, and brokenness—stepping closer, until we're nearly toe to toe. Electricity comes off her in waves. This was how it felt to be near her when she was writing or working on set. Those were the moments I believed she could do anything she wanted and no one could stop her—me, least of all.

"Business." I say it without the implications. Business means business. I feel nothing.

"Do you really believe that?"

No. I do not.

"Yes."

I'm more of a stunned animal than I realize, because she can't be this fast. Taking my face in her hands, she plants her lips on mine, leaving them there until I respond or push her away.

I can, so I choose.

CHAPTER 15

LYRIC

WHAT AM I trying to prove?

When I chose to kiss him, I knew, but when my lips meet his, I forget. It's a shock to the system that slows my breath and stills my body, as if I'm suspended in time while his tongue enters my mouth and circles, pinning my toes to the floor. His response sucks away all reason, leaving me a shell for him to fill with a purely physical, mindless response. A flood of high-voltage energy explodes from my heart and lands in my core.

I gasp, jerking away from him in a blast of sex-blindness. He looks down at me the way he used to before he fucked me. His promise of dominance is more of a guarantee. He will make me submit and I will like it.

The echo of staff clearing the lunch table reminds me where we are, and I remember why I kissed him in the first place.

"Business," I say. "Sure."

He breaks his gaze, wiping the corner of his mouth with his thumb. "That's not going to happen again."

"Bet on it." I walk out.

Let him chase me.

"Lyric," he calls.

I turn to face him, walking backward. "What?"

"Don't go anywhere without checking with me first."

"Yes, boss."

"No visitors. No parties. And I need to get into your house to secure your network."

My answer fits on the tip of my middle finger.

After I kissed him, he didn't chase me home, because I didn't run that fast. I wasn't getting into a wreck for him. But he followed, just as he did in the Mojave.

Once I closed and locked the door behind me, I realized I didn't have my iPhone. I had to switch to the Android because a dick pic guy said he was going to rape me. No one had the Android number yet. So I imported my contacts, texted Mandy to remind her about Liang, then called Mom to make sure she was all right and to assure her that Anton was sitting outside in his white Range Rover, watching my house as though it was his job.

Which it was, and late the next day, still is.

Did he pull an all-nighter?

If someone came and relieved him while I slept, I'd never know it, because he's still there in his white car, which now has a spotting of brown maple leaves on the roof and hood. If I was directing the movie of my life and wanted to show time had passed without the car moving, that's one way to do it.

It's business. He said it himself. There's nothing left to say.

My phone rings, and though I hope for half a second that it's Anton, it turns out to be Liang.

"Hey," I say, looking down at my block from the bedroom window. "How's it going?"

"I just got an invitation to a certain party."

"Would it happen to be the Masked Cowboy Ball at Club Amea?"

"Yes," he says excitedly. "I'm your plus one!"

"Uh…" I didn't say I was going, but now I guess I am. "Great!"

Being at my brother's party isn't a big deal. I can be ten percent less cool for a few hours, but parties, generally, are off-limits until we find dick pic man. I can't miss it.

Liang is a terrific actor, and if *Standard Deviation* had done what I'd hoped, he'd have more offers than he knows what to do with. But my movie sucked, and he has nothing but talent. He can't blow off a single opportunity to be where the right people are congregating. Unfortunately, they'll all be at my brother's dork party, so we either find dick pic man before that or… well, it doesn't really matter. I'm going with Liang.

"When is it again?" Pushing away from the window, I head downstairs.

"The twenty-ninth!" Liang seems beside himself. "I'm doing your face."

"You better."

"I can't go to Ozzie Dots today."

"Okay?" I feel out of the loop, and of course, I am.

Liang talks fast. "They're making the ten-gallon masks and Jake and Kelly are going today to order theirs, but I can't. I have a thing."

"And you want me to go?"

"Can you?"

I'm not sure I'm ever going to be allowed to leave the house again. It's been under twenty-four hours, and I already have to get out of here. A girl has to live her life and love her friends. That can't always be done from home with a guy watching from the street.

"Yeah." I open the fridge.

"Thank you!"

I gather bread, turkey, mustard, and lettuce. "I gotta go."

I slap together a sandwich, plate it, pop a pickle next to it, and put it on a tray. When I was working through the night, he always brought me the entire deal, so I do the same for him and add a bottle of Fiji and a cloth napkin.

After putting on my flipflops, I walk down the driveway and open the gate.

He's right across the street, hyperaware, starting the car and rolling down the window as if the beep of my code alerted him. "What are you doing?"

"You brought me sandwiches." I hold the tray to the window. "When I was ratta-tatting. Remember?"

"Writing like a machine gun. Yes." His stomach growls. I nailed this.

"Now I'm bringing you something, unless you had DoorDash deliver to your car."

He seems conflicted… and hungry.

"Have you been out here all night?" I ask.

He looks me up and down as if considering whether or not to answer. "Get in."

The locks clack open. I cross in front with the tray. He leans over and opens the passenger side door. I get in, lay the tray over his lap, and close the door.

"Thank you," he says before he bites into his sandwich. He does look really tired.

"Anton. You should get some rest. You're not going to do a good job."

"Roscoe's coming to relieve me. But you have to stay in the house."

"Okay." I cross my toes and watch the brown leaves fall from the maple tree.

"No sandwiches for him."

"No problem." I don't need to cross anything for that. I shrug an agreement and watch him bite into his sandwich.

"This is really good."

A hungry man will eat a shoe and call it delicious, but I still feel deeply praised and smile so wide my ears have to move out of the way.

"Should I make you another one?"

"No, this is perfect." He devours half the sandwich. He must have enough sugar in his blood now.

"How long am I trapped in my house?"

"Here's the plan." He cracks open the water. "Roscoe comes over here—"

"Did you hire him for having a cool name? Because that's a super cool name."

"I hired him because he's scary. He'll watch you from the street while I go to Mike's and pick up the sniffer."

"The who?"

"It's going to tell us if your signal's compromised. If it is, we have to look deeper, and that takes time."

"Yeah, but how long am I stuck for?"

He takes the last bite of sandwich. When he chews, his jaw gets even squarer. After swallowing, he points at the glove compartment. "There's a notebook in there."

I open the compartment and get out what he asked for.

"And take the pencil."

"Okay?" I fish it from the bottom and flip the door closed.

"I need an enemies list."

"My enemies?"

"Yes."

"I don't have any enemies," I say.

"Competitors, a nemesis, whatever you can think of."

"There's Insidious, who posted that I had four ball-bearings rolling around my skull."

"What did you do?"

"Ignored him. He went away. Now he's friends with Kelly."

"When did this ball-bearing comment happen?"

"Last summer." I bend my ring finger with a performative sigh. "RedHatGrl—that's g-r-l—called Liang a bunch of names that were not cool and so I dug around and found old video of her dropping a hard r, which finished her forever." Middle finger. "Leonard Rake wanted to debate me about feminism, which I'm not doing, so I got trolled for a week, then he got bored."

"These don't sound like serious people. I need real enemies."

"I'm not that kind of person. I'm not pointing a finger at everyone I ever got into a spat with and I'm not turning healthy, professional competition into 'oh, look at me you all want to stalk me,' okay?"

"Do you want to get rid of me or not?"

He asks it as if my reply should be obvious, but it isn't. I want to get rid of this situation. I want to be free to leave my house without a chaperone. But get rid of him? I'm not so sure.

I look down at the book, open to a fresh page, and write ENEMIES LIST at the top. "What if you found him right now?" I tap the page with the pencil point. "What if you didn't have to watch me anymore? If I'm not hacked, where are you?"

If there's an answer, it doesn't have words. It stays behind his twitching lips, teasing its way out like a grenade with the pin pulled.

I am weak without you.

Yeah, I don't need to hear this again.

"Forget it," I say, pulling my door handle. "Whatever. I'll write a list and get back to you."

"No." He reaches over me and closes the door.

"Look, I get it, okay? Here." I spread the book open on my lap and—under the heading ENEMIES LIST—I write the name ANTON. "There. This is where we are and there's no reason to move it just because some psycho wants to… whatever… and you 'happened' to be around."

"I was going to contact you."

"How long have you been skulking around LA? A month? You obviously had my number." I freeze while something that never occurred to me finally does. "Wait. You're with someone. You came here for her."

My heart stops beating while I wait for him to confirm. It shouldn't. His name is right there under ENEMIES LIST. It's fine if he traveled around the world for a lover as long as it's not me. Right?

"Not that it matters…" I add.

"No," he says. "It's more boring than that. My mother's here, and Mike wanted to be here for her, and…" Big sigh. "The beautiful women."

It takes me a second to realize he said women plural, not

one particular woman.

"He thinks LA women are more beautiful?"

"Sometimes…" The sentence ends with a shrug. "He makes me crazy. To experience life, he has women. Once. Twice. Never introduces them to me. Never fights with them or disrespects them, but never commits. He says life is too short."

"And has he figured out that we're all normal yet?"

He scoffs. "You're not normal."

"Okay, well. On that note, I'm going back into my cage to write down anyone who might hate me this much."

"Or like you. Or who you rejected or hurt. If you think you won a battle, the war might not be over for them."

"What about ex-boyfriends?"

"Write those down."

"Sure." I write NEVILLE right under ANTON. "How many do you want? I may need a bigger book." I don't need a single new line, but he doesn't know that.

"His last name." He taps the page but keeps his eyes on his sandwich.

"Bennett." I write it down in fat print. "It's not him."

"Date of birth." He sounds mad. I'm not going to call him on it though. It seems cruel.

"You forgot my birthday?"

"Your birthday is August twenty-first. I'm aware. Neville's."

"I have no idea. He's a Gemini. That's all I got."

He waves at the book, telling me to write that in. "Place of birth."

"Is Wisconsin the one with the cheese?"

He doesn't answer. He just keeps his head down and eats. I write Wisconsin under Neville's sun sign.

"Is that it?" I ask.

"Who else have you dated since—"

"Since you abandoned me?"

He looks up, reacting as if I just slapped him in the face. I wish I hadn't said it, but there it is.

Looking out the side window, he chews the inside of his cheek, then picks the tray off his lap and twists around to lay it in the back seat. A stall tactic so fastidiously epic it misses the subtlety it aims for. By the time he's facing forward again, his expression has been completely cured of emotion.

"Since you got back to LA."

This is really starting to piss me off. "How about you tell me who you dated between then and now."

"None of them are threatening me."

"*Them*, huh? How many of *them*?" I cross my arms and suck my cheeks between my teeth. Who were these women-plural? What did he see in them? How different were they from me? When they fucked, did he play a character? Did they make stories together? Would they act like a big baby across the front seat of his car?

The one reason I shouldn't act like I'm seething is that I actually am.

"You're asking me for a body count," I say. "Red flags wave both ways."

The satisfaction I get from diverting him doesn't last long. He swallows, then grinds his jaw.

I get out quickly, before he can reach over me and close the door. He beats me around the other side though, opening the back door as if he's going to retrieve the tray, but he doesn't. Instead, he looks as if he wants to punch through the window to get it instead.

"How many are there?" he asks with a tension that's

quadrupled in the time it took me to walk around the car.

It takes me a second to realize he's talking about the notebook-filling ex-boyfriends I created out of nothing in my head.

Yes. I could soothe him with the beginning and end of the list already being written, but he's way out of line.

"I told you, I don't do body counts."

"A lot?" He steps closer to me.

Not close enough to count the little creases in his lips, but close enough to touch them if I wanted. Close enough to run my thumb along his chin to feel the crackling scratch of his day-old beard. I don't know how I keep my hands to myself, but I do. Stealing one kiss at my parents' house is enough for the day.

"Don't worry, Anton. There are enough pages left in this little notebook."

"Is that why you want to get out of the house?"

"What is with you?" Stupid question. I know what's with him. He's a man.

He leans even closer to me, and I think for a moment that maybe, this one time, I should be afraid. But I'm not. I'm hopeful. I'm turned on. I'm so conscious of the shape of the space between us I can visualize the air displacement. But there's no contact. He moved so he could reach into the back seat and retrieve the tray.

"I was going to call you," he says, slamming the back door shut. "Every day, I opened my phone and tapped your name. But… I couldn't." He leads me across the street. "When I left that note, I was so sure I was doing the right thing, the right way. But every time I pulled up your name and had my finger right over that green circle, I wondered if maybe I gave up too fast. If I had stayed with you, I wouldn't have my inheritance, but a lot of things wouldn't have happened." He waves away all the things he's not going to say. "I don't like doubting what I can't change."

"And you say *I'm* exhausting." I punch in the code for my gate. "If you ever need to use the bathroom…"

"Roscoe will be here soon." He hands me the tray.

I put it on the little table under the mail slot. I'm about to close the gate when I stop myself. He and I haven't covered everything.

"About that kiss earlier?"

"Yes?"

"Don't take it personally."

Lightning fast, he's in the front yard, slapping the gate closed, and holding my face still as he pushes me against the fence by the mouth. He kisses me with the confidence I didn't have yesterday, as if he knows I'm going to kiss him back.

Which I do.

And when he bends his body so that the shape of his erection grinds between my legs, I grind back, throwing one leg over his waist so I can feel his hardness against my softness. Everything happening below should be a distraction from the kiss, but our mouths are locked in attention to each other.

Anton sips. He tastes. He understands the difference between lip, tongue, and tooth. He knows how to match the beat of his kiss with the rhythm of his body and hands.

If I'd appreciated that he kissed like this, I would have followed him into a war zone.

Then he pulls away. My foot falls to the ground.

He wipes a bit of moisture from the corner of my mouth and says, "You can take that personally."

CHAPTER 16

ANTON

ONE JOB. I have one job.

Protect Lyric Crowne.

That includes keeping my eyes on her and everything around her. My senses need to be attuned to patterns and changes. She sat in the front seat of my car for three minutes and became the world.

It was the unknown number of ex-boyfriends. For her own safety, I have to know about the men who have touched her, whispered in her ear, made her laugh, rubbed tension from the back of her neck, or fucked her the way she likes.

Remembering how she likes it adds ten pounds to the weight of my balls. My heart speeds up and my jaw clenches thinking of how hard she—

I cannot further entertain the snowball of choices I just made.

It was what it was and now it is what it is.

Win some, lose some.

I'm stronger for it. More in control. Or so I thought.

So, not at all.

Mike lives on a side street off the top of Western Avenue in a U-shaped apartment building that's painted something between bile yellow and shit brown. My mother's house is much nicer, and there's plenty of room for him. But he says when he brings a woman home, a regular apartment is less intimidating. Being good with them means making them comfortable. Letting them know they're safe. Can't argue with success.

Would it work on Lyric? Did any of the exes she wouldn't list live in a carpeted one-bedroom, one-bath with wall-heating and ceiling fixtures with dead bugs under the glass?

I park on the street and walk half a block to his place. Before I even know if he's home, I hear alternating popping and thwacking from the side alley. That's him.

A text comes in. Lyric's new number from Canada's upper reaches. Our messages before today are so old they're gone forever. They ended with her furious, unanswered texts, three and a half years ago. I can only remember a few, in no particular order:

Hey, what do you mean by this note?

Dude.

Are you all right? You seemed kinda sad.

Amy's taking me to get it taken care of. Thought you'd like to know.

Ugh. Cramps. I wish you were here making me a hot compress.

You're freaking me out.

Anton! You can't be this mad. Please. I love you.

We went to your apartment and it's literally empty? You're gone? What is wrong with you? I cannot believe you're such a fucking little bitch.

There were more in between, but that was the progression. Expectation. Mystification. Information.

Longing. Accelerating, justified rage. Then, bitch, period. Even the punctuation was final.

Her text today is one word.

—Hey—

It annoys me. *Hey* isn't a message. *Hey* doesn't have substance. *Hey* doesn't tell me what the fuck you want. *Hey* is what scammers and phishers open with because it invites information by offering none.

So I type a reply that returns what was given.

—hey—

Except I don't send it. I can't. Three letters? She throws the benefit of my protection in my face and texts three letters afterward, now all I send back is three? That leaves me in arrears by one insult.

Why am I so insulted?

Because I kissed her?

Fuck this. I'm not my own psychologist.

The gate's open. Mike's alone with a wooden paddle, smacking a little blue ball against the cinderblock wall that separates his building's property from the next. His brown hair's falling out of its slick-back. He's wearing a shiny black tracksuit with the logo of the Ukrainian National Soccer Team on the back of the jacket and down the legs of the pants. The left sleeve's tucked inside out.

"Hey," he says without slowing down.

"*Pryvit.*" I find another paddle on top of the wall.

"What's the frown about?" He sends the ball my way before I'm ready, but I just get it.

"Nothing."

He hasn't taken his eyes off the ball, but I believe him about my frown.

We don't say another word. I don't have to explain anything. We just hit that little blue ball against the wall. At first, it's friendly. I hit it so it goes to him, and he hits back the same way. Then it's faster.

I stop thinking about the three-letter offense. I don't wonder why I care. It's business. I've been professionally refused by people who thought they didn't need my services before. I've been hit. I've caused damage and been damaged. I've been refused and denied.

Mike raises the level of play without asking. He changes the speed, spins it, then with a smash, the ball flies by me, bounces off an empty bucket, and lands behind a row of garden tools.

I hold up my hands in surrender. I'm done.

"Getting soft." Mike gets a pack of Marlboros from his jacket pocket and pushes one out with his fingernail. "You want one?"

"No thanks." I retrieve the ball. "You should quit."

"Blah-blah." He lights it with a little blue Bic.

"Girls don't like it."

"They love it. Serve."

He plays with the cigarette dangling from his lips. I play with a frown he can see without looking at me.

"Did you sleep?" he asks after a smash.

"Did I call for relief?" I barely get the ball.

When Mike came to my car across her street to pick up Lyric's phone, he offered to get someone fresh on it. I refused. I couldn't give her to someone else.

"Could have."

I send him to the back of the court, where the cars are

parked. He sends a weak one back, then I drop it close to the wall. He runs for it—Mike runs for everything—misses, and smashes himself against the wall. He drops on his back, arm out, cigarette clamped in his lips as he drags on it.

"Did you look at her phone?" I ask.

"Yeah. Someone's going to a lot of trouble for a woman."

"Desperation makes its own trouble." I pick up the cigarette and toss it into a dirt-filled flowerpot with a dozen other butts. He offers me his hand and I help him up. "Those texts had the stink of desperation."

"Man, I hate this shit. I barely know her, and I want to castrate this guy. You must want to nuke the planet."

"Nah. Business."

"Sure." He claps me on the shoulder. "That's why you sat in your car all night."

We head up to his apartment, a one-bedroom in wall-to-wall beige carpet.

"Sorry about the mess," he says, getting beers from the refrigerator. I don't see anything out of place, but I shrug at him as if it's no big deal. "Had this girl over last night. Gorgeous. Wild, but..." He gives a chef's kiss while holding his beer with the same hand. "American women."

No new text from Lyric. Just —*hey*— and my unsent return volley.

I don't ever check my phone this much.

"Sure." I pocket the device, promising myself I won't look at it again. "They say 'hey' the way you like."

I remember another deleted text.

The abortion bothers you that much? You understand I just don't want to right now? I have to try again. One more movie. I can't accept failure after just one try.

She had access to more money. Her parents allowed each

kid to ask for one big thing, and her big ask was still untapped.

There was no second movie. I checked. There was just an increased Instagram presence and more care taken with the posts I consumed ravenously and selfishly, never wondering if I was the reason she never tried again.

"We can put Roscoe and Thomas on her." Mike tosses me a beer bottle. "You need to stay with me on digital."

Mike is right. But there's no way in hell I'm handing her off to anyone else.

"I want to see what's coming in and out of her network." I sit in the leather chair in front of the eighty-five-inch flat screen. "I need the packet sniffer."

"In the closet." He drops into his desk chair. "We need an office. I have nowhere to hang my shirts."

"Is there anything on this?" I wave my hand at the television. "Some football or something?"

"Always." He points the remote at the TV. A football game comes on. Some Italian league. "Why do you look like that?" He taps his keys, not even looking at me.

"Like what?" I reach into my jacket for the notebook.

"Like you give a shit about this match?"

"Stop looking at me and drink your beer." I wait before saying what's on my mind. "We have a name." I toss him the book. "I looked. Nothing actionable. Maybe you can find something."

"Neville Bennett of Wisconsin. I'll see."

My phone buzzes. I grab it. A lonely woman wants to show me her hot pussy if I click the link. I delete it.

—hey—

I don't know why I'm blaming American women. All

people are fucked in the head. They all want to say "hey" instead of anything meaningful.

"You know why I liked her?" I say.

"No?"

"Because she wanted more. Always more." I hold up the phone so he can see the dangling *hey*. "And now, this."

"Who are we talking about?"

I shake my head and look at the phone again like an addict.

—hey—

All she has for me is hey? I don't think so. Mike works on the guts of the phone I spent too long trying to get from her. I stare at mine thinking hey, hey, hey-hey-heyheyheywhyheywhy-why-why, why, why.

I got so twisted around about the length and depth of what she texted that I never thought about why. The horse is looking up the cart's ass. Why? Because no matter what either of us chose, I was going to fail her. I hit Send.

—hey—

—ok—

She's down to two letters. Next one's going to be the letter —I— if she wants to take responsibility, —u— if she wants to curse me, —c— if she wants to open my eyes to something she won't describe. Maybe then it'll be punctuation. A period if she's angry. A comma if she needs me to wait a minute. A whole emoji if her feelings are complex.

Running dots. The curse of technology. She's thinking something, but I have to wait to find out what.

As all this is zipping into and out of consideration, I type something, anything to avoid reaching a conclusion.

—I'm coming to check your network,
have your wifi password ready—

Dots stop. A player on the TV scores a goal. Dots again as he takes a victory run down the field. My body sinks into the recliner. I'm exhausted.

—password123—

—don't put it in a text and I know it's not this—

"Okay, so here's what we got," Mike mumbles from the other side of the universe. "Get off your ass and come here."

"Just tell me."

A small object impacts my head and spins away. A pencil. A planner lands on my chest. I catch a Bic lighter. I'm being attacked from the air.

"Jesus."

"Get up."

I drag myself off the recliner, grab the extra office chair, and sit behind Mike to see his screens. He points at a section of script.

"It's hacked as fuck, but the way it's done, it's like she hacked herself. Call's coming from inside the house. See this?" He points at a line of code. "Pegasus."

—You should have told me all
that stuff about why you had to leave—

I had reasons. Good reasons and every one of them was

about protecting her. Now I'm getting attacked—stabbed in seventy different places.

"The zero-click exploit?" I ask.

"Your guess is as good as mine. I guess yes."

My return text has to be sharp enough to open her smug satisfaction and venomous enough to poison the blame behind it. She texts before I figure out where to start.

*—But I guess that's how we
find out we were never good
for each other—*

I toss the phone on the couch and stand. "Which closet?"

He looks up from his screen. "The sniffer? Hall. Top shelf."

The closet is stuffed with boxes. The content and shipping labels are all in Ukrainian.

"Hey." He leans back in his chair to see me through the doorway.

"What?" I snap, because I don't want to hear that word again today.

"I know you guys have a history."

"This closet is like Jenga." I slide out a box. Wrong one. I put it aside.

"Don't fuck her."

"What?" I say again, but angrier. I'm deeply offended at the intrusion into what I fear I'll do.

"You heard me."

"That's the problem." Moving another wrong box reveals the correct one. I reach for it.

"If you're going to protect her, your eyes need to be off her and on the situation."

"Keep your eyes on the code." I crack the tape and open the flaps.

"We're, like, this close to getting this and bam, being exactly what we want to be. Do not let your dick get in the way. That's all."

"She's the principal. That's the end of it." There are three sniffers—serial, ethernet, and SPI—each half-a-sandwich sized and black-cased. Perfect. "I'm minding her because she knows me and I know how she is." I tuck the cardboard box under my arm and toss back the other boxes. "It's easier that way."

He makes a *hmph* sound and tips his chair away from the door frame as if he's satisfied.

"Do you have a clean laptop?"

He grabs a slim gray machine from a shelf behind him and hands it over. "Take care of yourself, all right?"

"Sure."

I'm glad to see I've placated him, because I'm not so sure I'm going to be able to keep my hands off her.

By the time I park on her block, I'm sure I'm in control. One hundred percent. I wave to Roscoe in his minivan. He rolls down the window so I can see his gray beard and shaggy hair in all their glory.

"Anything?" I ask.

"Quiet."

"All right. I have it from here."

He waves and drives off. I ring her bell.

I'm going to enter her house, tap her signal, and keep at least six feet away at all times.

I ring her bell again, and when she doesn't respond, I peek between the fence slats. Her little car is in the driveway.

The breeze flicks a few brown leaves against the tires, where little slopes have built up over time.

The car is here, and those little piles of leaves would be there if she was home.

Somewhere out of sight, there's a slap and clap of a gate closing in the wind. It's not on this block. I look through the slats again, between the car and the house, a slit of backyard and the slap and clap of her back gate swinging in the wind.

She's not here.

Fury rises like gasoline soaking a rag. It's too soon to be this angry, but it's not too soon to be this worried. She could have slipped out to pick up milk, or he could have her. The first option is dangerous but forgivable. The second is critical, and I'll never forgive myself.

This job was a mistake. Personal security isn't my specialty, but I don't want anyone else this close to her. I can't fail her. I won't.

—I'm here—

The jumble of questions, scenarios, and worries flow out of me, but the gasoline stench of anger stays. Three dots roll while I look at the oak bough hanging near the edge of her roof. That's not going to work.

—where?—

Is this him, texting as if he was her, while she lies on the floor, bound and gagged? I'm not giving any specifics until I know who I'm talking to.

—where you're supposed to be—

I pace the width of the property, noticing things I should

have taken into account already. The fence has a design that allows it all to be breached once a loose slat is wiggled out, the driveway gate can be easily rendered useless once someone's inside, and this entire place is a security disaster.

—oh—
—well, I didn't think you'd
be back for awhile sooo—

She adds an emoji of a woman shrugging. It's her, and she's not tied up on the floor.

Somehow, all the panic turns into fuel for the anger, and her next line is the spark on the gas-soaked rag inside me.

CHAPTER 17

LYRIC

—oh—
—well, I didn't think you'd be
back for awhile sooo—
—I'm at Ozzie Dots rn—

THE OFFICIAL STORE for the masque is Ozzie Dots, a warehouse in Los Feliz that has the thickest array of outrageous vintage wear outside of eBay. I was looking at the cowboy hats with the masks attached when Anton texted, and now I feel as if I've been caught diving into the pool from the roof when we've explicitly been told not to… except that I'm a grown adult and if Anton wants to babysit me, he's going to have to go where I go.

—where is that?—

—Hillhurst—

I don't know whether to apologize for being where I want to be or tell him to fuck right off. Except that I did sneak out the back and meet Kelly around the corner. That's consciousness of guilt, right there.

—I'll be back in 30-40min—

He doesn't answer. No three dots. No nothing. The status under my text says *Delivered.* I put the Android in my pocket.

"So," Kelly says, flicking through the rack. The place smells like wet concrete. Everything they sell is washed when they get it, but it can hang around the cellar for God knows how long. You have to shake the clothes before you buy a spider's nest in the armhole of your new/old shirt. "Anton." She draws out the o, waggling her eyebrows.

"What about him?" I hold up a tan leather vest with a big silver zipper pull at the bottom of the V-neck. "This is kind of cowgirl."

"You had a thing and…" She shrugs, clicking through the hangers without really looking. "Is it still on?"

"Nope."

"So, New York, that was what, three years?"

"And change."

"You past it?" she asks coyly. "Or no?"

I know what this is about. I've known since the moment she laid eyes on him. She thinks she's asking for permission to shake her ass in his direction, but what she's really doing is injecting a syringe full of Anton right into my veins. My cheeks get hot and my heart beats a little faster. I usually have more antibodies against jealousy.

"I'm not sure what you're asking, Kell." I put the vest away, then grab it back. I can't tell the difference between what I like and don't like. How am I supposed to know what to tell her? No, you're not allowed to call him because I have a feeling left with his name on it. Go out with him and I'll scratch your eyes out?

"I think these?" Kelly holds up a pair of pink cowboy boots.

"Please don't mix your pinks."

Agreeing, she puts them down. "So, what do you think, Lyr?"

She doesn't have anything in her hand. I could pretend I forgot who we were talking about. One more line of dialog so I don't have to imagine his hands on her, his smile for her, his eyes on her body the way they used to be on mine.

"You're asking her about that guy?" Jake says, strolling over from the menswear side with a finger-hook full of cowboy shirts.

Kelly invites Jake around all the time, insisting he's a friend and it's cool, and he always comes as if one day, she's going to sleep with him.

"She's deflecting." Kelly pouts.

"I have reasons." I flick and click through outfits without really seeing them.

"Such as?" Kelly feigns casual, clicking hangers on the other side of the circular rack.

"I talked to my brother," Jake says. "About your Instagram problem."

"The white hat hacker?"

"Yeah. He says to look at that security guy."

"You might be right." I flick faster. Jake just stands there, waiting for me to explain, but my comments about Anton are for Kelly. "Which only supports the point I'm deflecting. He's not your type. Reasons."

"Spill it," Kelly says sternly. "Or I'm going to humiliate myself and ask him out."

"Okay. You asked for it." I hold up a polka dot shirt and shove it back. "Back east, I hired a guy I knew at Tisch to be UPM. Really organized. Knew the business. Grew up in the city."

"Wait." Kelly stops shopping for a second. "What?"

"Unit production manager," I say. She nods and works her way around the rack. "Coordinates everything. Manages the budget. It's a big job. He was also a pretty good director at school. He just didn't have the rich parents so he couldn't make his own movie, which no one did except me. Is what it is. Anyway, so it's fine, until we start shooting. He goes rogue. He starts calling me princess. Undercutting me. Like this one time he changes the schedule because it quote-unquote, makes more sense. When I tell him to change it back to what I want—because I want fresh actors in the morning and tired actors for the night scene—he tells me I'm being emotional."

"Fuck that guy," Kelly says.

"Were you though?" Jake asks. "Emotional?"

"Are we getting to the Anton part?" Kelly asks before I can tell Jake to fuck himself.

"Yeah. So. I tell my boyfriend what's going on. Just sharing, you know? And he finds my UPM on set and says to him—which, so you know, I didn't find out until we wrapped —Anton tells him sixty-two percent of the budget is a Russian mob investment. Bratva. Friends of his. And they're going to look over the books when we wrap, so he oughta keep his head down and make sure it all lines up. And if anything's a penny off, he shouldn't go above the third floor of any building alone."

Jake scoffs. "He believed that?"

"Pushed against a window on the tenth floor?" I shrug. "I

guess. Maybe if the window had been closed, he wouldn't have? I dunno."

Telling Kelly this story is my way of putting scary red flags between her and Anton. It's supposed to make her back away from him. But when I look up from the rack, her wide eyes and parted lips tell me I made a mistake.

"What a dick," Jake says.

"Sexy dick," Kelly adds.

"See?" Jake looks from one of us to the other. "You girls always say you want a nice guy, but you don't."

"Don't try to understand it." Kelly goes to the next rack over and says to me, "Girls are going as saloon sluts or, like, Calamity Jane style. You'd look awesome in this." She holds up a gold-and-black bustier. "And, like, a ruffly skirt with a slit up the middle."

"I'm just saying." I check out the bustier. "He's a handful."

"Man, I feel sorry for that guy he tried to throw out a window," Jake says. "What was his name?"

"Whatever. I forget. Bart something."

"Winthrop." Jake snaps his fingers and points, clicking his tongue on the back of his teeth.

"How would you know that?" I ask.

Jake turns a slightly pinker shade of beige. "I have the DVD of the movie." He flicks through women's shorts just to keep his hands moving.

"It was never released."

"My dealer got a promotional copy off eBay." Only Jake would have a DVD dealer who finds the most obscure movies ever made. Anywhere in the world. Any language. Jake had it. "I didn't want to tell you because you're so sensitive and weird about it."

"I'm not…" I stop myself because I have been sensitive

and weird about anyone seeing it. But honestly, I do not care what he thinks about my movie. Even if he loves it, I just don't care.

"Can I watch it?" Kelly asks. Normally, I'd distract her or find a reason why she shouldn't. But... I just don't mind either way.

"Ask him." I snap the bustier away from her and head for the fitting room. "It's fine with me."

Kelly chases me with another one in solid black. I take it.

"Don't forget to shake them out first!" she cries. Good advice. Always.

I hurry past the attendant, who has a million questions about my every need and desire, and get behind a closed door.

I've already told Anton that Kelly wants to fuck him, but now I have to seriously bring it up and ask if he's interested back. It's that or give the impression that I'm not over him, which I am. Hundred percent. Never looked back.

Unless he'd say he was interested. Then my mind's gonna launch itself back into the exact moment I found that note.

This is unbearable.

I am weak without you.

I am useless with you.

I can casually ask him if he thinks Kelly's cute, and I can say it like... I think she's cute too, so he doesn't feel weird about agreeing?

I can just flat-out say Kelly's going to call. Heads-up! Incoming!

Or I can tell the truth.

Nope.

The phone buzzes in my pocket.

The text can wait. I shake out the black and gold corset,

get visual confirmation that there are no spiders in the seams, and try it on over my rib tank. Turning in front of the mirror, I tuck and adjust until I have a realistic amount of cleavage. I guess I look all right, but all I can think about is that text.

Flinching, I check the preview.

—Where are you?—

He just asked me that in the last text. It's right above, so why is he asking again? There's only one Ozzie Dots on Hillhurst and he's just going to have to wait until I get back to hear me tell him how I gave the shaggy-haired guy I'm assuming is Roscoe the slip.

My reply is half-tapped when I hear his voice, but more stern than I ever experienced when I was with him.

"Where?" he asks. Kelly answers, but I can't discern the words and they must not be definitive enough, because he barks back at her, "Which one?"

"Listen, buddy."

Buddy? That has to be Jake puffing out his chest. We need to find him a girlfriend or something. But not today.

"You let her in there alone?"

I run out in my corset and jeans to find Jake with his back to me and his arms across the entrance to the hall. He doesn't stand a chance against Anton, who's eye to eye with him, pointing over Jake's shoulder at the row of dressing room doors.

"I'm right here," I say. "Yes, alone."

They both turn their attention to me, but while Jake has a hangdog look, Anton is a wolf. He'll rip whoever's in his way to absolute shreds to get to me, and when he does... well, he'll shred me too. My chest heaves as his gaze tears the corset into satin scraps.

I guess I'm going to have to buy it now.

"I told you," Anton says, "to stay home."

"You said so many words. Words, words, words."

He pushes past Jake and stops two feet from me. I put my hands on my hips and stick out my chest. The effort to not look down reveals itself in the tightness of his shoulders.

"You heard every one of them."

"Honestly, Anton, I didn't give it that much thought, but—"

"Is he bothering you?" Jake says from down the hall.

"I'm fine," I call to Jake without breaking Anton's feral gaze. His metabolism is running on a cocktail of adrenaline and testosterone right now. I should be scared of him, but I'm not. I'm turned on. More firmly and softly, I repeat, "I'm fine."

"You're not doing this again, Lyric."

"Not doing what? Living? Breathing?"

Anton comes a step closer. I don't break my gaze, but it's hard not to look at his body—the same one I held so many times, but bigger, harder, stronger.

"I told you," he says. "You go where I say, when I say."

Anton is not a stranger to me. If someone asked about him, I'd admit to knowing him. But he's never spoken to me with this combination of confidence and force. Add in the fact that I'm sure he'd never hurt me, and it's a recipe for my solid parts melting into a warm puddle of lust.

"Or what?"

"Don't test me."

"You turned into a complete asshole."

"I'm following you home."

He steps out of the way. Jake and Kelly stand at the end of the hall. Jake is closer, tilted forward as if he was thinking of jumping in to protect me, then—out of cowardice or common sense—decided against it.

I roll my eyes at Kelly, then address Anton. "I should change. Do you need to tell me to go in the dressing room now or can I self-direct this one?"

"Go ahead." He says it like a commander allowing a soldier to stop marching long enough to tie his shoe. Or a high school science teacher letting a kid run out to pee. As if he doesn't like the responsibility of issuing hall passes, but it's his job so he might as well get on with it.

When there's a closed door between Anton and me, I take a second to breathe.

God damn, he's terrible, and I want him terribly.

CHAPTER 18

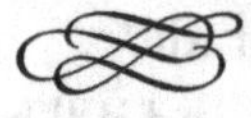

LYRIC

As promised, his Range Rover follows me the entire way—even through rush-hour traffic on Sunset. Though you can never find a spot on my block, he pulls in two doors from my house. Incredible parking karma. First rate.

Stopping in my driveway, I'm confronted with my life all over again. The raping text isn't on the Android, but now that I'm home and not running around distracting myself, I wonder if—or when—one's going to show up. Nothing's changed. I have no social accounts, and somebody wants to hurt me.

Everything was fine, but suddenly it's as though, in the past twenty-four hours, I've been racking up a fear debt and the bill has just come due.

I don't know how to gauge my fear. Should I be more scared? Less?

Anton knows. I'll ask him the exact level of terror I should feel then subtract ten percent.

I gasp when my peripheral vision catches someone next

to my open window, and exhale in relief right after. It's just a wall of turtleneck. I didn't even register him getting out.

"Christ," I say. "You scared me."

He leans his elbows on the door. "You don't have to be afraid."

"Funny you should say that, because I haven't had a bodyguard since twelfth grade."

"Just do what I tell you and it'll be fine."

Leaning my head back, I close my eyes and sigh. "I'm not used to being constrained."

"Hey." His voice is tender and closer, as if he's leaning into the car. I feel him take my face with the crook of his finger under my chin and his thumb over, turning it to him. "Look at me."

I open my eyes. He's taking up the entirety of my vision, making himself the only thing in my world. I'd shoot this tight, with a longer lens, and it wouldn't even hint at how intense his presence is.

"I know I was raised into all this money," I say. "It made me feel invincible. But I have the same body as everyone else. It's got the same ways to be hurt and like… just now? I feel every inch of myself. Like I'm soft and weak everywhere."

"You're going to be all right," he says, letting go of my chin to touch my cheek. He believes it. I should too.

This is unbearable.

I am weak without you.

I am useless with you.

Different time. Different situation. I shouldn't compare the abandonment of the past with the maybes of the future.

"I'm not going to ask you to promise," I say.

"I'm here to be scared for you. It's my job."

"Business. I know."

"Think of it like this. You do what I tell you, and I'm less worried. Do it for me."

He drops his hand and taps the hood before he steps back. The sun falls below the edge of the port-a-cochère, throwing a glare into my sight and casting his face in shadow. I'm supposed to open the door now.

"I don't think I can get out of the car."

"If I stand here any longer, I'm going to have to ask for your license and registration."

"Oh, like Officer Everhard?"

The outline of his face changes when he smiles. "Mrs. Longbottom, do you know how fast you were going?"

I laugh, remembering the stories we made up together. They were all clichés of power and servitude. The games were a way to lose myself for a little bit, and a way for him to gain himself back from the sedentary intensity of all the coding he was doing.

Can I escape this nagging fear by living in someone else's vulnerability? Yes. I want that, and I want him. But I don't know if he'll play along or how far he'll take it.

"I was rushing home to cook my husband dinner," I say. "But I'm sure I was going the speed limit."

"You were not."

I exhale rattling anticipation and inhale a glowing heat that settles in the bottom of my lungs. Lyric isn't here. Neither is Anton. There is no painful history between us.

"Please, officer, if I get another ticket, Larry's going to be so mad. That's my husband."

"I remember."

"What else do you remember?"

"That Brenda's a dirty little slut." He strokes the skin along the neck of my T-shirt.

"I am."

"Brenda has an OnlyFans account she thinks is secret." I tingle everywhere from the new twist he's adding to the story. "But I know she opens her legs and shows off her pretty cunt."

The way those words are so comfortable in his mouth... I forgot what it does to me. "That's not illegal, officer."

"The speeding is."

"Maybe there's a trade we can make." My voice quivers. "You look like a nice man."

He bends forward at the waist, blocking the sun. "I am not."

I swallow. My lungs feel too small for the size of the breaths I need to take.

Are we doing this? I want to, but internally, I flinch at the thought of him stopping after I've committed.

"I'll do whatever you want," I whisper.

His eyes skate over my body. If he's playing around and wondering when he should stop, he's not showing it. This is Anton in full Officer Everhard mode.

"Open your legs," he commands.

Every nerve ending goes into red alert. My palms sweat. My mouth goes dry.

"Or maybe I should bring you in for trying to whore yourself?"

We're here. This is happening. I can't even breathe.

He stands. His face is above the top of the window. He's a torso with a huge boner right at eye-level. I part my knees. Just doing that sends a fresh wave of heat between my legs.

"Like this?" I say with an innocent lilt.

"For now. When I fuck you, I'll need you to spread them wider."

"Yes, officer. About that ticket?"

He reaches in and opens the door. I put a foot on the ground.

"No," he says. "I didn't tell you to get out."

"Oh, sorry." I pull my foot back in.

"I didn't tell you to apologize."

"I—" My mouth clamps shut. The porch lights flick on. The sun's dropped below the rooflines.

"I didn't tell you to put your leg back into the car either."

Everhard always was impossible to please. Mrs. Longbottom always tried anyway, and always failed.

"This is too hard," I whine.

"Complaining. Another thing I didn't ask for."

"Can't I just suck your johnny-come-lately?"

"Bargaining." He's trying not to laugh and doing a better job than me. I hope I'm not making this an impossible task, but this is funny.

With a deeply childish pout, I face forward, hoping the hot cop with the ticket book fucks this pout right off me.

"Sulking," he says. "That's six times you didn't listen to instructions."

"But there were no instructions." I put my fingers over my mouth. "Oops, is that seven?"

"Get out of the car, Mrs. Longbottom." He roughly guides me aside when I obey, then closes the car door. "Hands on the car."

Slowly, as if I don't want to, I turn around and put my hands on the roof. He puts his hands on my shoulders, patting me down.

"That wasn't so hard, was it?"

"Well, no, I guess."

He runs his hands under my arms, under my jacket, to the

front where he finds his way under my shirt. "Are you armed?" He runs up under my bra.

"Just the two you see." I gasp when he finds my nipples.

"So, you're a wise ass." He steps back, pats my hips, and kicks my feet apart. "Let's see how wise that ass is when it's pink."

"Can you just do it? I have to cook dinner."

"You sure you're not hiding any weapons?"

My clever denials come out as a squeak when he grabs between my legs, rubbing the center seam of my jeans.

"I'm sure."

"You moved twice without being told to." He presses hard, circling with flattened fingers. "You'll get those for free. But the other five will be punished. Apologizing. Complaining. Bargaining. Sulking. Counting. Repeat that."

"Um, I moved twice, those are free…"

"The five punishments."

"Right. Okay. Apologizing, bargaining—"

"In order."

"How about you make it six and skip the 'in order' part? Oh, poopie, I'm bargaining again."

He stops. I look over my shoulder. His head is bowed and his shoulders shake slightly, but he doesn't time out. He straightens with a mask of distant, dour command.

"Stand here." He points at the ground a few feet from the car.

I go there. I look around, same as Mrs. Longbottom would, but I'm also looking for the real Lyric, who's willing to time out to avoid a show for the neighbors. No windows from this angle under the carport overhang.

"This okay?" I ask.

"Take off your clothes."

With a swivel of my hips, I start with my shirt and toss it to him. He plucks it out of the air and tosses it on the car.

"I didn't say 'strip.' I said 'take off your clothes.' Don't forget—this is a business transaction."

Why is that so hot? The play at cold cruelty. The utter lack of emotion or enthusiasm.

And yet… it's not really cold. It's not a lack of anything. It's control. I can feel the heat coming off him. The raw desire. I'm not supposed to want those arms around me again. My nipples shouldn't be hardening against the bra. I try to remember that I hate him. He may be made of muscle now, but when push came to shove, he was weak.

But this is a business transaction, and it's been a long time since I felt a man inside me.

Yes, I decide again. I want what he's offering.

Reaching behind my back, I unhook my bra and slide it down my arms. He takes it and drapes it over his arm, nodding for me to continue. He comes around me as I pull off my shoes, slowly circling while I undo my fly and pull down my jeans and underwear in one move, until I'm naked as a baby, with nothing but the intensity of his stare to clothe me. It's chilly—but that's not why my nipples are hard furls.

I hold out my pants and he takes them.

"Good girl."

He can't be impressed by the fact that I just did a thing any five-year-old can do. And yet, his approbation is a balm on a wound I didn't know I had. A place in me is soothed. A moment ago, I was starving, but now my belly's full because he just fed me a Happy Meal.

Or, actually, he fed Mrs. Longbottom a Happy Meal.

Right. We're doing a thing.

I hold one arm over my breasts and use the other to cover

between my legs.

"Come here." He draws me to the front of the car and turns me to face the windshield. "Bend down. Tits on the hood."

Butterbomb has just enough front to bend onto, but I have to stop.

"Time out." I make a T with my hands.

"Yes?" He holds up his palms to illustrate that he won't touch me until we're not in time out.

"I'm glad I had an abortion, but I'm not in the mood for another."

"Okay."

"So, condoms. Every time."

"Agreed. I have."

"Cool. Time in. Now…"

"Tits on the hood, Brenda." He puts his hands on my hips.

I bend at the waist and press my hard nipples to cold steel.

He kicks my feet apart. "Now, first. Apologizing."

With an open hand, he slaps my ass, and I gasp at the impact. That's surprise. The groaning exhale is something completely different.

"Two." He slaps the other cheek. "Complaining."

My body buckles and blooms like fireworks on the Fourth of July. I have never felt so good about being humiliated.

Before Mrs. Longbottom can answer, he spanks me on the first side, but lower, almost on my thigh. I can barely breathe under the force of my arousal. Then he slides a hand up the inside of my thigh and I'm sure I'll never breathe again.

"If you remember the third"—one finger runs along my

seam, barely touching it—"I'll make you come."

"Sulking?"

Please God, let it be sulking so I can feel his approval, but also, let it be anything else so he can punish me.

"Bargaining." He spanks the other thigh. "And now." He hits that same place again, and it burns so hot it almost scorches away the last bits of doubt. "Sulking." He keeps his hand where he spanked me last, letting the burning sensation linger under his palm. "And last, counting." He gets me there a third time, and it's such a fire ripping through me that I let out a grunt. "Are you wet?"

"Yes, officer."

He slides his fingers between my cheeks and down, pushing two inside me. I shudder and groan, cheek to the car.

"Does your husband know what a slut you are?"

"I'm not a slut, officer."

"You sure?" Two fingers circle my clit.

"Yes."

"A slut would come for me even if I tell her not to." Side to side now, my nub is tight with fluid, wildly sensitive to his touch. "A good girl only does what she's told."

"I'm a good girl."

"Prove it." He flicks my clit faster and faster.

I think of my feet on the gravel. The possibility of Larry getting home and catching me here. But the pressure between my legs grows bigger than my body and hotter than summer beach sand.

"God!" I spit. My mind is utterly clear. Maybe there's a cricket bouncing around in there.

All I want is him, leaning over me to kiss my neck before he whispers in my ear, "I didn't tell you to pray."

He didn't. Is that another spank? I hope so. I want more, but Mrs. Longbottom also wants to be good for him. To do the deal, but also to bathe in his approval.

He waits for me to answer him. A part of me knows he's looking for a sharp retort or a pearl-clutching joke, but I can't say a thing. My eyes meet his in the half-dark, and he understands. Thank God because I have no idea what would come out of my mouth.

"Time to pray." He backs up.

I stand and turn. He takes his jacket off and lays it on the ground in front of him.

"On your knees." He undoes his belt.

I kneel on the jacket. His cock is out, and what was a throb between my legs turns into a pulsing need. I hold myself up against his hard thighs, face to face with his open jeans.

"Take it out."

Reaching for the rigid heat beneath that last layer of fabric, I am a powerless housewife letting a man in authority use me. I release his cock, inhaling its wonderful musk. I hold it and look up at his shadow against the moonlit sky.

"Open your dirty mouth." He takes me by the back of the head.

I tell myself I don't want to, knowing I do, so when I take him against my tongue, I can almost believe I'm being defiled. I suck him, surrendering to the fantasy that when he pulls me back and forth by the hair, he's degrading my every pretension to status I'm trying to maintain. Stroke by stroke, he's the one stripping it away. Not me.

But I know him. He's going to make sure I don't want to time out. I need to get in front of that.

"But, Officer Everhard, Larry will be home soon, and it

takes me forever to… you know… with my um… mouth?"

He knows for a fact that's not a real Brenda problem, so he presses my mouth open and shoves himself in. I open my throat for him. He keeps it there for a moment, then pulls out slowly before going back in, then out.

"I own you," he says, holding himself deep. "No one else. This mouth is only mine." He pulls out. I have spit dripping down my chin. "Tell me whose mouth this is."

"Yours, officer."

He takes me by the bicep and pulls me up gently. "Are you cold?"

"I'm fine."

"Good." He reaches into his back pocket and takes out a condom. "I'm going to fuck you now."

He pushes me against the car. I wrap my legs around him, aligning his cock where I want it.

"Oh, not again."

"Don't 'oh, not again,' me." Looking me in the eyes, he gets the rubber on. "Your filthy little cunt wants it. Say it."

"My cunt wants it."

He pushes inside me, hard and deep, and I'm already so close I nearly burst right there, arching into him.

"You come when I say." He pounds me with hard, methodical precision. "This cunt is mine."

"I'm so close."

"Whose cunt am I fucking?"

"Mrs. Long—" The rest of the word turns into a long groan.

"Look at me." When I open my eyes, he stares into them, fucking me in short strokes that push me closer and closer to the edge. "What if I couldn't keep away from you?"

He grinds into me, pushing to the root, my back against

the car door.

"I won't speed… any… more."

"No matter how fast you go, I'll—"

"How fast?"

He reads my mind and speeds up. I wrap my arms around him as he buries his face in my neck.

"Do you hear me? I'm not staying away. Not when you sleep. Or eat. Or go out. I'm there."

"Will you come to my house and take me away from Larry?" It's hard to stay in character when my whole body feels like a balloon being inflated.

"I'll murder him and burn down your entire street." He pauses to catch his breath. "I'll break the world to have you."

A little voice in my head suggests that maybe Anton's character is slipping, but it's drowned out by the thinning membrane between me and the orgasm as it gets wider, and wider, until it's almost too big to contain.

"I'm going to—"

"Yes. Now."

With that, he starts to come, and his loss of control puts me over the edge, naked and writhing against him. The balloon bursts. I claw at the back of his sweater, and he pushes his fingers into my skin with a groan. We come together, the way we used to.

"Good girl," he says, pressing his lips against my jaw.

I let out a sigh of contentment. He pulls back a little to look me in the face.

That's all it takes to break the spell. I can't tell if this man is pretending to be a cop with a ticket book or my ex-boyfriend from New York, and it doesn't matter.

Larry's wife is gone. I'm Lyric, and I already know I'm a good girl.

CHAPTER 19

ANTON

As I realized who I was, what I was doing, why I shouldn't, how I had no choice, and it all went back to normal, I asked myself—was normal always this wrong? Did it ever feel this right?

I grabbed her clothes and carried her inside, put her gently on the floor, told her I'd be right back, then walked right out to my car.

The back door of the car automatically resists me slamming it shut, slowing it with a whisper of hydraulics. Going too fast, pushing too hard—things get damaged that way. People get hurt.

She could get hurt.

I am filled with a blank, wordless terror.

How many times will someone get hurt because I don't think clearly? Mike lost his arm because of me. I swore I'd never do anything like that again, and now here I am, doing the same thing, like a fool, thinking I can act outside the rules without consequences.

Next time I'm tempted to fuck her, I'm going to take a

breath. Count to ten. Realize how fucked up this is. How much I don't want to look Ted Crowne in the face and tell him that I went too fast and pushed too hard when I should have been watching out for his daughter.

In the end, I have to live with myself, and if she's hurt in any way, I won't be able to.

With the box and laptop under my arm for the second time, I cross the street. This time, she's waiting by the open gate in sexless sweatpants and clogs. She looks as fuckable as she ever did.

Officer Everhard needs to go back to the donut shop of memory, forever.

"I need your wifi password." I come through the gate.

She locks it, falling behind me as I go up the driveway. I don't look back at her. Without breaking my stride, I pick my jacket up from the ground.

"Can't you hack that or something?"

"I could brute force it," I say from her porch, finally turning as she climbs the steps.

She meets me by the door. "Don't threaten a girl with a good time."

Punching in the code, she lets me into her house.

It's pristine old school Hollywood. Dark wood floors and white walls. Original art. Fresh flowers. But the furniture is a riot of color. Hot pink. Lime green. Lacquered cerulean. The photos of family and friends are stacked three deep on the mantel with frames that match the furniture.

"What?" she asks at the bottom of the stairs when I take in her décor for too long. "Too much for you?" She seems sincerely, if inadvertently, concerned.

"I expected more pictures of you on the walls."

"I have a couple a friend took in the hallway upstairs."

Is she inviting me?

I could. But I won't.

"Where's the modem?" I ask, laying the sniffers and laptop on the dining room table.

"In the hall closet." She points. "The password is taped to the router. Have fun in there. I'm getting in the shower."

She heads upstairs.

I have it under control. I feel the same as I did yesterday. She's not who I remember. She's gone from a creative force to a flattened version of herself. This is not a woman I can feel anything for.

The pipes hiss. She's in the shower.

At her place on Thompson, the pipes would bang loudly enough to shake the walls. Her poster for The Lobster fell. I put it back, went into the bathroom to tell her I'd get an anchor bolt and rehang it. But she was talking to herself, playing a line of dialog over and over, testing it for weakness like a guy kicking the tires on a used car.

"Shower inspection!" I'd said, snapping back the curtain. She stood, soaped, open-mouthed, shocked, then pleased. "Ma'am, this shower is not up to code."

"But sir…"

I plug in the ethernet sniffer to the modem cable then to the laptop and wait for it to connect, remembering how I stripped down while reciting made up zoning restrictions on the wetness level. Then I fucked her so hard the poster fell again.

The photos on the mantel of her house in West Hollywood are not Instagram-ready. They're unfiltered and of-a-moment. Her and her brother Dante at an amusement park. Her parents and one of the brothers in a backward baseball cap at Jules Verne, Paris stretching out beneath them. An ancient woman who must be her grandmother holding a baby. Profile of Lyric at about five or six being booped by a black cat. It's a visual collage of a happy, uneventful life.

It's easy to see what's there. Harder to notice what's not.

College in New York.

Directing a full-length feature.

Me.

As far as she's concerned, I left her, pregnant and alone, with a note about my own, pathetic frailties. I haven't earned a place here. She's right to erase me.

This is not a good use of time. I have to get the scan going and figure out what's coming into her house and going out. I distract myself setting it up, and by the time I'm done, she's down the stairs in bare feet, loose jeans, and a hoodie.

"Hey," she says, going into the kitchen area. "What did you find?"

"Nothing yet." I stand, watching her over the bar as she bends to reach the back of a shelf.

"Technology so advanced, it takes forever."

"It's not that simple."

I expect her to ask for an explanation. Instead she asks a question. "Coke or Sprite?"

The light from the refrigerator makes her skin glow. The huge metal zipper ring on her hoodie swings when she bends, taunting me. It would be nothing to pull it down a few inches, expose a little more soft, glowing skin.

"Water." I sit down again. "This is a nice house."

"Thanks. Oh, I have Fresca too."

"What is that? Apple?"

"Grapefruit, I think? Liang likes it." She holds up the can. It looks inoffensive enough, and I like grapefruit.

"I'll try it."

She puts the Fresca and a Coke on the counter and stretches for the cabinet. The hoodie rises a few inches above the edge of her waistband, exposing another patch of soft, secret skin.

Didn't I just fuck her twenty minutes ago? What's going on with me?

"You a glass-and-ice guy or a right-outta-the-can guy?"

Does she not remember, or has everything changed?

"Glass." I stare at the laptop, punching in the settings to catch all the incoming and outgoing signal.

"I'm a buy-the-can but drink-from-a-glass person. The metal can keeps it extra cold and then with the ice..." She cracks open the cans. "It's as close to fountain as you can get." She gets the bucket of ice from the freezer and drops the half-moons into the glasses. "And honestly, there's nothing like a 7-Eleven big gulp full of Diet Coke with a ton of crushed ice."

I try to keep my mind on my work as she fixes the drinks and speaks about absolutely nothing, but she threw the hoodie on over her bare skin, and all I can think about is how I was too impatient to give her breasts the attention they deserved.

"I was thinking of getting a soda fountain thingie and crushed ice, but I can just go out and get it. Do you want lemon in yours?"

"No."

"Yeah, that makes no sense in a Fresca. Duh. I'm a no-lemon girl myself." She chucks the cans in the recycling.

"You surprise me."

"Because I don't take a lemon in my soda?"

"Because you're this nervous."

"I'm not. Do you want a straw?"

"No, thank you."

"Me too, I—" She stops herself short. Shrugs. Takes a sip. The way she stopped herself as if she realized that she's babbling through nerves is as much of an admission as I'm going to get from her. "Whatever."

She brings the drinks around to the dining room table and stands above me, condensation dripping into the seams between her fingers and the glass.

"I'm working for your father," I say. "And now that part of my job is you."

She hands me my glass. "You're sitting here like it's your whole job."

"I shouldn't have touched you."

"You didn't. Officer Everhard did."

"I'm not playing games, Lyric."

"Fine. Look, have you heard of Nelson Fried?" She sits in the chair diagonal from me. "The congressman-slash-actor-slash-wingnut?"

"I've been living in another country up until a month ago."

"Come on. Moustache?" She puts her finger over her lip. "Eyebrows?" A spread hand goes over her eye. "Never met a book he didn't want to ban? Bangs things when he talks?" She puts her fist to the table as if she's pounding it.

"Actually, yes. My father associated with him, I think."

"Yeah, well, he and my father were not buddies, let's just say that. Whatever. I went to high school with his daughter. She had a driver and a bodyguard and the whole nine yards. Let me tell you, Nellie was fun as fuck. This one time—it was before the family moved to DC, obv—I was at Dougie Corn's wrap party after *Dear Evan Hansen,* and it was a rager. If he hadn't hired security, someone would have peed on the Monet… anyway… Nellie got lit up like the Vegas Strip, which—her dad, being into performative piety and all— should have gotten her grounded for life. But her bodyguard, I think his first name was like a last name… like Smith or Jones or something… he got her home and never said a word about it."

"Is there a point?"

There's always a point. How could I forget her stories with the point written in Sharpie and slipped under the door?

"She wasn't careful, but her bodyguard? He had secrets. Tons of them. He said nothing. He just zipped it. That was his job."

The sniffer beeps to let me know it's finally online. A series of connections and protocols rolls up on the laptop screen.

"My job isn't to 'zip it.' My job is to protect you. I can't do that if I'm fucking you."

"Sure, you can. But I'll tell you what. Let's make it easy on you." There's a smile in her voice, even if I can't see it because I'm looking at the screen. "You can stay outside, in your car, staring at my door and wishing I'd come out and bring you a glass of Fresca. And when I go out to a party, you can—"

"No parties."

She knows that, so I don't remind her again, because looking at the packets as they roll up, there's something wrong here. Too many protocol adjustments and an anonymous pipe that shouldn't be there.

"Yeah, parties." She leans closer to look at the screen with me.

I stop the scroll. Copy a line. Screencap just to be sure.

"Listen!" I didn't decide to shout, but my demand echoes off the walls and she flinches. I've never seen Lyric Crowne flinch. I don't like it. I want to punch the guy who made her afraid. "Just…" I have to breathe before I remember what I wanted to ask her. "You have just the one modem?"

"It's a small house, so… yeah?" She shrugs and stands.

"No. Listen, I need to get Mike in here. He has to see this."

"Okay." She walks to the living room area and throws herself on the couch where I can't see her.

"He's going to bring equipment."

"Fine, I guess."

"Lyric. You've been compromised a long time."

"Fix it and let me know."

The TV flashes on. We should have talked about what happened, but I'm shut out, and I have to call Mike right now, before this gets any worse.

One thing is for sure, I'm not leaving this house if she's in it, and she's not going anywhere without me.

CHAPTER 20

LYRIC

"Pack a bag."

I'm trying on big, clunky shoes. Terry, my old shopper from Bendel's, holds up the Dior tote I carried around my first semester at NYU—before I realized hauling my books in a four-thousand-dollar bag wasn't making me any friends.

"Lyric," Terry says in a man's voice.

Ah. I'm dreaming. Okay.

"You need to get up and pack."

Anton. I fell asleep on the couch to the chatter of *Big Brother* season seven and Anton and Mike saying shit I couldn't understand. They went in and out with stuff for hours.

"Excuse me?" I rub the goop out of my eyes.

"Please." He's a fuzzy black turtleneck against the white ceiling. "Get some things together."

"Why?" Blinking, I get up on my elbows and look around.

Mike, Anton's half-brother, is at a bank of monitors and boxes on my dining room table. He looks like he's managing a space mission at NASA.

"Good morning," he says when he sees me looking over the back of the couch at him.

"Morning. You can make coffee if you want."

"Tha—"

"Someone's in here," Anton interrupts. "In the house."

"What?" I'm awake now.

"Not…" He holds up his hands and takes a breath. "Not physically. Someone's using your signal to watch you."

"My internet? Like what I click?"

"Maybe. Can you please…?"

"Maybe? What's the alternative?"

"Buttons," he says softly. That's my nickname, and I'm sucked back in time, hearing it from his lips. Part of me wants to melt into a puddle of contentment. The rest wants to punch him in that time-traveling mouth.

"You can't call me that anymore."

"Pack. Up," he demands without acknowledging the boundary he just leapt across. "You're not safe here."

I look around my house. Everything I placed here is mine. It makes me feel as safe as he thinks I'm not.

Anton's not kidding. He has dark circles under his eyes. Drawn cheeks. He hasn't slept.

I should take him seriously.

"Okay." I throw off the blanket. "Okay."

He nods and goes back to the equipment. I make a mental list at the top of the stairs but stop when I hear him on the phone.

"Bring Peter. We need to sweep down to the studs."

"You packed enough for a month," Anton says, slamming the back of the Range Rover. Frustratingly, it won't let him slam, slowing itself like a nanny telling the kids to wait until she's finished cutting their carrot sticks.

He unlocks the car and opens the passenger side door.

"Well, how long is it going to be?" A maple leaf flies into my hair. I pull it out.

"Get in."

"Don't worry about it, Lyric," I say in a fake deep voice. "Everything is going to be okay. We have it under—" He slaps the door closed. When he gets in, I finish. "We have it under control."

"We have it under control," he repeats. "You'll be home soon."

"When?"

"When it's safe."

"Where are you taking me?"

"You have two choices. One, your parents' house."

"No. They're going to treat me like some damsel in distress and I'm not."

"Two, then. I can take you where I live."

"Oh, fucking great."

"There's a guest house in the back. It's all yours."

"Fine. I give up. Whatever."

"Believe me, I'm motivated to get you out. The sooner this stops, the sooner I can get on with my life instead of fucking with all this past-life shit."

"That can be over like this." I snap my fingers and leave the middle one straight up.

He nods, confirming he sees it, but that's all I get out of him. He turns on the car.

"So, you don't think you're bringing me to your house and, like, trapping me, do you?"

"You won't be trapped. And I don't live in my own house."

"Okay?"

He pauses. Checks his side mirror. Adjusts his ass in the seat. "I live in my mother's house."

"Great." I laugh. "I'll finally get to meet her."

"This isn't a social call." He whips the car around into a K-turn, pulling right up to my driveway gate.

"Fuck." I rub my face. This sucks. Everything about it sucks. I did want to meet his mother, but now we're not even together and this is one hundred percent not a social call. "You know what? It's fine. For the best. Can we not tell Dad, actually?"

"Tell him what?"

"Whatever. That you saw some... code? I don't know. What did you see?"

"Things that shouldn't be there."

"Fantastic. Yeah, you can't tell him that. He's going to get me a police escort to take a shit and my mother's going to die of worry. Forget it. Don't say anything."

"I'm not sure I can do that." He throws his arm behind my seat to look behind him when he backs up, cutting the wheel confidently. If I lean forward enough, I could just about kiss that scruffy jaw. Bury the entire bottom half of my face in that spot where his neck meets the hard angle of his face—if I wanted to, which I don't, even if I do.

"You can." I hold a finger up to him because what I'm saying is absolutely correct. "You totally can." My phone rings. It's Kevin from Meta. "You start by shutting up whenever you're tempted to say anything to them."

Anton isn't looking at me. He's looking at my driveway gate.

"Give me a second." He gets out without further explanation.

I shrug and answer my phone. "Hey, Kev. You're on speaker."

"Hi, Lyric, just calling on a recorded line. This call may be—"

"Whatever, Kev, you don't have to—"

But he goes on his spiel anyway. Meanwhile, Anton's standing in front of my gate—a solid wall of wood—and taking a picture of it.

"Got that?" Kevin says.

"Yes."

Anton turns away from the gate and walks back to the car. My eyes follow him. They have no choice. The way he moves is like a rock-solid agreement between his body and the area it occupies. Space folds around him, and he moves through it as if he owns it.

The driver's door snaps open.

Right. I'm here. Kevin's talking. "Our head of security has a possible solution to your problem. Would you like to come in to discuss?"

"Yes," Anton says, pulling down the block.

"That's... um..." Saying he's my ex isn't going to help anyone, so I dig his actual title from the back of the closet. Anton stops at a light, opens his mouth to answer, but I find what I'm looking for before he makes a sound. "He's digital security for Crowne Industries."

Kev pauses, then puts the customer service voice back on. "Great! Will he be joining us?"

"Yes," Anton says, turning west on Sunset.

"You heard the man."

"Sure did."

We make arrangements and I hang up.

I try to make stupid conversation, but Anton's distracted. He's all grunts and hmms. I sigh and watch the city whip by.

North of Sunset, the estates are either behind hedges too thick for a machete, or deceptively, daringly open. Which am I getting?

"I forgot all about my account being shut down," I say pensively. "It seemed like the worst thing in the world. But it wasn't."

"No?"

"Getting yanked out of my house is."

"It's going to be all right." At a stop sign, he looks at me, then squeezes my hand. "We have it under control."

"It doesn't seem like it."

He takes away his hand and turns onto a dead-end street.

"We do. Trust me." He turns into the driveway of my new home for the foreseeable future.

CHAPTER 21

ANTON

Lyric deserves my attention, but I can't give it to her. I'm convinced she saw what I saw on her gate and she's so terrified she's babbling, but when she tells me the worst thing about all this and it's not someone jerking off onto her house, leaving a trail of translucent spooge, I snap out of it.

"Trust me," I say, creating a lie of omission. If she didn't see it, she doesn't need to know about it.

Vlad greets us. I introduce Lyric and let him take care of the bags.

"Come," I say to her, guiding her around the side of the house to the back.

What if this doesn't work? If she's threatened again, where will I move her? What if something happens to her while she's here?

"You look really uncomfortable," she says.

There's no way I'm addressing what she thinks she's seeing. "My mother's back here."

"I promise not to say anything really dumb."

"I'm not worried about that." I open the gate to the backyard before she can ask what I'm worried about and I have to make up something.

Lyric hangs back as Mom runs to me… robe flowing behind her, holding down her wide-brim hat. She loses a slipper, and when she bends to aim her foot back into it, her sunglasses fall off. By the time we reach her, she's properly shod and clutching the glasses in one outstretched arm.

"Anton!" She's hugging me before I even say hello. She unwraps herself.

"Mom, how are you?" I kiss her cheek. We both speak Ukrainian and Russian, but even in the house, we communicate in English.

"And who's this?" she asks.

"This is Lyric."

"The one you talked about?" Mom looks at the new arrival as if she's inspecting a melon at the market. "From New York?" They shake hands.

"He talked about me?"

Shit. I am not going to encourage this particular exchange of information.

"You can sleep in the guest house," I say, walking toward the back house. "I'll get your bags after—"

"All the time," Mom says.

"Really? When he was in New York?" Lyric asks.

"Is it open?" I ask. "Because I want her to get settled."

"Yes. And Kyiv, constantly. And Mariupol, which was…" She laughs as if it's funny. "Over the bangs and booms. It sounded like a war zone, more or less, and wasn't it, sweetheart?"

She's looking at me. I wish she wouldn't. I don't want to answer or even think about the war in front of Lyric.

"That sounds terrible," Lyric says.

"Sofia!" I call in the general direction of the house.

"You said you were a propagandist and computer guy." A knot appears between her brows. "You didn't say you were in the war part."

Sofia's in front of me later than I'd like but as quickly as humanly possible. She's lived in our houses in St. Petersburg and Crimea since I was shorter than a fire hydrant, and she came to America with us when I was ten.

"Can you make sure there're clean sheets and towels in the back house?"

"Changed on Monday."

"Can you do it again?"

"No," Lyric interrupts. "That's fine. It's not even a week."

I'm about to insist, just to get Lyric off the subject of the war and my place in it.

"Can you get us something to drink, dear?" Mom saves me.

"We have iced tea," Sofia offers. "I'll get it before anyone refuses." She's on her way in before I can assure her she doesn't have to serve us anything.

"Lyric, come sit!" Mom takes my charge by the arm and leads her to the patio table, throwing herself into a chair so hard it almost tips over.

I'm going to have to control this conversation until I can get my mother aside and tell her to put a lid on it.

"Where's Sabrina?" I ask.

"Insists on working." Mom sighs and tosses her sunglasses on the table. They skitter and slide onto the chair across from her. "Leaves me here to my own devices all day."

"As long as she comes home, Ma." I retrieve the glasses and hand them over. "That's what's important."

She turns to Lyric. "I thought being in love with a woman meant an end to male bullshit."

"Having a job is male bullshit?" I sit on the chair formerly occupied by her sunglasses.

"What job does she need?" Mom spreads her arms at the absurd wealth she's offering, then waves her hands when I start to answer. "Don't say it. Never mind. I know." She clicks her sunglasses on the table. "I'll never get used to Americans. They ask for trouble."

"That, we can agree on," Lyric says.

I don't have to look at my mother to know she's a little charmed.

Sofia brings the tea in a pitcher and one glass with an orange wedge, the way I like it. My mother gets something clear and bubbly with a lemon. When I was a kid, it would have had enough vodka in it to give an entire frat house a hangover, but not enough to even slow her down. Once Sabrina entered the picture, the vodka magically stopped flowing.

Americans. They ask for trouble and get their heart's desire instead.

"I do wish we'd met earlier," Mom says to Lyric. "You were all I heard about, and I said, 'Well, when are you bringing this lady around?' We were right in Philadelphia, but all I got was a story about how busy you were."

"I would have made the time." She doesn't even turn my way.

"I was busy too," I say.

"At some startup." Mom waves me off, fully intent on Lyric. "Did he call you the entire time he was over there?"

"No."

"Not even from Mariupol?"

"No." Now Lyric shoots me a glance, and I'm not sure how to read it. Is she annoyed? Questioning why? "We'd broken up, so."

"Well, you'd think he would."

"Mom, she doesn't want to hear about this."

"What woman doesn't want to hear a man is mooning over her half a world away?"

Lyric hides behind her iced tea. I love my mother, but I want to kill her.

"Did you spray the orchids today?" I ask about the high-maintenance flowers she loves, because it has nothing to do with the mooning I never did from anywhere.

"Of course I did."

"They look good."

"Thank you." She turns back to Lyric, and though I hunt around my head for a follow-up, I don't come up with anything in time. "Did he tell you about the day his brother lost his arm?"

"No, he didn't."

I kick my own mother in the foot, but it has no effect.

"They both moved east to do some technical stuff to the Russian communications. Right into a war zone! Who does this?"

"Brave men?" Lyric offers, shocking the hell out of me, but I can't bask in her appreciation while my mother's mouth is a loose cannon.

"It was nothing," I say, then start to get up. "Lyric, we should move your stuff."

"The building they were in was shelled. Mike bled and bled." Mom puts her hand on her chest imagining it, and

Lyric doesn't take the hint that it's time to run away from this conversation. "Anton saved his brother's life, but he called me from the hospital absolutely beside himself. He had your hair tie on his wrist."

"I mean, that's reasonable. It all sounds pretty traumatic." Now Lyric looks at me as if wondering why Mom thinks this is abnormal. It's not.

But the loose cannon goes off with a detail I was keeping to myself. "He kept saying he lost you and Mike at the same time."

"Mom!"

She looks at me as if there's nothing revealing or humiliating in what she said. I'm about to tell her to shut up in Ukrainian, but that would only hang a lantern on what she's already said.

"What? She's right here. Not lost."

Life is full of uncomfortable moments. This one will live on after we're all dead.

"Ah, you know." Lyric clears her throat. "I read somewhere that when someone has to keep their wits about them during a really traumatic event... when it's over, they can fixate on a really small thing. A meaningless thing can seem huge, you know? It's a survival mechanism."

"Well, he should have just called you." Mom sips her drink.

I avoid looking at either of them.

"Can we get my bags?" Lyric asks me. "I want to change into something warmer."

"Yes. Good," I say, eager to get out of there.

Mom gets up, pushing the chair back into the tower heater. I grab it before it tips over.

"It's good to finally put a face to the name." Mom takes Lyric's hand. "Come into the big house any time to say hello."

"I will."

"Let's go." I walk toward the guest house gate before Mom can offer to tell her more over dinner.

CHAPTER 22

LYRIC

ANTON'S MOTHER seems really nice, and I could see how proud of his decisions she is, even as she questioned them. She told the story to show me how strong he is. How brave. How levelheaded in the face of danger. I'm not sure that's what he heard.

He unlocks the back gate with a code.

"It's locked in both directions," he mumbles, not looking at me. "Code is 1991. Your bags should be there already."

"Are you okay?" I ask, walking behind him through a garden and little patio with a table and two chairs. A huge oak casts shade over the entire space. The house itself has wood shingles and a red door. It looks like something out of a fairy tale.

"Yeah. The house code is 1917." He punches it in. "That's the door and security system."

He opens the door. The musty smell of a summer house in May hits me. My bags are in the front room by a soft-cushioned couch and a dark wood coffee table. The kitchen is in the far corner, separated by a short bar.

"It's cozy," I say, then fear I may sound as if I'm complaining about the size. I don't care about that. "I mean homey."

"It's temporary." He strides to a door and opens it. "Bedroom's here. Bathroom's down the hall. If you need anything, this button rings Vlad and Sofia."

"I'm sure I'll be fine."

He doesn't seem ready to leave. He looks around frantically as if there's another part of the house to introduce me to and he only has three seconds to do it.

"This is a good place to write," he says, indicating the breakfast nook.

"I don't write anymore, Anton. I thought that was obvious."

He clears his throat, straightens. "Okay. You'll be safe here until we find this guy."

He tries to pass me, but I grab his arm before he can.

"Can you slow down? I'm getting motion sickness."

I wait for him to say something about what his mother told me, but he's both too distant and too deep inside himself to disclose how it upended his mood.

"You'll be fine," he says after a long pause, then heads for the door.

"I missed you too," I call. He stops with his hand on the knob. "And you were in a traumatic circumstance. So, whatever. We cling to shit, you know? But if it helps you to know I missed you, I did. And then I didn't. Now we're here, and it's now, and we've both moved on. I'm not mad. You're not... whatever you were. We've been with other people, life went on, and what happened yesterday was fun but not a big deal so..." Why am I still talking? "I just don't want you to think your mom told me a story about anything but a brave man she's proud of. I'm not building a city in my head, if you know what I mean."

Finally, I shut up, but my monologue slowed him down. He doesn't seem as if he's in such a hurry now.

"You can't tell anyone where you are. You can't go anywhere without me. Not until you're safe."

He's so hard and demanding I'm not sure if I should be scared or turned on. His assumption that I'll obey him is carnal, and powerful enough to overwhelm the temptation to disobey.

"When will that be?"

"When I say."

I want to please him as much as I want to be made to please… but Lyric doesn't bend or submit. Lyric is strong and independent.

I tighten my lips, point a toe, twirl my earring while I take him in from head to toe.

"How long are you going to trap me here?" I use my play voice. Mrs. Longbottom is powerless and free to be compliant.

Anton comes a step closer.

"It's for your own good." He gets it. I know from the hard eyes and half smirk.

"All alone? What about my husband? What will he think?"

He smells like sex and manhood. The scent is thick, deep, an unbroken line from brain to bones.

"Why should I care what a man with such an unfucked slut for a wife thinks?"

"How dare you, sir," I coo, playing the part of a woman torn between her values and her desires. I can't help but smile, despite the deep offense I'm trying to act out. "I should tell him what you just said."

Anton comes closer. "I've jerked off to you so many times already."

"Sir!" I gasp and clutch at the pearls I'm not wearing.

"You spread your legs and open up your pink lips for the camera. Your clit's hard and your cunt is wet."

Ah. I can imagine them. I know why I posted them. For men like him. He is the culmination of my every secret suburban desire.

I am not Lyric Crowne. I have no history with this gruff, strong man. I'm a bored housewife with a secret life. He isn't Anton Markov. He's the security man who stumbled on my OnlyFans account. He will ruin my life unless I do what he wants.

"You. Disgusting. Animal."

Roughly, he takes my jaw in one hand to growl in my ear, "Do you know how many of us disgusting animals want your pretty little cunt? We should all visit Larry and show him what you look like with your fingers deep in your pussy."

His voice is laced with a threatening undercurrent, and it's both the presence and distortion of the threat that makes my heart thrum hard enough to send every drop of blood in my body right to my clit. He's not going to hurt me, he's only going to pretend to be someone who would, and I'm going to pretend to be a woman who doesn't want to be hurt.

"I'll do anything for you not to tell him."

"Anything?" Still holding my jaw, he picks up my shirt and pushes up my bra. "You'll let me do this?" He pinches my nipple.

My bones turn into lava and flow to where my legs meet. The cable between his fingers and my clit jolts so hard it's almost painful.

"Yes."

"Like you mean it." He's so commanding I lose the ability to want anything or anyone but him.

"Yes. Anything."

"Pick up your skirt."

"You filthy monster," I whisper as I gather my skirt and pull it up over my knees.

"All the way. I can't smell your cunt." He sounds like a brute and my spine shivers with the thought of such a beast taking me right here.

The bedroom. Sheets. Who did Sofia listen to?

"Time out," I say when a single shot of sense enters my mind.

"Okay." He loosens his grip to a caress.

"Condom and is the door locked from the inside?"

"I have one, and yes, they won't come in if it's bolted."

"Time in." I take a breath. "Is this what you want, sir? To see it?"

"It's a start." Reaching between my legs, he grabs the crotch of my underwear. I shudder and groan. "You're soaked, you dirty little bitch."

"I do not appreciate that kind of language!" Sounding shocked and offended isn't easy when every word out of his mouth triggers new pulses of arousal.

"Turn around."

"Why?"

He spins me and pins my elbows behind my back. "There is no 'why,' do you understand?" He pushes me forward into the kitchen area and bends me over the breakfast nook. I feel my skirt being pulled up again, and my underwear down, then a sharp, burning smack. "Do you understand?"

"Yes."

He slaps my ass again. This time, it really stings. Then he

slips his fingertips in my seam gently, like a man who knows how to tease. When his touch disappears, I squeak in disappointment.

"Now, show me one of the pictures you posted. One of the ones I got off to."

Of course, there is no picture. Just the permission to make it as filthy as possible.

Stepping out of my underwear, I leave it looped around my right ankle, then hitch my right knee onto the table. Reaching back, I spread myself open and look over my shoulder. He's taking a condom out of his wallet.

He smirks and lays the condom wrapper on my backside. "That was a good one." He undoes his jeans and takes out his cock. "So much prettier in real life."

"Can you just do it?"

The condom's removed from my back. "Show me another pose." He pushes me so I roll onto my back, legs open, exposed to his eyes and his opinion, which is, "Fucking beautiful. I always wanted to know if this tastes as good as it looks."

With that, he bends down and kisses between my legs.

"Does it?" I ask.

"Larry's a fool if he doesn't tell you how sweet this is."

He sucks my clit and I throw back my head in ecstasy.

"Look at me," he says.

I bend back and I watch as he teases with his lips and tongue.

I'm close to falling off a cliff when he asks, "Do you want me to fuck your cunt?"

"God, you're so dirty." I say it as if it's a compliment because it is.

"Is that a yes?"

"Yes. It's a yes."

Dick already out and covered, he pushes into me, and I stretch into a delicious burn. In a few strokes he's deeper than I thought possible, fucking slowly and angling himself so I feel it where it counts.

"You feel so good, I may keep you here." He licks his thumb and puts it to my clit. "Fuck you again. I'm going to fuck you the way that poor bastard won't."

"I hate you." My nails dig into his arms. "Go faster."

"I don't take orders from you."

"Please."

He handles my clit roughly and expertly, until I shudder, clench, cry out, bucking against the kitchen table as he bends to me and, in a long exhale, lets himself go.

A few breaths later, he's pulled out with two fingers holding the condom in place. I'm burning sore and dripping.

"Hold on." He drops the condom in the trash and spools paper towels around his hand.

I pull my skirt away from any potential staining agents until he gets back, cleaning me gently and reverently.

"Thanks. I'll give the table a wipe before I eat off it."

He takes a deep breath and checks to make sure I'm spick-and-span, then lets my legs drop. "We… I shouldn't do this anymore."

My hurt is more from shock than insult. I cover my legs with my skirt.

"Why?" Before he can answer, I jump in with why not. "It doesn't have to mean anything, right?"

"It doesn't."

I nod as if that's good, but I'm hurt. This time though, it's not from shock. It's the confirmation that he's as empty as I'm pretending to be.

"I'm trying to build a business with my brother." He buttons and zips his pants.

"Don't you have it already?"

"We want it to be big. World-class. And if I'm fucking the clients… as much as I like it…"

"Is that all I am? A client?"

He bites the inside of his cheek, then shrugs. "We don't need to be more than that, do we?"

"I guess not." I hop off the table. "I guess we already tried that and it didn't work, so. Yeah." I shrug. "It's fine. Can you kinda go? I have to unpack and whatever."

"Yes. I'll be at your place, checking the… ah… signals and… I guess if you need anything from there, let me know." He puts his hand on the doorknob.

"I will."

"Stay here." He opens the door. "Don't go anywhere."

"Anton. Get the fuck out already."

He waves and heads down the path to the front house. I close the door and lean my back against it.

Should I be happy to finally have had extremely satisfying sex? I should.

Should I be glad he and I are on the same page about developing real feelings? Absolutely.

Should I be hurt that he had to clarify the utter lack of romantic feelings with words? And that I had to agree wholeheartedly, out loud?

No. I should not be hurt, but I am.

I don't know why, but I am.

CHAPTER 23

LYRIC

THE NEXT DAY, I'm still staring at my bags. Even when I go on overnight trips, I unpack completely. But I didn't last night because I'm not sure how long this will be. How much unpacking should I do? This threat could be over in a day, or two weeks. Can I get away with what I put in the day bag, or do I need to hang the linen shirtdress before it's wrinkled permanently?

Starting with the things I need for the next few days, I pull out a couple of pairs of shoes. Underwear. Night makeup, as if I'm going anywhere. Then I get to the winter outerwear, and fuck it. I just put it all away because I hate it when things are left half-done.

I really want to be good. Mr. Rapey is real, and I'm not going to play into his hands. But without my Instagram account, there's not much to do. I watch a little television then order lunch. Sofia brings it to the back along with some groceries.

Pacing around my outside area, I pull a few dandelions,

find a broom to sweep cobwebs, and unspool the hose to do some watering.

That's when I find a six-inch high plant in a playing-card-sized patch of broken concrete.

"Oh! Yay!"

It's a volunteer tomato plant. They're like weeds that grow anywhere, but this one isn't going to thrive in this mean, shady crack in the paving.

Finding gardening tools in the shed, I dig a hole in a sunny spot and transplant the little guy. I pat the soil and water it. Then I'm done.

It's not that I love garden-grown tomatoes that much. For ten minutes, I had something to do. Ten minutes stretches into thirty when I find two more tomato plants growing from under the neighbor's fence and a sprout that could be a cucumber but could be complete trash. After all of those are transplanted, I make eggs for breakfast, eat them while scrolling through Insta like some kind of anonymous lurker, then it's almost noon.

Twelve more hours to bedtime.

The UN considers solitary confinement literal torture, and just because I can't go anywhere doesn't mean I can't make a call.

"Liang!" I cry when he picks up my call. "What are you doing?"

"Ozzie D's, where are you?"

"Home." A lie, but close enough. One day—if I'm not found dead in a ditch sometime soon—we'll all laugh about this.

"I'm getting on video."

Liang rarely leaves the house with an unmade face, but today seems to be one of those days. Without makeup, he's still devastatingly handsome, with glowing, well-cared-for skin and highly defined facial features. His cheeks and chin are rough with scruff. His hair isn't slicked back but falls loosely over his high forehead and ears. His hoodie is half unzipped, revealing a ribbed tank top.

"Do you like this?" He holds up a silver lamé jacket and matching pants.

"Um, it's a lot."

"Really?" He holds the outfit at arm's length. "You're right." He hangs the silver suit on a rack. "I don't have silver boots."

"I forgot to get the mask thing," I complain as if I'm going.

"They're putting them together here and at Fred Segal." He moves the camera to a Styrofoam head on the counter. There's a cowboy hat on it, with a mask dropping down from the brim and attached to the bottom of that, long fringe to cover the rest of the face—Orville Peck style.

"Okay, well, I have absolutely nothing to wear." I know because I didn't buy the corset and I've unpacked every single article of clothing I brought from home and none of it is flashy enough. "Can you order me a hat?"

Before Liang answers, I hear giggling. He turns around and says, "No, absolutely not."

Colleen steps into the frame with a long, spotted cow-fur coat. "It's cute!"

"No." Liang is definitive. "It's not."

"*Mooo,*" Jake intones, though I still can't see him in frame. I guess he didn't find anything last time, so he went to try again.

"Shut up!" Colleen scolds, then holds the coat against herself. "Lyric? What do you think?"

"Meh?"

"That's Lyric?" Jake grabs the phone from Liang. His face fills the screen. "Why's the video off?"

"My hair's a mess."

"You oughta come down here."

"I can't."

He peers into the video as if that's going to make me appear. "Where are you?"

I look behind me at all the old cozy things I'd never have in my actual house. I'm not supposed to say where I am, but these are my friends. "I'm hiding out."

"Where?"

The fact is, I don't want them to know I've lost control of my own life and I especially don't want them to know Anton is taking care of me.

"I could tell you, but I'd have to kill you."

"I'll rescue you anyway, princess."

"Put Liang back on, dipshit." I joke with everyone like that, but sometimes, Jake gets a hurt look on his face. It's unpredictable, and of course, this is one of those times. I don't know why I constantly forget he's more sensitive than I expect. I ask nicely. "Please."

The video blurs, swings, and lands on Liang.

"She's putting the cow thing away."

"Thank God," I say.

"Hey," Liang whispers. "Can I come over? I'll bring you some stuff to try on."

Anton said no one could come over, but come on, he knows Liang.

"When? It's kind of late."

It's not that late, but if I stall, I might have a chance to ask Anton if it's all right.

Because I'm a child asking permission.

"Tomorrow morning?" he asks. This is important to him. It's in his voice.

"Sure."

We hang up. It takes me a good twenty minutes to figure out the exact address and how to get around the back way.

I feel fine about having him over. I'll tell Anton what's going on when I talk to him. It's just Liang, after all.

CHAPTER 24

ANTON

A MINIATURE CITY of equipment sits on Lyric's kitchen table. It's been a long night.

"The whole house is a mess." Mike's unlit cigarette bounces up and down as he speaks. The ceiling creaks as our men scour the upstairs. "The stacks of signal surveillance are layered like… they're a lot."

I expected to find something, but I did not plan for this. I wasn't prepared to feel personally affronted by what's already been done to her while I wasn't looking.

"This individual," Mike says, "whoever they are, has been setting this up for a long time."

"It's someone she trusted enough to let inside the house," I say, trying to stay professional while bile fills my gut. "Cleaning person, handyman…"

"Friend," Mike adds.

I look over his shoulder so I can see the logs. I know what they mean, but not with the fine-tuned sense that Mike has. I'm glad for that. It gives me one step of separation from the desire to burn this house down so she can start over.

I point at the screen. "What's this? Audio? Video?"

"Audio pickups."

No. She cannot get out of my sight. There's a man listening. Wanting. Coveting what's mine. I won't have it. I've been so busy congratulating myself for keeping her safe I didn't bother with the simmering heat of fear bubbling under the surface.

"Where?"

Did he hear us? We can playact housewife and cop all we want, but my body was still inside hers. That act was not for his consumption.

"Everywhere but the bedroom."

I should be grateful. I should be relieved. I am neither. I'm angry her bedroom is even a consideration.

"So, not the cleaning person," I say.

"And not an ex-fuck."

For a guy who brings women home as often as he does, he's naïve. Or maybe he knows women better than he knows men, because a man will think he has a woman one minute, and the next, he finds he's lost access to her bedroom. He might not develop an unhealthy obsession until it's too late to act on it. I should know. All too well… I should know.

"I'm going to talk to her." I snap my jacket off the back of the chair.

"Anton," Mike says sharply. "She's not yours anymore."

"She's mine to protect."

I leave before he suggests any differently.

She's not mine anymore.

Thanks, Mike.

Master of the obvious. She's not mine, and I don't need her to be. This is business and I'm not a moony little weakling trying to find himself.

My history with Lyric is a list of stupid decisions, mismatched intentions and outcomes. Maybe I had to run away to get it right. Paint my face in my brother's blood. Tease death by less than an inch. Maybe I had to grow up and learn that opening my heart made me do stupid things.

Putting her up in the back house is the smartest thing I've ever done with her, and it was only possible because I left her and became a man instead of a simpering weakling. Now I know what's right, and I'm willing to do it.

Now I can ask her who's been in her house, which of them have used the bedroom and which haven't without hearing an answer over the noise of betrayal and jealousy. Now it'll be easy. Direct questions. Clear-cut answers.

I head down the driveway, past the pool, toward the back gate. The angle of the morning sun, along with the oak's overhanging branches, casts a twilight of shade onto the back end of the yard.

The laughter must be the television. That's my first assumption. But it goes on too long, and one laugh is definitely Lyric's. The other is a man's.

The gate is suddenly too far away. My legs are too short. I don't have a gun. How did I leave the house without a gun?

I'm getting soft.

I'll kill him with my bare hands.

She's laughing. She wants him there. That's worse. So much worse.

No. It's better. She's not in danger if…

So much worse.

Then he shouts, "How could you!" with an incredibly

booming rage that would confuse me after the laughter, but I'm not confused.

There's me, and her, and everything between us.

I have to punch the code into the gate twice.

How do I not have a gun?

I grab a shovel that's leaning against the back of the fence, walking shoulder forward to the half-open door. Back to me, Lyric's wearing gold bellbottoms and a vest, hands on her hips. There's a man leaning over her. Hoodie. Jeans. A short beard. Holding a sheet of paper.

He's not molesting her. It's not an attack. She's *smiling*, looking down at her own paper.

"Do you know what you did to me?" he roars.

"Louder!" she demands. "Drown out the demons in your head!"

The words mean nothing. She's not fighting him. But nothing about her smiling consent is any comfort. The sky is whistling. Los Angeles is being shelled. There are explosions everywhere. Dust. Flying rock. A blast so loud my eardrums are shattered and all I hear is a constant, high-pitched ring as I lose control.

CHAPTER 25

LYRIC

THERE's a man with a shovel in the doorway, then there's a man holding the shovel over his head in the house. I shove Liang away from the arc of the swing, and it *thunks* and rings on the wood floor.

"Anton!" I shout when I recognize him, but then again, I don't recognize him at all. His face is beet red, yet cold. His expression is tight, yet unconflicted. "Stop it!"

Anton raises the shovel. Liang's in a defensive crouch, arm arced over his head.

"Get in the bedroom and lock the door," Anton growls, barely looking at me. We were together almost two years, and I never met this guy.

"No!" I lean down on the inside of his elbow. "Look at him!"

"I got you, fucker." He's spitting mad.

"Got what?" Liang chokes out.

I can't stand seeing this. Liang's never hurt anyone. Now I'm so mad I can't even think straight.

I kick Anton in the shins as hard as I can, and I'm wearing

cowboy boots, so though it's not enough to make him put down the shovel, it's enough to get his half of his attention. I kick him again, harder. He turns fully to me.

"It's Liang, you stupid fuck!" I shout. "Look at him!"

He does. Liang takes down his hood. After a second, Anton's arms loosen. The shovel drops a few inches. He steps back. Liang scuttles back and stands when he's out of arm's reach.

"He was yelling at you!"

She holds up her paper. "I'm helping him with his acting class."

"I said no one in this house!" Anton's enraged, but I can see the seeds of shame have been planted, and good. He should be ashamed of acting like this.

"I was going to tell you, but you didn't call me." I feel my cheeks tingle with the heat of a half-truth. I could have called him. I could have texted. I did neither because I didn't want to hear him say no. I didn't want to have to decide between obedience and danger.

"Do you understand what can happen to you?" Anton says, still breathless.

"Better than you do." I stay between him and my friend, though that seems unnecessary right now.

"What's your deal?" Liang asks Anton. "Do you really think I sent her that shit? Come on."

Anton swallows. The undulation of his throat is a reminder of the guy I knew. The vulnerable human man who only wanted to do good and be good.

"What happened to you?" I ask.

He opens his mouth to speak, then shuts it, deciding instead to turn around. He grabs the shovel and storms out the door, slamming it behind him.

I face Liang, "Are you okay?"

"Untouched." He zips his hoodie all the way up. "He wasn't like that before, was he?"

"I don't think so. Are you sure you're okay?"

"Oh, please. Look at me. You think I haven't dealt with worse?"

"You're shaking."

"Well, duh."

"Yeah, duh." I look at the door, where Anton was last seen. "When he left, he went to Crimea and stayed for the war."

"Please tell me he fought on the right side."

"Duh."

"I really never thought I'd see him again."

"Me neither. And I thought he was totally rear-viewed, but… here we are."

Liang squints one eye, looking at me at a three-quarter turn. "Did you? With him?"

I shrug.

"Oh, God, really? Babygirl, why?"

"Because…" I really feel like a baby with my beggy voice.

"Do you even remember what he did?"

"I do but—"

"He broke my heart too, you know. He was part of *us*." He makes a circle with one finger. *Us* is a tight group. *Us* includes the talent I promised the world. *Us* is everyone in New York I left disappointed. "And then he wasn't, and you were too broken to see it, but I wanted to pick up a shovel and bash his head in. Difference is? I didn't."

"Well, he wasn't around."

"He has tendencies. We always knew it, but at this point?" He slings his bag over his shoulder. "Honestly, I think you should come over to my place. We'll bring Jake and whoever else to get your stuff tomorrow."

Implication being we should bring a man in case Anton flips out, but Jake's no match for my ex.

"Maybe just for the day," I agree. I'm not sure where I'll sleep tonight. I'm trapped like a caged animal. Still, the only safe place is the zoo, and I'm increasingly concerned about my keeper.

The sun dips to the western side of the sky. No word from Anton and I'm not reaching out to him. I watch TV and snack on junk with Liang while wondering why a guy who was so concerned about my safety is okay with me being so far off the leash. Then I look out the window. A bald white guy with big ears stands across the street. He was there, in that exact spot, before lunch. I take his picture and send it to Anton with a text.

—this guy work for you?—

"I have class at six" Liang says, stuffing paper wrappers into the trash. "You're staying here, right?"

—his name is Thomas. He's a vegetarian—

Is that supposed to make him more harmless to me? I know some pretty tough vegetarians. My phone dings with the punchline.

—In case you were thinking of
bringing him a sandwich—

Right. Anton thinks I'll bring any rando lunch the way I did for him when he was outside my house, in his car, watching me.

Thomas can do that as well as Anton can.

"I think I just want to go home."

CHAPTER 26

LYRIC

LIANG DRIVES me back to my house. I don't check to see if Thomas is following us. I'm sure he is.

My driveway gate slides open, revealing my little car alone under the carport roof and my little house with all the lights off.

"See you later." I kiss Liang on the cheek. "Ugh, you need to shave."

"Didn't have time," he says, waving off my question. I don't call bullshit, though I could. He always has time. "Tomorrow morning, I'll have cheeks like butter. Now shoo. I'll pick up some stuff at Ralph's. We can pig out and fall asleep on the couch."

"Thank you."

"You're welcome, now go."

He shoos me and doesn't drive off until the gate clicks closed behind me.

As I approach the house, the motion sensor lights flick on.

Anton is sitting on the porch steps.

Shit.

I'm not afraid of him, even though a sensible person would be. I'm more annoyed that I have to deal with him.

"Okay." I step up to the porch. "What?"

"I wanted to apologize to Liang."

"I'll ask him if he's interested, but don't bet on it." I go right past him and open my front door.

"And I want to apologize to you."

"Can an insane person give a sincere apology?" I flip on the lights. "Jury's out."

My dining room table is covered with black boxes and computer monitors. There are wires everywhere. One screen flickers and glows against the wall, diffusing the blue light.

"If you knew what I knew, you would have gone insane too."

"But I don't." I get the rest of the six-pack of Fresca out of my fridge for Liang. "And if knowing means you run my life, then my father can send Earl or whoever to babysit me."

"You're not safe here." The glowing screensaver lights half of his face in alternating colors. "This entire house is a broadcast station. Audio pickups everywhere. Signal interception."

My fingers go cold from the inside. I put down the Fresca. I can't feel my face. "What?"

He didn't just say my house was bugged. He must have meant something else.

"We cleared the audio, but there's a signal tracker we're still working on."

What have I done in this house? Who heard it? I feel as if the walls are pressing in on me. The room is too small. There's no air.

"How?" I say, losing breath before I get out the last sound.

"All planted. Physically planted." Leaning over a keyboard, he taps a space bar, and the monitor comes to life. The screensaver turns into rolling code and bouncing bars. "Inside the outlets. Every power strip was compromised. And the smoke detectors. You have to *be here* to do that."

This isn't my house anymore. I bought it with my own money, but the name on the deed doesn't even matter. Someone who hates me has ripped it out from under me.

"I have to get out of here." I rush to the door and grab my key fob and purse.

Anton's right there, not quite blocking my way, but definitely in the way. "Where are you going?"

"You lost the right to even ask that when you tried to bash in Liang's face with a shovel!"

"Put it together, Lyric. One of your friends is doing this."

I look away and up. There's a hole in the ceiling, like an open mouth puking wires.

"How do I know it's not you?" I ask. He hasn't been around, as far as I know, but maybe I don't know anything far enough.

"You don't. But it isn't. All I want to do is protect you."

"You can't ever go apeshit like that again."

"And you can't ever defy me like that again. If I say no one visits, no one visits."

"I'll think about it." I slide past him and walk out, hurrying to my car. I get in the driver's seat, but a second later, he's in the passenger seat beside me, bent into a pretzel to fit in the tiny seat.

When I open the door to get out and away from him, he reaches over me and snaps it closed. "Starting now, you don't do anything until I tell you to."

"Can I breathe?" It's more than a rhetorical question. I

can't breathe without forcing down my diaphragm to get air into my lungs.

"You have to." He squeezes my hand. "Lyric, I won't say I don't know what came over me because I do. The thought that someone wants to hurt you... it made me crazy. I went blind."

"Obviously."

"Yeah." He lets go of me. "I'll make it up to Liang. I swear."

"You will." I stare at our hands together, unable to wonder about what our connection means without the context of my life, my house, my place in the world.

"Listen," he says. "We're going to fix this. The house is clean now. The only problem is he knows you live here." He takes me by the chin and turns my face to his. "We've protected diplomats. Politicians. We cleared the entire Georgian embassy in Kyiv."

"Like you got everyone out or got rid of a bunch of bugs?"

"The bugs. Exterminated." He smiles when I laugh a little. "Mike and I—we have this."

I believe him, but I'm none of those things. I'm not important. I'm a dopey lifestyle influencer.

"What does he want?" I ask.

"We'll ask him when we catch him." That seems a million miles and a billion years from the current reality.

"I'm scared."

"I know." He cups my face in one strong hand. I used to marvel at the size of his hands—how one could practically touch both my ears at the same time. Now, I'm not marveling. I'm just grateful.

"Is he getting off on me being scared right now?"

He strokes the top of my hand then squeezes it again. The touch lights every nerve ending like a fuse that sparks in a line leading right between my legs. Somewhere, in the helplessness I feel, is the thickly warm, sticky call of sex. He starts to pull his hand away as if he knows what his touch does to me, but he couldn't help himself. My thumb catches his index finger before it leaves and holds tight.

My fear was simple a moment ago, but it's reshaping itself—folding into an origami of rage, annoyance, terror, and recklessness.

"When you find him, give me ten minutes in a room, slapping him over and over. Just for the inconvenience," I say.

"As long as you leave him alive for me. I want him to feel his dick getting ripped off."

"Did you castrate the guys who bugged the embassy or is that perk just for me?"

He smirks, looking away for a moment. He strokes his lower lip, then stands right in front of me. His eyes are camphor. Cold at first, then deeply hot.

"Get out of the car." He opens his door, gets one foot out and stops to say, "Mrs. Longbottom."

Before I have a second to pick my jaw off the floor, he's on my side, opening the door to hustle me out. He firmly, but gently pushes me against the car.

"Don't get smart with me." His breath is warm and wet on the side of my neck. "Feet apart."

I am Mrs. Longbottom, free to fuck with only the disapproval of a nonexistent husband to worry about.

"How wide?" I ask.

"Wide like the cheating slut you are." With his foot, he kicks my feet open. "How does Larry make you come?"

I shrug.

"So." Anton starts pulling open his belt. "He doesn't."

"He says it's not his job."

"Looks like it's mine then." He looks down at me as if I'm his favorite meal. "Take your pants down so I can fuck you."

"I can't."

"Why?" He takes out his cock and fists it, aiming it at me.

"My legs are open and you're standing between them so—?"

He yanks up my knees, pulling them apart and leveraging me against the car window. "Like this?"

"Yes, I can't… it's not… oh…"

With my legs over his shoulders, he bites inside my thigh, through the fabric of my jeans, to a dull, delicious pain.

"You think clothes can keep me from making you come?"

"It's just…"

He continues biting inside both thighs, and it's so good, I want to get these pants off more than I've ever wanted anything. So I unbutton and unzip, but he runs his teeth along my center, and all I can do is groan when he bites down. The denim dulls any kind of pain and turns it into so much raw pleasure.

I pull his head into me, whispering, "Yes."

"I think," he says, looking up at me, "Larry doesn't eat your pussy often enough."

"He doesn't believe in it."

"Luckily, I do."

Anton takes absolute control, holding me up to get his mouth on me. He kisses between my thighs, bites, sucks the tender skin through tough fabric, dragging his teeth along the center seam. He is truly savage. I've never been eaten through jeans by a starving animal.

"Now, I'll taste you." He drops my legs. We wrestle my pants down to my knees. "Hands on the hood. Fast, Brenda."

I turn my back to him. He pulls me to him, bites my bare cheeks, spreads me open, continuing the ravishing of his mouth.

By the time his tongue touches my clit, I'm collapsing in on myself. He sucks on it as if he doesn't have the self-control to tease, and my orgasm is so brutal, hard, and all-at-once, it's like a bludgeoning.

I jerk and cry out, and when I look behind me, he's watching me with smiling eyes as I come against his mouth.

Once I'm able to breathe without panting, he pulls away my pants, twisting the shoes off only when he has to. He tosses it all aside, fully dressed with his dick hanging out like an angry red soldier who's ready to fight.

"Time out." I make the hand gesture. "Condoms in the night table. Time in." I change back to a damsel in distress. "Do what you want, but please be gentle with that thing." I point at his dick.

"You mean this?" He's trying to stay tough and not laugh.

"Yes. It's going to hurt."

He pushes my legs apart at the upper thigh, pinching my labia open so he can see.

"Probably. Yes." He slides two fingers inside me, and I'm immediately wet again. "You're tight, and I'm going to fuck you very hard."

Removing his fingers, he pulls me up by the arms and crouches until I'm over his shoulder.

I put my elbows on his back and fold my hands on my lips. "I'm praying for your salvation, you brute."

"Officer Brute."

He slaps my ass so hard I yelp.

"You animal!"

He slaps me again as he takes me up the stairs.

"Show me where Larry fucks you," he demands with another slap.

"Left."

Carrying me to the bedroom, he drops me onto the bed and stands over me.

I start to remember things Mrs. Longbottom wouldn't know about. The tender days. The soft words. The trust with things that hurt just enough.

The days and weeks and months he was gone. Checking hospitals and police stations. The worry turning into a simple, bitter loss.

Officer Everhard has a rod sticking out of his jeans. Brenda's worried it will hurt. She's worried it'll stretch her out for Larry's needle dick.

Brenda closes her legs and covers herself with cupped hands.

"Don't pretend you're not a slut, Brenda." He pulls his turtleneck over his head, leaving his hair mussed and the tight musculature of his body exposed. "Pull your shirt over your tits."

Exposing myself to him, I wonder how we managed to not spend sixteen hours a day fucking. I'm an object under his gaze. An expensive cut of meat. He's considering which corner to cut off and consume first as he undoes his belt. His pants fall away, releasing a throbbing, thick cock that terrifies Mrs. Longbottom as much as it excites Lyric.

"Just finish with me. Do your filthy business."

"That's not how this works."

"I have to make dinner."

"Close your eyes, Brenda." I do it because he's Brad Everhard. I feel him take out a condom and put it on while he speaks. "Keep your legs open so I can see what I'm about to destroy. Now open your eyes. That's right. Look at me."

Pushing my hips off the bed, he takes his time spreading my cheeks wide, inspecting everything. I'm so turned on I barely need him to touch me.

"You ever take a cock so deep you could taste it on the back of your tongue, Mrs. Longbottom?" He sits with his back to the headboard and his sheathed cock sticking up like a flagpole.

"Oh, dear, no, Larry can't reach that far, but you…"

I let my eyes drift between his legs. He reaches that far.

"Come here." He grabs my arm and pulls me to him, then turns me so my back is to him. "Leg on either side. That's right."

He guides the head of his wrapped dick along my seam with one hand, then with the other, he pushes down my hips, impaling me on him. He pushes me down slowly, then stops before he's all the way. I drop to get another inch in, but he holds me.

"Please," I whine.

"Begging already?"

"Please fuck me all the way. Do all your dirty things to me. Go ahead."

He reaches around to put his hand between my legs. "Who's doing what, Brenda? If you want to take it all, just take it."

I push down, and he doesn't stop me this time. He's buried deep. In the mirror, I see us. Me with my T-shirt pushed up, and him with his right hand over my clit. Our eyes meet in the reflection. For a moment, he seems like my old Anton, with all the warmth and passion he used to show me. It's terrifying.

Then his expression goes hard. His left hand grips a handful of hair.

"Get to work." He pulls my head back and murmurs in my ear, "Earn it."

He lets go. I jolt up and down on him, fucking him while his fingers circle between my legs. He thrusts hard, burying himself, and I'm immediately so close to orgasm I let out a shout and grip his legs like a lifeline.

"I can. Take. It."

He rocks against me, then shifts, hitting new places every time, pressing his lips to my cheek.

"You want to come?"

"I'm going to."

"No, you're not. This is business. You don't get to come until your boss says you come. You got that?"

"Please."

"Say your name."

"Lyr—"

"Brenda."

He must know how close I am to coming, so he's making me talk to distract me. I don't know how much longer I can bear it.

"Mrs. Brenda Longbottom."

"Say, 'I am getting used like a filthy slut.' Say it now."

I repeat the words, and they're freeing. I am nothing but that. I can just fall through this thick pleasure without worrying about when I'm going to hit the bottom. He's going to orchestrate that down to the precise moment.

But it's too far. Too much. I'm about to start crying in frustration.

"Use me more," I say, gripping his neck. "Use me harder."

"Like this?" He pounds into me once.

"Yes. Please."

Again. "Will this make you come?" Again.

"Yes."

"Good woman."

Three more strokes like that and my entire body fills with molten fire. I tighten, clench, pulse around him, grabbing the muscles of his arms when I scream.

He lets out a long exhale into my neck, and says, "You are good. So good," as if it's the most complex sentiment he can put together.

I appreciate that. It's the most powerful one I can hear.

"Anton." I say his real name, assuming we don't need to time out.

"Lyric." Reaching over my shoulder, he takes my jaw tight in his fingertips and murmurs into my neck, "Please come back where I can watch you."

CHAPTER 27

LYRIC

CLEANED UP, clothed, and ready, I'm faced with the question of where exactly I'm going.

"You're going to tell me I shouldn't stay with Liang."

"You cannot."

"He's not the hacker, you know. Like, I'll eat my Jimmy Choos."

"You eat one and I'll eat the other. But I'm playing the odds anyway, and knowing what I know, I'm a little on edge."

"A little," I scoff. "You owe him a dozen yellow roses."

"Yeah." He clears his throat. "If you want to stay with your parents—"

"Are you trying to kill my mother?"

I sigh and take out my phone to tell Liang I'm not joining him. I don't tell him why. The thought that my whole house has been a Lyric Crowne surveillance station is too much to explain without bursting into tears. He's going to have to trust me for now.

We pass Butterbomb sitting pretty in the driveway. I tap her hood to let her know I'll be back. Anton walks me to the street and we walk down the block to where his car is parked.

"If I go back to your house," I say, "there are going to be rules."

"Really?"

I'm not sure if he's deeply offended that I'm going to make rules for his house, or just surprised I'd attempt to.

"You don't come into that house unless you're invited. Pretend you're a vampire or something."

He raises an eyebrow. "You're prohibiting Officer Everhard?"

It's such a relief to laugh. Almost better than sex in a stranger's skin. Almost.

"And I come and go as I please," I say.

"No. Absolutely not."

"How long am I supposed to stay in prison?"

"You'll tell me where you're going, and if I say you don't go, you don't go."

"What kind of bullshit is that?"

"Security bullshit. Safety. My job."

I scoff. His job. Sure.

"Was spanking me and fucking me your job?"

"It was a betrayal of your father's trust in me and completely unethical. I could lose everything we've built, and I'd deserve worse."

I want to ask him if it was worth it, but I'm afraid he'll say it was.

"Let's go." I start across the street for his Range Rover, but he stops me with a word.

"Buttons."

The nickname knocks the breath out of me.

"What?" I say with what little I have left in my lungs.

He meets me in the middle of the street.

"As long as my heart beats, nothing will happen to you. Do you understand? It's my job to make sure you're safe, but don't fool yourself. This is not just a job or business. It's everything. I won't have a world where you're in danger. It's incorrect." He opens the passenger side door. "It's offensive to me."

I get in and he closes the door. His words hang in the half-darkness.

I try to remember a time when I've seen him like this, and I can't. Maybe I was too wrapped up in my misery to notice, or there was never a situation that pushed him hard enough.

He gets in and starts the engine.

"You meant all that?" I ask.

"I'm not leaving you."

I wait for a qualifier. There is none. We're crossing into Beverly Hills when he finally speaks.

"We'll find him," he says more to himself than me.

"Can I help?"

"No." His answer comes too quickly, and he seems to know it. "Did you add anyone to the enemies list?"

"Ugh! Totally spaced it."

"Who had that much access to the house?"

"No one. I mean, I have parties, but the smoke detectors? I've never had a party *that* wild." I'm grateful I'm already sitting because my legs cannot support this level of betrayal.

"Have you had a house sitter?"

"No."

"What about the cleaning person?"

"She's been with my family forever. No way."

"Is anyone jealous of you?"

"Oh, for fuck's sake. Of course. But not my friends."

Am I being naïve? What about Liang, who I'm helping but who's always chasing my followers? Or Jake, who gave up finally? Or Colleen, who's always telling me how much prettier I am than her? What about Cole, or Kelly, or Rachel, or anyone in the entire universe?

"I need you to think," Anton demands.

"I am thinking," I say through a tight jaw. "I'm thinking of everyone who cares about me. Who got me through the worst time of my life by just being fun and happy. I came back here, and my old friends accepted me without asking a ton of questions that made me feel bad and I made new ones from social media who don't even know what a failure I am. So, yes, but everyone loves me, okay?"

He sighs. "Everyone does. One person, just a little too much."

CHAPTER 28

ANTON

IN MY ROOM. In bed. It's quiet. I am physically comfortable. Lyric is safe in the back house, and she understands the danger she's in. I should be able to sleep, but my mind is racing.

Whoever's after her is going to see the depletion in signals. I shouldn't deduce away half the population, but I'm sure it's a man. A woman wouldn't threaten to rape her.

More than anything, that's the threat that keeps me up. The specter of her violation fills me with electric rage and I'm too exhausted to cool it down.

In the dark, I huddle with my phone and navigate to Instagram, where I have an account under a fake name. There are no posts. All I do there is consume the content of one woman. I turn up the volume on a year-old video. Her longest one.

"Hey, Luxies! Lyric Crowne here by the rooftop pool at The Standard Downtown. It's a gorgeous day, but duh, of course it is. Check out this view. Right there is Dodger's Stadium where they're setting up for the Elton John concert tomorrow night. I have four tickets and I'll be taking my besties to the show. A little to the north and wow… it's so clear you can just see the snow on Mt. Baldie…"

And on and on. Nattering about this and that, narrating what we can clearly see.

This video was such consolation to me when I was in the hospital with Mike. It was the only thing that soothed me. She existed in a peaceful place. She was happy. She was safe.

It's not working now. It's agitating me. The source of my comfort is the source of my anxiety.

Just before I shut it, a message from her drops into the frame.

*—We have the appointment with Kevin
and a woman named Tanya tomorrow at Meta—*

I sit up.

—What time?—

—Yikes. I didn't think you'd be up—

—Well, I am—

—11:30—

—I'm going with you—

—Already established duh—

She added a rolling-eye emoji. She may not like that it's my job to protect her, but she accepts it. I can live with that.

—I talked to Liang—

—What did he say?—

**—He said he'll forgive you but
you have more red flags
than a communist parade—**

Texting with her directly is much more calming than watching a video. I get out of bed and look down at the back house. Through the trees, there's light. Her shadow floats across it. She's right there. Safe.

I message her back.

*—let me tell you about living in
a country run by communists—*

She responds with another eye roll.
—You can explain it to Liang too—
There's that, but I'm already tapping my reply.

—you have to do what you're told or you disappear—

—what if I want to disappear—

*—Trust me. You don't want that.
You'd be wishing for Officer Everhard—*

—try me—
Lyric and I didn't always pretend we were other people, but when we did, we always played the same characters. I'm not sure if she's trying to change that or if she's just being a brat.

Only one way to find out.

*—You posted anti-government
propaganda. This is a problem for you—*

There's a pause. Rolling dots. Below, her shadow has stopped moving. Is she considering the game?
—but it was true—
This is too easy.

—what is truth?—

I don't wait for an answer, because none exists, and I'm not trying to role play a philosophical discussion.

*—it's what I decide. Now I decide truth
is you taking your clothes off—*

Her shadow disappears, leaving an uninterrupted yellow glow on the yard.
—Where should I put them?—
I smile at her obedience and nod at the unexpected and reasonable question.

—the floor—

—Okay—

*—Now, you will do as I tell you. No more.
No less. Because you're a filthy
propagandist whore—*

**—I never imagined that particular
insult on my list of turn-ons, but here we are—**

—There's a chair in the bedroom.
Blue. Floral. With upholstered arms—

—Yes—

—straddle the left arm. Put your
cunt right on it—

—Left facing it or left if I was the chair?—

She's a pain in the ass. It's irrelevant. Or at least it should be. The only way it would matter is if someone was looking in the window. That can be arranged.

—You are the chair—

I throw a hoodie over my bare chest and run downstairs in that and pajama bottoms. At the back door, I jam my feet into sneakers and go outside. I take one last look at my mother's bedroom window. It's dark. Good. I don't feel like getting interrogated.

—okay—

—wait—

Hard as a hammer, I get through the gate and slink around the little house to the back, where the bedroom window looks onto a slit of bushes. I can see her there, in the dark room. Her bare back is lit by the moonlight and her legs are on each side of the arm of the blue chair.

She was doing what I told her to, and that sends even more blood to my cock.

—are you wet, little slut?—

I expect her to just say yes, but she's a good girl. She leans back on her left hand, which is holding the phone and, with her right, reaches between her legs.

—yes. What do I have to do?—

—for this first infraction, you will rub
your dirty cunt clean on the chair—

—but the upholstery—

—do it or that's another infraction—

She moves her hips back and forth. I have never seen anything so hot, but I'm not supposed to be able to see.

—confirm you're doing what I told you—

—I am—

—for the second infraction, you will take
off your clothes again. You will put your
hands on the back of that chair and I
will beat your bottom while you sing
the anthem of the fatherland. When you are
sobbing hard enough, I will pull your ass
cheeks apart. I will place my cock at your
open pussy and tell you to sing it again.
When you start, I will fuck and
when you are done I will come—

Her body moves faster as she reads, and I match her rhythm, watching her ass move back and forth on the chair. Not slowing for a second, she picks up her phone and taps.

—?—

I am so close, I cannot type a response longer than one letter.

—y—

Her body jerks and I come in the bushes like a filthy stalker.

I'm not supposed to be here.

—tomorrow, I will sniff that chair and
make sure you did as you were told—

She gets up and texts me back, naked in front of the window without looking through it. She doesn't know I'm right in front of her. I suddenly feel ashamed and guilty.

—God, Anton, I knew you were
filthy but damn—

I stand and wave, but she's turned to the side, naked, curved exactly the way I like.

Why do I keep getting into this with her? One minute, we're two complicated, but normal people. We talk about things normal people talk about. We unravel past hurts and have emotions and say things we regret. We're two of tens of millions who do.

Then we turn into other characters with simple pasts and immediate physical needs. It's already a pattern, so I texted to avoid this exact outcome. But like clockwork, we started playacting a cheap porno with characters burdened with less knotty personalities.

This is a compulsion. *She's* a compulsion.

I'm not sure I can stop sliding into these scenes with her. It's so pleasurable, so entertaining, that my thoughts slide down a greased ramp and my mouth follows, bypassing logic, sense, and self-preservation.

Reaching forward, I put a knuckle to the glass to let her know I'm there. I don't want to rap too loudly and scare her, but before I can make a sound, there's another text-ding from her side, but I haven't texted anything else.

She looks at her phone and cries out a single vowel of despair, stepping back in wide-eyed shock.

CHAPTER 29

ANTON

THE GUILT over looking at her without her knowing disappears and is replaced by action. I run to the front door and bang on it.

"It's me!" I shout. "Let me in!"

The door swings open. The horror on her face keeps me from appreciating her nudity. I shut the door and lock it.

She hands me the phone without asking how I got there so quickly or how I even knew to show up.

There's a new text from an unknown number.

—where did he take you?—

She collapses into tears, and I catch her. I silence her notifications then drop the phone so I can hold her with both hands.

"Why?" she cries.

We're huddled on the floor together. I want to cover every inch of her body, but I only have the width of my arms.

"Okay," I whisper, clutching her. "It's okay."

"Why is this happening?" She's sobbing fully now.

There's a buzz in my hand as another text comes in.

—*I know what you did with him*—

I slide the phone into my pocket. "You're safe with me."

"It's the Android! It's brand new!"

"Who did you give this number?"

"You. Kelly. My parents. Um… Liang?" I'm sure there's someone else, but I can't think.

"That it?"

I nod, still thinking about it, but I come up empty. No one else has it.

"You'll get another one."

"I don't know what to do." Her breath hitches and gasps, letting the words out in broken pieces. "I've never felt like this before. Like a really bad thing can happen and I can't do anything about it? Like I don't even exist. I'm invisible and all alone in a cage with a monster. And when it eats me, and I scream, no sound's going to come out because there's no one to hear me."

"I'm here." I let her tears fall against my neck, holding her shuddering body. "You're not alone."

I don't know how many times I reassure her, but I keep doing it until the sobs slow enough to let her breathe. I loosen my grip. My arms ache from holding her so tightly.

She touches under her nose and it comes back connected to sticky, clear filament. "Sorry, bad snot management."

"Here." I pull my cuff over my hand and wipe her nose.

"That's the most gentlemanly thing anyone's ever done for me."

"Well, I wasn't such a gentleman a minute ago. I was watching you through the bedroom window."

"Yeah. Duh."

I can only stifle my inappropriate laugh down to a breathy chuckle.

"Can I take you to bed?" I wipe the new tears away with my thumb.

"I don't think I'm in the mood for another round."

"That's not what I meant." I get my feet under me and crouch to pick her up.

She lets me gather her in my arms, tucking her head against my shoulder as I carry her to the bedroom and lay her down. She pulls the covers back and gets under them.

"Can you stay?" she asks.

I shouldn't, but I've broken just about every boundary I've promised myself I'd keep. She just keeps finding new lines and I keep crossing them.

I get between the sheets with her.

"Thank you," she says.

"My pleasure."

"Did you lock the front door?"

"Yes."

"Are you sure?"

"Do you want me to double check?"

"No. Stay."

We lie facing each other for a few minutes, the way we did in her apartment in New York, talking for hours after fucking. When the reviews for *Standard Deviation* started coming in, she'd tell me her hopes for the next screening, the next write-up, the next meeting. Those hopes got smaller and smaller, until I had no more to listen to. All my comforts became physical.

"Turn around," I say. She rolls over onto her stomach, facing me. I shift close, swinging my leg over her and moving her hair away from the back of her neck. "I'm right here."

"If I fall asleep?"

"I'll stay." I rub between her shoulder blades and up her neck the way I used to.

"The whole time?"

"I'll be here when you wake up." There's more tension under my hand than I'll ever be able to massage away.

"I have the camphor stuff," she says. "But it's in the bathroom, so forget it."

"I can get it and be right back."

"No."

"What if I have to piss?"

"Hold it or get a new mattress."

"You're a tough nut."

"I'm not. I'm a stupid baby. I hate this," she says. I stop the massage. "No. I love that. I hate that I can't take care of myself."

"I'm going to tell you a secret," I whisper, rubbing her neck.

"Mmm?"

"No one takes care of themselves. We all need help."

She scoffs, her mouth half-smashed against the pillow. "Says you."

"It's true."

"When was the last time *you* needed help?"

"I'll tell you about one time."

"No cheating. No diapers or whatever."

"As a full-grown man, I needed help."

"Tell me."

"It was me and Mike. We were working with four other

guys... one of them was a woman... on the fifth floor of an office building in Mariupol."

"What were you doing? And how did you get there from Crimea?"

I sigh. This is going to be a longer story than I was ready to tell.

"I met with some old friends while I was waiting for the bank to clear. They could use my skills, and I had both Russian and Ukrainian passports. I could move between without trouble. In one way, out the other. Equipment. Papers. People."

"You were a smuggler?" Her eyes go a little wider. "The possibilities." She bites her lip. I pull it away from her teeth with my thumb. "You have to get me over the border. I could be a young virgin promised in marriage."

Yes. She could be. And yes. The possibilities.

But she's talking about taking the time to build another world between us. We didn't agree to a future, and I'm not sure I can give her one.

"I stayed and learned how to crack wifi. Hack cellular signals. And also, I guess you'd call it messaging. Before the Russians invaded, there was a propaganda war."

"I love that you're on the right side of this."

I scoff. "Mike and I used our father's funeral as an excuse to meet with a contact in St. Petersburg. That's not *right*."

"What. Ever," she whispers. "Get to Mariupol."

"They invaded, that's how I get there."

"Okay. You were hacking. Jamming."

"Listening in on calls. Sad fuckers." For a moment, I think of all the dead men talking to their wives for the last time. "And there was a missile. Dead of night. Came in like this." I take my hand off her neck and make the whistling sound of an incoming shell before it lands between her shoulder blades. "It was… chaos. Dust. Rocks. The floor was hot to the touch. My ears blew out. Couldn't see through the dust in my eyes. Lights were gone anyway, and it was so dark." I clear my throat. I have to get to the part where I needed help, and this isn't even it. "I got the dust out of my eyes and used my cell phone as a flashlight. I found Mike."

I stop.

"Was he okay?"

"No." I shouldn't have started this stupid fucking story. Thinking about it makes me physically ill. Speaking it into words might kill me. "He was bleeding from the artery in his arm. It was… a lot. The blood. So much of it. I wasn't thinking right, and I'm not a medic."

"You're not. But you did your best, right?"

"Maybe. Yes? But probably not. The blood soaked through everything I put on it, so I made a tourniquet. I ripped up my shirt, but there was this sleeve dangling. So I held it down with a hair tie I had on my wrist. It took us hours to find help. Too many hours." I rub my eye. Sniff. Turn away for a glance at the ceiling. "When the doctor came out to tell me Mike was alive, he returned the hair tie. It was cut open. He said I saved my brother's life but the arm?"

I stop for so long she has to finish it for me. "They couldn't save it."

"Because of me. The tourniquet was too tight, and it was on too long. I didn't know what I was doing."

"I'm sorry that happened."

"Me too."

"It wasn't your fault," she says.

"Sure."

"You can't be everything to everyone, all the time."

"I only needed to be one thing, one time."

She makes an mmm sound and her eyelids droop. Her back rises and falls in steady rhythm. I will stay here, as I promised, and watch her dream. Then her lips move, even as her eyes stay closed.

"Why would he return the stupid hair tie?"

"It had a little silver buckle on it."

"Like the Hermès ones."

"Yes."

"Those are cute."

She's going to ask if it belonged to a woman I was with. I'll have to explain that there were women, some who were important to me, all of whom I liked and respected. Some could afford an Hermès hair tie, but none had one. All of them asked why I wore the same one on my wrist, day and night, and I didn't tell any of them the real reason.

When Lyric asks, I'll tell her. She'll know everything.

Instead, she falls asleep.

CHAPTER 30

LYRIC

Twelve years.

Meeting with Kevin down on Silicon Beach makes the time I've been on Instagram seem extra-long. Glacial. Eons. Measured in tectonic shifts and space relativity. I was on Instagram before Facebook bought it in 2012, when I was 15. There was no Los Angeles office at all.

I am not old. My body isn't deteriorating in a way I can perceive. But pulling up to the guardhouse at Silicon Beach with Anton next to me, I feel the flow of time in what changes and what never will.

"You all right?" Anton asks. He stops at the last light before the turn onto Silicon Beach.

"Yeah, just felt like… the presence of death for the first time ever. At Meta HQ, no less."

"He's everywhere. Just ignore him."

He doesn't elaborate, and I can guess why. Death must have been breathing down his neck a hundred times. I grunt some kind of understanding, but the presence of death isn't just about the number of years I've had a social media account. It's about how much time I have before I get murdered and how little I've done up to now.

"I don't want to go," I say, both hands white-knuckled into fists. "What's the point? Like, I don't even want this stupid Insta account anymore. They can shove it for all I care."

"They might know something that helps us find him."

I sigh and look away, then down at the little dashboard pocket under the radio. It's empty. Anton has my Android since I never want to touch it again.

"I don't want another phone." The light changes, and he makes the turn. "Ever. I want to live in the forest next to a babbling brook and just make stuff I can be proud of, so forget any kind of career, much less directing, but it's fine." The car stops at the guard gate, and I root around my bag for my wallet. "I'll do interpretive dance or make animation no one sees."

Finding my driver's license, I give it to Anton. He hands both of ours to the guard, who takes them to the little house to make sure they match. I used to resent this kind of inconvenience. Not today.

"That's something," Anton says.

"What?"

"That's the first time I've heard you talk about yourself as a director since I've been back."

"Well, if a bad director lives in the forest and no one hears her—"

"You're not bad."

"Oh, Anton. Really?"

"Yeah. Really. You made a thing no one wanted, and you couldn't sell it to them. That makes you bad at your own propaganda."

After a short laugh, I punch his arm. "You're nuts, but I like you."

Our IDs gets handed back.

Using his finger to draw lines across the map on an iPad, the guard shows us to the right parking lot, and we go. Anton skirts pristine white sidewalks bordering verdant native gardens. Each building is the result of a dick-swinging architectural contest. Most glass. Most trees. Most colorful. Most daring. Tallest. Curviest. Ballsiest.

"Here we are." He parks in the spot the guard circled on the map.

Kevin's already here with a paper cup in each hand, messy blond hair flopped over his ears and down his neck. He's wearing the Meta winter uniform. Hoodie. Jeans. Allbirds shoes, which went out six months ago, but Kev won't know for another year.

"He looks like a twit," Anton says.

"That used to be two buildings over." I open the door to get out. "That was a joke," I whisper. "A pun."

"I know," he whispers back.

We get out at the same time.

"Hey!" Kevin P. hands me a cup, watching Anton as he comes around the car. "I got you a yaupon with avo-milk. I forgot you were bringing someone or I would have gotten another."

"We can stop at the caf and get him one."

"I'm fine." Anton looks around as if he expects snipers on the rooftops.

I wait for Kevin to realize that Anton's with me and will receive the same courtesy. If he makes me spell it out, this is going to be a long meeting.

"We can pick up a latte or... anything else?"

That's better, Kevey.

"No thanks." Anton makes eye contact this time.

Smiling, Kevin walks along the sidewalk to the huge entrance, slowing down to give us the rundown on their expansion, the new kitchen, and the waiting list for the pickleball court. We take glass stairs to the mezzanine, where the wraparound balcony overlooks the atrium.

"Right in here." He opens the door to a conference room that's glass on all four sides.

Three people already wait at the table. Only the woman avoided the Meta uniform and wears a white suit that contrasts with her bronze skin. That must be Tanya. We exchange the usual greetings and introductions.

Tanya's the VP. Brad's a security specialist—early thirties, sallow, and balding already, with a knot of curly brown hair tied at the base of his neck. Lyle's an intern. Our age. His soft hand shakes mine so gently, it's as if he's terrified of breaking me.

The six of us sit. Anton and I across from Tanya, who's bookended by the two younger men. Kevin the facilitator sits at the head of the table.

"Let me start by saying," Tanya says with her hands folded in front of her, "we at Meta are so sorry we allowed this breach of your security and peace of mind. We've been working day and night since it happened."

"We got right on it," Brad interrupts. "When Kev asked for the first tranche of logs, I knew something was up."

"I'm sorry," I say to Tanya. "You were saying since it happened?"

"When we got the first log request. Brad inspected your account."

"Just high-level, bird's-eye view." Brad shrugs. "There was a mess of troll activity in April."

"We took care of that," Kev says.

"And…" Tanya says, hands on the table, looking at each of the men she works with before going back to me. "We found no blocks or reports. The trust team had no reason to throttle the account. You have some fans in that department, by the way."

"Say hi to Debra for me."

"I will. So, as Kevin told you, the logs don't show anything unusual. Just that you stopped opening the account until an Android attempted a sign-in on…" She checks a piece of paper.

"That was me," I say.

"You're confirming you got in." She places the paper on the table. "And you didn't post or comment?"

"Couldn't. That's what I've been telling Kevin."

"I told—" Kevin starts to defend himself, but Tanya holds up her hand slightly in a subtle gesture that stops him in his tracks.

"You did," she says. "I wanted to hear it from the user."

"Okay, you heard it. I tried everything on my side. I'm here. Now what?"

Just leave it.

Stop using it.

It's not safe to be an Instagram personality.

Then what am I?

Anton clears his throat, demanding attention. His elbow is on the chair arm, and his finger curves over his lip while the hand closer to me is braced against the edge of the table as if he's going to leverage its weight against his when he lunges across it.

"I'm afraid there's not much we can do," she says. "We've seen this hack before—on smaller profiles. We're developing a workaround, but for anyone hit in the meantime, we've never been able to recover the account."

"I wasn't here before." Lyle waves away her concern. "I bet I can figure it out. I've unspooled worse than this."

Tanya closes her eyes and opens them slowly, then smiles. I really feel for her surrounded by these human turnips.

"So," she says, "yes, we'll figure it out, but until then, we're prepared to start you a new account and move your followers over. All on the back end. It will need approval one level up, but I think we can get it through."

"She's in immediate danger, and you're talking about redoing what put her there in the first place." Anton sits straight, folding his hands in front of him to mirror Tanya's position. "We need the PEG logs."

Brad rolls his eyes. Lyle scoffs audibly. I'd very much like to punch both of them, but Anton doesn't give them a moment's worry, maintaining his attention on the person in the room with the most authority.

"Those are proprietary." Tanya's clearly taken aback by the request but handles it like a pro.

"Excuse me?" Anton's not asking for a pardon. He's making a threat, and I kind of love it.

"They're for marketing and they're siloed. I can't even see them."

"Wait," I say. "This is a log of my actions, or actions on my account or whatever? How can that be a secret from me? It's my acc—"

Lyle, who's a twenty-something-year-old fucking intern, interrupts me, leaning forward as if he has something to say to me. "If you read the terms of service, it clearly states that ownership of—"

Anton slams his hand on the table. Everyone jumps except me. Somehow, the thick *whacking* sound is neither scary nor shocking.

"She was talking," he says. "When she's talking, you're silent." He turns to me. "Sorry. Go ahead."

"Your terms of service were a lot shorter when I created that account. Now they wouldn't fit up an elephant's ass. Some people might say that's not actually fair, adding on rules in the middle. Your lawyers might say it's legal but go press them on it and tell them Crowne Industries has lawyers too. See what they say. Then go look at your growth areas. Oh wait, you have none, because nobody trusts you, they trust me. They trust me on Instagram, and they'll trust me standing on a fucking box of cat food." I stand. "He wants those logs."

"Ms. Crowne, you don't know what you're asking," Tanya says.

"Maybe not, but he does." I'm doing my level best not to throw a tantrum and ask if they know who I am. "Anton and I will sign an NDA for the logs. We'll sit in a SCIF and read them. I won't understand them anyway." I make the promise with as much professionalism as I can scrape off the sides of the bowl. "This is my security that's being threatened. My life. Please. Don't fuck around with it."

Tanya stands across from me. Her smile holds no derision, and her nod is not dismissive. The knowledge that she's so much smarter and calmer than I'll ever be is a dead weight on my chest. I want to be the most competent person in the room someday.

"I'll see what I can do," she says, then turns to Anton. "But don't count on it."

"Thank you."

Anton's already at the door, opening it for me before I even announce I'm leaving. I walk past the cubicles, along the mezzanine rail, cutting through the lunchtime sounds of the atrium below, and descend the glass stairs with my head high.

When I reach the bottom, I turn and find Anton. He captures my attention so completely, I'm not sure if anyone from the meeting is behind him.

"You're good?" Anton's words are both question and statement. He wants to know if I'm all right, and wants to reassure me that I am.

"Of course. My content built this fucking campus."

Kevin appears behind Anton. "Hey, so." He claps once and rubs his palms together. "Our executive café has a quinoa salad today and it is incredibly fabulous."

"Thanks," I say. "You should go ahead. We're gonna bail."

"I uh, rules. I have to show you to your car, so…" He holds his palm toward the exit, which is big enough for a cathedral.

We let him lead us, chattering about the glorious wonders of the Meta empire.

Anton leans into me and whispers, "You were perfect."

A smile spreads across my face and my cheeks get hot. I'm literally blushing over three stupid words—partly because they're the exact opposite of how I feel, and partly because they're coming from the International Man of Mystery. I have to put my hand over my mouth because I'm grinning like a fucking idiot.

"Here we are," Kevin says when we get to the Range Rover. Anton opens the door for me. "Have a good ride."

"Thanks, Kev. Let me know when the logs are ready."

"Will do!" He steps back and points at Anton. "Nice meeting you too, sir."

Anton waves. I'm about to get in when Kevin throws one more nicety.

"See you at the Amea Club party!"

I wave to Kev, and I hear Anton, just at the lower edge of his breath, mutter, "Like hell you will."

Kevin turns his back to return to work. Anton and I are finally alone.

He demanded the impossible when I didn't know what to ask for. He slammed the table so I could talk. The rush of gratitude for his protection is ridiculous, but overwhelming.

I twist in the seat, throw my arms around his shoulders, and kiss him. He makes an immediate *mmnn* sound, holding his hands away from my body, but he doesn't push me away. He takes a deep breath through his nose and opens his mouth, putting his hands on my back to draw me closer.

The kiss is like being in the ocean with no idea which way is up. I lose all sense of direction, but I'm safe, floating, surrendering in the sense that the water will carry me to where I need to go. When he pulls away, my head thinks I'm still in a directionless sea. I close my eyes to catch up to my physical place in the world. Anton takes another breath and exhales it slowly like a man who can control his own body when everyone else is lost in chaos.

"We should go," he says, starting the car. "I have to get you back and go to the east side."

"You could just take me home. I can get Butterbomb," I suggest. He looks at me sideways, as if I'm not trustworthy, which I guess I'm not. "Please? I swear I'll just drive back to the guest house and not make any stops."

"I'll get someone to follow you." He puts the car into reverse. "And we should keep our hands to ourselves until we find this guy."

"Then all bets are off?"

"All bets are on." He backs out, arm behind my seat.

"One more," I say, then quickly kiss the space under the angle of his jaw. It is as rough and delicious and all-consuming as I hoped. "Okay." I sit back. "All done until we find him."

When I make that promise, I really and truly intend to keep it, but he looks at me as if he doubts he can win the bet he's made with himself.

CHAPTER 31

ANTON

Kissing her again. Tasting her tongue. Holding her face in my hands to feel her every move. I wasn't playing a game in these cramped leather seats, and if I had to guess, neither was she. No games. No playacting. We were who we are.

Which is why I stopped it.

She's in profile now, with the city streaking behind her as I drive.

On the New York subway, I stood over her while she sat, quiet together in the crowded train. She asked me if I'd ever seen the Masstransiscope. I hadn't. *Wait for it*, she'd said. The artwork appeared in the tunnel like a giant, lit-up flip book. Colorful shapes became a man. A rocket. A knot. It was beautiful and unexpected. A treat in an otherwise uneventful trip from point A to point B. But all I could see was her, profiled against the flickering stop motion. Then it was dark again and she turned to me with a smile. I can't remember what she said to me. I only remember a love too big to bear.

Stopped at a light, her Android chimes from my pocket.

She swallows. Looks at the center console, then sets her gaze forward again.

"Last night." The two words are a complete sentence. "Thanks for staying with me."

"You're welcome." I say it as if I've held open the door for a polite stranger.

The phone dings again. The light changes, I drive without checking it.

"The hair tie. In the story." She glances at me finally, then turns back to the road ahead. "Was it mine?"

Of course it was hers. But what would be the point of answering?

"Lyric," I say before I can explain that I can't get too close to her. I'm supposed to protect her. I can't fail. I need to be a man in control. Not a boy in love. "We can't go back to what we were before I left."

"Yeah. Duh."

"I won't be able to protect you. I'll be distracted, blind to pattern changes, overreactive to threats. Useless."

"Anton. I asked about an Hermès hair tie, not our future."

"The games are fine but…" I stop the rest of the thought because it's bullshit. The games are not fine. Pretending we're made-up people with old world powers and hang-ups used to be fun. Now it's a way of tricking myself. We're going back to the guest house together, and I'll walk her to the gate, and we're going to fall into something we shouldn't.

Her phone buzzes with notifications.

"Can you just look at it?" she barks.

At the light, I open it with her code. A quick scroll tells me who's talking to her and what they want. Liang. Jake. Colleen. Kelly.

"Don't tell me," she says before I open my mouth to tell her what the notifications are about. "I just…" When she lowers her gaze, I realize she's terrified. I should have seen that, but I was too busy building cities in my mind. "I don't want to know."

"It's fine," I say about the texts. "Just friends talking about the party at Amea."

"Ah." It's an exhale of tension.

"Tell them you're not going." I hand her the Android and move forward at the green. She doesn't take it.

"I have to go."

"No, you do not."

"Liang's my plus-one. If I don't go, he won't go."

"It's just a party." I pull up to her driveway gate and tap the button on her phone to open it. The spooge has been cleaned off, but it's forever burned into my brain.

"There's someone there who wants to meet him, and I told him I'd help him. How am I supposed to back out now?"

"He'll live."

"He lost his first career because of me. Am I supposed to kill the second one for him?"

"No crowds, Lyric."

I'm about to put the phone in my pocket when she snaps it away, tapping out a response.

"I appreciate you, Anton. But I'm going. Figure it out."

She's looking at her screen when the gate's open halfway, and the only way to close it before she looks up is with the phone she has her attention on.

"Lyric," I say. "Don't—"

When she looks up, her eyes aren't on me. They're forward, at the driveway. She gasps and drops the phone into her lap.

Butterbomb is covered in a bloodbath of dripping red paint.

CHAPTER 32

ANTON

ROSCOE WAS NEARBY. I held her close in the front seat until he arrived. She buried her face in my chest while I watched her car disappear behind the closing gate.

I have never been this angry in my life. I can barely breathe. Even after Roscoe reports that he got Lyric back to the guest house without incident, I am red hot.

Mike whistles when he sees it.

"This is fucked up,"

"Yes, Mikhail, it's fucking fucked." I pace the length of the driveway. "Last night she got a message to the new number, and now this. Fuck!" I almost punch the hood of the car, then stop myself. "How am I letting this happen?!"

"She's safe. That's what we need to—"

"No. I need to end this and I'm nowhere. She's miserable. She's trapped and she's…" I take a deep breath, but only get a teaspoon of air in. "She's so unhappy."

"Hm." He takes out a cigarette but won't light it in the driveway.

"Opening a text, or the gate… anything… it's like a trap.

It's just like opening another envelope and finding a rejection, or a review, or anything she's already been through. But worse. So much worse."

"Come on." He claps me on the back. "At least this time, there's shit you can do about it."

Mike follows me to the stripped-down Echo Park warehouse where this masquerade party is happening.

It's a two-story box. Ten thousand square feet, give or take. The freshly painted mural of nausea-inducing waves of black and white check is unbroken by windows or doors.

"Painted right over them," I say on the street side at the chain-link fence. "It's totally blind."

The building is set back from Glendale Blvd by three car-lengths. Four stories of matte black condos tower over it to the south. A narrow street with a ten-foot cinderblock wall stretches along the north wall. On the west side, a dilapidated two-story Craftsman can serve as a parkour jump to the flat roof.

And how would he get her out?

Five underground parking spaces means he's using street parking. That's a negative. But he'll be a block from the freeway entrance. That's where cars disappear.

"You spoke to the promoter?" Mike asks as we walk around the side street, imagining every possible way this can go wrong. "Her brother, right?"

"Yeah. The ex… Neville. He's not on the guest list."

"I think he's out."

"I don't. And I don't like this space."

"Come on, man." He lights his cigarette. "Her car threw

you off. We dealt with spaces that a bomb rearranged. This is nothing. We have two days to figure it out. Easy."

He hands me the cigarette. I take it without thinking so he can lodge his foot into a crack in the cinderblock wall and his hand over the neighboring six-foot wooden fence around the Craftsman, which—for all intents and purposes—renders the cinderblock wall so useless, a man can get over it with one arm tied behind his back.

I jam the cigarette in my mouth and follow him up, inhaling when I'm stable at the top of the wall. My lungs shudder and my blood runs harder with reawakened delight.

"Cameras are worthless." I point at the surveillance unit on the building's corner and hand back his smoke. "Whoever's looking can watch her get stuffed into a van."

"It's not that big a deal. We get Thomas on this side. I'll station on Glendale. You go in and make eyes at her all night."

"Fuck you."

"Then you should be the one standing around Glendale Blvd. like you're looking for a hooker."

The thought of her inside this solid block while I stand outside it makes my chest tighten.

Already—with no imminent danger—she's sitting behind my sternum, pressing against the back of it, asking me where I am and why I'm not watching her. The walls are closing in, trapping me until I can't get from Echo Park to Beverly Hills fast enough. The space where she existed will be a vacuum in my brain, sucking the rest of the world away with her.

"I'm not going back to Ted Crowne and telling him I lost sight of his daughter," I say. "That's the fastest way to fuck up what we're trying to do here."

From the other side of the club building, a door opens

and closes. Mike and I stay on top of the fence as a shadow moves around the corner and into the backyard.

Dante Crowne shades his eyes. "Markov Group?"

"Yes." I jump down into the yard and shake his hand.

"You did the penetration testing on Crowne HQ."

"We did." Behind me, Mike takes a little longer to get down to our side. I let him arrive on his own clock.

"Keeping track of my sister... you're a brave and tenacious man."

"I just want her to be safe."

"Don't we all."

Dante Crowne takes us through the building as it's being prepped for the party. The length and placement of the halls is unusual because it used to be a small warehouse, but otherwise it's unremarkably up to code.

Meaning, I can't find an excuse to keep her away.

"We good?" Dante says, signing for a palette of linens.

"Yes," Mike says. "Thank you."

"Not good," I add, quickly. "The best way to keep her safe is to keep her away from this party."

"You want me to, what? Deny my own sister entry?" He scoffs. "Have you met her?"

"It's the only way."

"Okay, look," he says. "The fire department cleared us. There's a pat-down on entry. Mags at the front with my guys. Cams on the exits. Anything more and I start to look a little nuts." He looks at me with half a nod—which is to say I'm the one who looks nuts.

"Hold up," Mike says once we're back out on Glendale. "You've done these jobs. What we just saw in there is fine."

He's right, and he's also wrong. I can't deny our experience with guarding politicians and diplomats, but Lyric is neither. She's everything else. That's the problem and I'm smart enough to know it. I'm also stupid enough to not do anything about it.

"She's not going to this thing," I say as if my word is final.

"It's not your job to stop her."

He's right. Even if I win the argument, that doesn't make him wrong.

"You saw her car. Whoever it is, he knows her." I check up and down the block, along rooflines, into windows. It's all wrong. The world is too porous. "Our guy's going to be in that room unless we stop him. We find him before then, and she won't need us."

"You can go as her date."

"She already has a plus-one." I know what he's trying to do and I'm not going to be baited.

"But is she fucking him?"

The question is a slap in the face I manage to dodge, because she's not fucking Liang. In an attempt to see if he's fishing, I look at Mike directly, which allows him to see that he's hooked me.

"I've got it under control," I say.

"You never got over her. Not for a single minute. And you're going to tear your eyes away long enough to see the guy coming for her before it's too late?" He scoffs and shakes his head. "I don't think so. Did she even give you a list with more than one guy on it?"

"No." I unlock my car with the fob and walk toward it. "I'll get it."

"Keep your dick out of her," Mike calls to me.

"No problem." I wave without looking back. Too late for that. He knows I'm lying anyway.

CHAPTER 33

LYRIC

CURLED up in the fetal position in front of the couch, I do a eulogy to my Butterbomb. I love that car. I love the creamy color. The way it's so cute and small. I love driving it. Now I guess I have a choice. Drive it looking like a crime scene or have it towed away forever.

Anton gave me back the Android, but I took off all the apps and shut all the notifications except for voice calls.

Okay. In the end, it's just a car. That's what Dad said when I got into my first fender bender. Just a car. The vulnerability and shock of the accident is what really hurt.

But I'm fine and I can get another car.

I need sun. I go outside with a can of Coke. But the oak tree shading the yard with brown leaves has been alive for a hundred years just to keep me from getting skin cancer. I should climb it, just for fucks and yucks. I step up to it, thinking, whatever, maybe I will. But there's good old Roscoe, scraggly hair camouflaged by the tree bark and shade, looking like a paper cut-out of a generic bodyguard you'd never be able to pick out of a lineup.

"Hi."

He nods. I sigh.

I feel cut off from the workings of the world. Staring at the tomato plants won't get them to grow. The black widows didn't weave any new webs. I could rake the leaves, but a splashing noise comes from the other side of the fence and dots of water spray above it.

"Jorge!" a woman's voice scolds. "Why do you have to do it like that?"

"Because it's fun, Ma."

Someone named Jorge is doing cannonballs into the pool and Mom doesn't dig it. That's a completely unexceptional drama but one I could really use right now.

Grabbing my can, I open the gate that separates the back house from the house in front.

"Oh! Look who's here!" Anton's mother waves me over from the table where I met her. She's sitting next to a dark-haired woman in her mid-thirties who's holding out a towel for a skinny teenage boy who's shaking with cold.

"Hi," I say, putting the can on the table.

The gate clicks. Roscoe stands in front of it with his hands folded in front of him.

"Honey," Anton's mom addresses the other woman, "this is Lyric." She spreads my name out like frosting on a cake. "This is Sabrina. My fiancée."

"So nice to meet you," I say.

"And you. This wet mess is Jorge."

"Hey." He paces to the other side of the patio, towel over his shoulders, looking down at his phone.

"Hey. So, um…"

"Sofia!" Anton's mom cries. "Oh, you're right there. Sorry. Can you get Lyric a big glass with ice?"

"Do you like a lot or a little?" she asks me.

"A lot. Thanks. So, um, I don't—"

"Sit!"

I obey and say what I have to say before she can distract me. "I know you're Anton's mother, but I don't know your name or what I should call you, and I don't want to be disrespectful."

"Oh," Sabrina says with one perfectly plucked raised brow. "I like you."

"You should call me Natalia."

"Mrs. Rojas," Sabrina corrects.

Natalia playfully slaps her fiancée's arm. "Hush."

"You haven't told them yet?"

"Oh, look who needs a little snip-snip!" Natalia gets up and approaches her orchids.

"Told what to whom?" I whisper, leaning forward like a woman starving for gossip, which is exactly what I am.

"She's getting rid of that idiot man's name. It follows her around like a dead dog on a leash."

"I can hear you!" Natalia sings back, pinching away a bit of something on the stem.

"The sons living in Russia will not approve," Sabrina continues at low volume. Anton has two brothers, besides Mike, that he barely talks about. "They're kind of..." she mouths the word *assholes*, then glances at her partner.

I'm borderline high from the juiciness of the gossip.

"It's a surprise," Natalia says, coming back toward us, bumping into a chair. "I don't want to ruin it."

"I wish we could see their reaction, *mija*."

Natalia leans into her fiancée, who puts her arm around her waist. It's sweet. I could almost feel safe here. I'm not thinking about the bodyguard by the gate, watching everything. I'm just here with a nice family.

Then my phone vibrates on the table, and that's that. Mood murdered.

"I'm going to throw this thing in the pool."

Gingerly, I flip it so the glass side faces up. It's Anton. I answer.

"Hey."

"Where are you?" He doesn't even say hello.

"By the pool?" I state it like a question because I can't help feeling like he's being stubborn.

"Which pool?"

Natalia sits. Her cushion falls through the space between the chair back and seat. Sabrina reaches down for her lover's cushion.

"Your pool, Anton."

He hangs up. I put down the phone. A minute ago, I was having fun. I'd forgotten I was one text away from getting abducted, or raped, or whatever.

I also forgot I'm right in front of Wow-Dude's mother, who clears her throat and scootches in her chair.

"Tell him we invited you over," Sabrina says.

"Oh, it's fine. Roscoe's right there"—I wave at the quiet man with all the hair—"and I haven't left the property."

With a shocking *clack*, the back gate swings open and smacks against the fence. Anton stalks around the pool, waves to Jorge—who barely looks up—gives Roscoe a glare, and stands at the end of the table, casting a shadow as black as his turtleneck.

"Roscoe's been there the whole time," I say when Anton's in earshot. I don't like him giving the guy a hard time just because I slipped away once.

"What are you doing here?" he asks.

"We like her," Sabrina cuts in. "So you can take a seat and ask your next question nicely."

"Sofia!" Natalia calls. "Can you bring Anton a Zivchik?"

"I don't want any."

"You love the apple soda," I say. "You said so."

"I just went into the back house." He puts his fists on the table and leans over me. If he's trying to scare me, he can take notes from the guy who bugged my house, cut off my socials, and found my new number. "The door was wide open, and you weren't there."

"Because I'm here."

"Anton," Sabrina whispers, soothing, as if they're the only people here. She stretches her arm across the table, palm down, and clicks her ring against the glass twice. "I don't know why you're acting like a fool, but sit the fuck down."

Sofia comes out with a tray of soda and ice for Anton. He thanks her, then looks at each of the three of us before he sits, his gaze lingering on me.

"I need to know your location at all times, or I can't protect you." He takes a drink of his soda and wipes his upper lip with his fingertips.

"I'm here."

"I'm aware that you know where you are."

"You could just AirTag me."

Anton sucks on his teeth. His knee bounces like a piston. I can't tell what he's thinking, but he's sure thinking a lot of it.

"Why do all that?" Natalia says sweetly, putting her hand over his. "You have Roscoe right there."

"He's been great," I say. "And I like sitting here with these guys. For, like, five minutes, I wasn't afraid my phone was going to ding or that someone was going to climb the fence. I didn't feel trapped or confined or isolated."

"That solves it," Natalia says. "You're staying for dinner."

"Oh, that sounds nice."

"I'm making my Texas chili recipe," Natalia says.

"Come for the beautiful Ukrainian women," Sabrina says, touching her fiancée's face. "Stay for the authentic meals."

Everyone laughs except for Anton, who's hidden behind his bubbling glass. Didn't we just fuck? Was it yesterday, two days ago? Or three years ago and thousands of miles away? He seems like a man who never kisses anyone, or at least never enjoys it. I try to remember him in New York, pounding code, frowning, too serious for his own good. When I kissed him, the frown would break into a smile and his piercing gaze would open as wide as the sky.

"I like chili," I say with a shrug. "I'm kind of tired of being trapped in that back house anyway."

"We have reservations," Anton says, then stands with his soda in hand. "At seven. Be ready." He points at the fence with his glass in his hand. "Back house."

He takes his empty soda into the big house without looking back.

CHAPTER 34

LYRIC

ANTON DRIVES HIS CAR, since Butterbomb looks like a crime scene. Not that a criminally gorgeous sourpuss in a Range Rover shouldn't be a felony on its own.

"Where are we going?" I ask.

"We're almost there." His eyes are on the road and his gaze is somewhere miles deep inside. "About Neville."

"Still jealous of nothing?"

At a red light, he looks as me with a mix of displeasure and lust—as if he wants to spank me for my behavior, then fuck me as punishment, and I can't say that sounds unappealing. If we were in a comic book, he'd have wavy lines of intensity coming out of his eyes and I'd have hearts popping out of me. If it was a dirty comic, there'd be little gremlins poking between my thighs. This isn't either. It's real life, and I can't look away as I turn into a puddle.

"I need to know everything." He glances at me for a split second, then back at the road. "I checked. You have no posts about him."

I let out a little laugh. "There's one post. There were more on his account, but they got taken down. I guess if you were better at this, you'd find them."

His lips tighten and he stares forward, his gaze as heavy and hard as a statue. If he's mad, I don't know why. But I think, maybe, he's weighing what to say next more carefully than I would.

"Let me tell you," I continue. "I will never, ever date a guy with that kind of reach again. I mean, I kind of knew he was shallow and self-absorbed. It comes with the territory. But he really *was* mad I had more followers. And, dude, if you keep pimping energy powder, yes, you're going to lose people. That's not quality content. That's loser content. You're supposed to be entertaining them, not sucking them dry. You know? And he couldn't hear that. He kept saying oh, let's do another beach day! And so I said yeah, I'd go with him and post from the pier, but he was like, 'no, no. The *beach*. And wear that bikini,' so yeah. Okay. Fine. Like, I can see that the first beach shoot we did, he got a ton more interaction, and the pic where I had a little cleave went viral. But the comments can get super gross and what does he do? Nada. Doesn't get in front of it at all. Then his next post drops dead. Like duh. Nobody. Wants. Your. Shit. Powder. Whatever. End of summer, I say, 'Okay, fine. The beach.' And you know what he did."

"I don't."

"It felt like everyone saw it in the little time it was up."

He shrugs. "You don't have to say. I'll just assume it was bad."

"While his douchebag idiot friend was making a video, he undid the string on my top."

He makes a sound that's half-cluck, half-hiss, shaking his head in disapproval.

It's more powerful than any strongly worded reply.

"He posted it with a bar across my nipples, and it lasted on IG for about fifteen minutes. But when I got mad at him, he was all, 'It was just a joke, baby, take it easy,' so I posted a video saying that wasn't cool and apologizing to anyone who saw it. Then he realizes he fucked up, so what does he do? Directs his douchebags to his website where the full tits had no bar." I pause to grind my teeth and take a hard swallow. "It lasted like two weeks, but I thought maybe I was moving on from…" I wave in Anton's direction. I don't want to tell him how hard it was to move on from him. "I thought… I don't know. He was cute. We had fun. I couldn't see how he was."

"A man selling energy powder?"

"I have high-end self-esteem and bargain-basement judgment. So, lesson learned."

"Is he going to be there? At this Amea Club party you insist on?"

"Hell no. He's finished now."

"Are you sure?"

"I destroyed him, Anton. My lawyers got him on a trademark violation. The Chinese powder factory closed. He moved back into his parents' house… in Castaic, for fuck's sake. We broke him and left him for dead."

"Jesus Christ." He rubs his jaw. "I asked you if you had any enemies."

"I don't."

"He's been seething… for how long?"

"He never spoke in complete sentences. I doubt he could pull off an 'exploit' or 'hack' or whatever."

He's silent for a minute, working his jaw, fisting the steering wheel as if steadying himself against it as he slows down to get in line for the valet serving a courtyard of seven restaurants.

"I should have told you everything. It was just… I don't know. Kind of humiliating."

"No." He turns into the line for the valet. "You did everything right."

"Doesn't feel like it."

"You destroyed him." He squeezes my hand and leans into me. "It's exactly what I would have done."

CHAPTER 35

LYRIC

HIS CHOICE SURPRISES ME. The name of the restaurant is Ne10, the symbol and atomic weight of neon, and it's lit up and down, corner to corner in… shocker… neon. The food is all reflective white so the hot red and purple light doesn't trick your camera into thinking your meal is an uninstagrammable black blob.

"Ms. Crowne!" the maitre'd says, scuttling over as soon as we show up. The staff wears black turtlenecks, like a little army of Antons. "You're back!"

"Hey, Henry." I don't know why I'm embarrassed. He has to know no one shows up for the food.

"I haven't seen you post in… hm… did I miss something? Two weeks?"

It's been less than a week, and I'm not sure if I should correct him or just slink into a corner and die. Anton breaks into my shame like the Kool-Aid guy.

"We have a reservation."

Henry waves for us to follow, leading us to a corner table.

"This is super romantic." I hold up my phone and open

the camera toward my face. I'm red with a flashing yellow and green edge on my forehead. "I look like a traffic light."

"You said you liked this place."

"It doesn't matter what I *said*." I'm hunched and scratching out my voice low enough to just be heard over the music. "It's branding... like this turtleneck thing you have going on."

"Do you ever mention the places you do like?"

"Sure. All the time."

"So." He leans forward, elbows on the table. "If I want to know where you might be, I can play the odds. I find out which nights you go out. I find places you've been to more than once. I do the math. Then imagine me in here, wearing this, where everyone is dressed the same."

He'd still look better than any of them, frankly, but he doesn't need his ego stroked right now. What he needs is me, listening.

"Could be the Noho Room on a Thursday. Could be here. Or the new Instagram-ready pop-up that's been sending out meal vouchers to every influencer in LA?"

"Hey there." A waiter appears, dropping square white napkins in front of us. "On the house." The two drinks on his tray are in glasses ringed with battery-powered neon bulbs twisting up them. They have straws, which are totally normal, but imagining Anton, a full man, drinking from one of them seeds some deep mortification in my soul. "Henry wanted you to try them."

"Thanks," I say.

He pauses, waiting for further instructions, and when he gets none, he leaves.

Henry waves from the front. A woman my age takes a picture. It may be of me, or I may be in the frame. A man at the bar looks in my general direction. Suddenly, it's all threats.

"I don't know what you're trying to say." I slide my drink toward me and whip off the paper at the end of the straw. "I've been leaving the house and going places for years already."

"I'm telling you that whoever is after you probably expects you to be at your brother's club."

"See, but I have you there. I don't usually go to his dork parties."

"The odds, Lyric. He's going to play the odds."

"If he can get an invitation."

"Or a job slinging lemonade." he growls, then takes a deep breath, speaking more calmly. "Mike and I checked out the venue. It's not secure."

I take a long pull of my drink. It's sweet enough to hide the alcohol and smooth enough to drain halfway without a pause. Lemonade.

"What does secure mean even? Does it mean you're hanging over me? Bossing me around?"

"No, because I'm not confident I can protect you there. I spoke to Dante. He's not confident he can either. Let me tell you what's going to happen if you continue to insist on going to this party." He locks his eyes on mine, dead serious. "I will wait outside. You'll have a good time. You'll dance and talk to your friends. You will need to keep your drink in your hand all night and that may or may not keep him from drugging it. He will try to lure you away with a text. He'll use your friends to trap you. Isolate you. If there's nothing in your drink, there may be something on the napkin. He may slip something into your friend's drink, and he'll be there to help you with them. He'll have a way out the back, so you don't have to go through the crowd. You'll have a problem and he'll be there to solve it."

"I won't drink, or breathe. Or… help." That's a lie. I'm definitely doing at least two. "I'll be extra careful if I do."

"You won't see it coming, Lyric." There's no insult in the words. He's not calling me oblivious or ignorant. I don't even have a chance to put in a good counterargument before he goes on. "What he can do to you is going to make those texts look like love notes." He drinks his water for a heavy-pause effect that's utterly transparent, and very effective at giving my imagination time to work. "If he touches a single hair on your head, I will kill him. This is not an overstatement or some metaphor for siccing lawyers on him. I will commit murder. But if you're hurt… or worse… what's that going to matter?"

I gather my bag in my lap. "I've managed without you for a long time. And I'll keep managing." Standing, I look down at him, slinging my bag over my shoulder. "I'm going to the ladies'. You'll be amazed at how I can do it myself."

Turning with military precision, I head for the ladies' room, passing casual interest and short, intense stares. I am recognizable in a place like this. Exposed in three dimensions, unfiltered, made of flesh instead of light.

As always. I've always been this vulnerable, and I've always done what I want. The change is throwing me.

The bathroom's locked, so I wait in the hall and look at my phone.

Message from Jake. He wants to talk but won't get more specific.

Message from Liang with a funny meme comparing racists to roller skates.

Email from Kevin P. I'm just about to open it when Anton texts.

—*do you trust me?*—

That's a full question. Its depth and breadth should require more than a simple yes or no. But in this case, if I'm being honest with myself, it doesn't require more than one word. And if I'm going to be honest with myself, I can be honest with him.

The latch clicks and the bathroom's empty. I lock myself in.

Yes. I trust him. I trust his intentions and his abilities. Do I trust him with my heart? Maybe not, but he wasn't asking that and doesn't need confirmation of what he already knows. After I wash up and dry my hands, I text my answer.

—yes—

I fluff my hair, get my bag, and unlatch the door. I'm immediately faced with pressure from the other side. Pushed backward, I gasp as Anton enters and locks what I just unlocked.

"What—?"

He grabs me, turns me around, and puts his hand over my mouth. "You see how easy this is?" he hisses in my ear.

In the mirror, we lock into a stare. My grunted response is both fuck you and let me go.

"I can fuck you right now."

His hand wedges between my legs. I try to wiggle away, but he's strong, and the more I resist, the tighter he holds me. I'm not scared. I'm both annoyed and turned on.

"What if there had been something in that drink?"

I roll my eyes. He increases the pressure of his fingers and I groan into his palm.

"You'd be half unconscious already." He unbuttons my jeans. "You'd be slumped in my arms like you had too much to drink, and I'd just carry you out like a knight in shining armor." He unzips me. "I'd be at the table waiting. Then what?"

"Mmph," comes out when I tell him I don't know. He gets his fingertips just past the top edge of my underwear.

"Time out if you want to." He runs his lips along the ridge of my neck, melting the skin under them into warm, yielding flesh.

My hands could come together. I could time out. Instead I shake my head against his hand.

"You want me to take you like this?"

I nod, looking at him in the mirror.

"Like it's the first time I'm touching this pretty pussy?" He slides his hand down as I nod again. "Like I've wanted to take what you refused me?" He moves his hand from my mouth so I can answer.

"Yes."

Pushing deep, his fingers dig between my seam. He's rough and careless. Pushing his erection against my ass while he jams inside me.

"You're wet." His other hand circles my throat. "I knew you wanted me. It was all a game for you, this whole time."

"Let me go, you pig."

He pulls me close to him by the throat. I couldn't get away even if I wanted to. I am powerless to stop the arousal pulsing through my veins.

"I'll let you go when we're done." He bites my earlobe and

tugs it, my earring clicking against his teeth. "Pull your jeans down so I can fuck you."

I struggle to get away. Maybe not as hard as I would if he was really the man stalking me, but hard enough to force him to pin me to the vanity with his hips. He holds my head against the mirror with his hand.

"Fine," he says. "We'll do it your way."

He pulls down my jeans and underwear, easily matching my twists to keep me still. I fling my arms behind me, but my blows are weak. Nothing's going to stop him but a time-out, which I won't give. I've never wanted any man inside me so much. There's no fear, only desire.

When his head is poised to enter me, he asks, "You timing out?"

"No."

Roughly, he holds me down to thrust inside me. "You love this."

"No, I don't!" But in the mirror, I nod. Yes. I love it.

He pulls out, then slams back in. The edge of the counter digs into me and he pushes so hard it hurts. I shudder, blown apart with pleasure.

"Condom," I gasp.

He grabs my hand and pulls it behind, putting it at the base of his dick, where I can feel the tight ring of rubber. I have no idea when or how he got it on, and trying to figure it out goes nowhere when he takes a handful of hair and jerks my head back. We're eye to eye in the mirror.

"Watch me fuck you." He holds me by hip and hair, thrusting behind me with gritted teeth.

"Is that what you're doing, loser?"

He tightens his grip, pulling my hair harder, as if I'm his

toy to use and abuse. "I'm fucking Lyric Crowne and she knows it."

"Do I? Maybe you should try harder."

"Maybe I should." He pulls out and whips down my pants. "Turn around."

I put my back to the vanity. He lifts my left leg. My loose pants fall to the floor, and he puts my leg around his waist. We're face to face when he enters me again.

"That's it." We're nose to nose. Open mouth to open mouth. "A-plus for effort."

"Haven't even started."

He fucks me as if he's trying to kill me, and yet the deeper he drives, the closer he gets to touching the places I've closed off for so long. He puts a hand behind my neck and puts his face to mine, breath to breath, eye to eye, as he says my name.

"Lyric."

It's just my name. One of the first words spoken to me, and from his lips, it's the world. It's freedom, and refuge, and a prayer in the dark. My name like this doesn't call me. It calls us, together. I crack from the inside and contentment spills out, flooding my veins with well-being and peace. The more that gushes through the cracks, the fuller I become.

"Anton. It was always you."

"Always."

When I hold his face and kiss him, I'm safe under a dragon's wing.

I try to keep my eyes open to see how a man so strong can be so soft—how fucking me this hard can feel like a form of protection—but I'm swallowed in wave after wave of pleasure. I close my eyes with the explosion of heat.

My mouth opens to cry out, but no sound comes as I

release when he's deep inside, rigid with overwhelming pleasure. I feel the pulse of his orgasm against me. His lips fall on my throat in a slow kiss.

"You okay?" he asks.

"Very." I pull his face to mine. He kisses my cheek and pulls out. I hop off the vanity. "Thank you."

I pull up my pants while he buttons his, and as he turns on the faucet to wash his hands, I remember that I just washed mine. I was getting ready to go back to the table. This all started with him showing me how easy I was to isolate.

"I guess you made your point." I wash my hands next to him, and we share the warm flow of water. "I shouldn't go."

"You should not." He dries his hands while I shake the excess off mine. The doorknob jiggles. Someone's been waiting. "Unless we get him first."

He shuts off the water.

CHAPTER 36

LYRIC

We didn't end up eating at Ne10. Anton threw a bunch of money on the table, and we left in favor of the In-n-Out drive-thru. With our bags in my lap, he parks in a corner of the lot. I reach into the bag and hand him his burger.

He takes it with one hand, and with the other, he snaps open a napkin and lays it across my lap. I do the same for him, then set the French fry bag in the center console as he opens my burger for me.

Once we've each taken a few bites, Anton nods. "These are better than I remember."

"Meh. They'll do."

"Why is this one party so important to you?"

"Because." The entire episode with *Standard Deviation* is so blocked in my mind, I almost don't tell him, but he was there the whole time. He saw the whole nightmare as it happened. "Because Liang had to quit school to be in *Standard Deviation*. I promised him my agent would sign him, which he didn't. Then I promised when the movie was released, more work would come, and it didn't. He quit trying and I can't blame him. I promised him what I couldn't even get for myself—a literal career—and he never got mad. He trusted me with his acting career, and I fucked up so bad he left New York, and now I have the chance to help him do something else."

"Maybe you should stop promising things."

"Fuck you," I whisper, cursing the fact, not the messenger.

"Lyric Crowne," he says, softly, eyes on mine without the piercing bite I've gotten used to, but something warmer that I recognize from a lifetime ago. "The only thing you fucked up at was dreaming you could make a movie and control what people thought of it."

"Yeah," I scoff. "They—the film professors and every industry douche they brought in—were like, 'oh, it's really about the process,' but none of them ever said what that actually means. Like, does it not matter if I finish? Does it not matter what people want to see? If I want to keep working, I should maybe check the market before I start this quote-unquote process they worship so much but can't fucking define?"

He shrugs, chews, scans the parking lot a moment before planting his attention back on me. "Maybe that's the process?"

"Sure. It's everything. That's why they don't bother explaining it. Meanwhile, I've got on clown shoes and a big honky nose. And Liang, who's going to have a hard time as it is for reasons I don't have to list, is stuck pulling on my bowtie to make it spin. I won't ever disappoint anyone who believes in me again. I won't put them in that position."

He shakes his head slowly, as if I don't understand shit and never will. "I think I grew up with different clowns."

I wipe my mouth, trying not to laugh. "Just let me suck in peace, Anton."

"No." He grabs my hand and squeezes. I stare at our clasped hands, mine with a French fry between two fingers, shocked at the sudden, intense intimacy. "I will never leave you in peace or otherwise."

He did already though. Apology notwithstanding, he may think he's somehow better than any other man I could be with, but he did it.

I pull my hand away. He clears his throat, then crumples up his packaging. He eats faster than I do, and I'm not rushing. In the silence, my mind takes a review of the night. Back to leaving Ne10, the sex in the bathroom, the conversation at the table about how I couldn't go to the party.

Wait. I'm missing a part.

When I first got up from the table, in the hallway outside the bathroom, I was looking for something before Anton texted me about trusting him. There was an email.

"Oh!" I say. "I heard from Kevin." I wipe my fingers and reach into my bag, finding the phone. I unlock it and hand it to him so I can eat. The device glows on Anton's face, cutting the edges of his jaw at a sharper angle while his skin glows. My jaw stops moving, unable to chew and appreciate his beauty at the same time. When he looks at me, I feel as if I've been caught peeking in his window while he undresses. I pop the last of the burger in my mouth and crumple my packaging. "What does he say?"

"The PEG logs have arrived." He starts the car. "I'll drop you back at the house. Someone will be there to watch you."

"Ah. Okay." I try to hide my disappointment. I didn't realize I wanted to take him to bed for real until it was clear he wouldn't accept the offer. "I should probably scrub the upholstery on that chair anyway."

"Buttons." Taking the bottom of my chin, he tilts my face up to him. "I have you. You have to trust me."

I do—with everything but my heart, and that's the one thing I'm starting to lose control over.

CHAPTER 37

ANTON

It's not that late. Mike's car is in the lot under the building. There's light filtering past the edges of the blinds. I can see he's home enough to answer the door and sure as fuck home enough to answer a text.

I'm about to punch the door again, but he opens it in nothing but pajama pants. I can see where his shoulder ends in a long, ugly scar.

"What the fuck are—"

"Get dressed." I brush past him into his apartment. "We have to go."

"You can't call?" He indicates the bathroom door. "I have someone here."

"I did call. And I texted. You don't pick up."

"I was busy."

"You just answered your own question." I look at my watch even though I know the time within five minutes. "Meta's on coder hours, but they won't be there all night. We have half an hour to get to Mar Vista. They'll put us in a room with her PEG logs."

"Oh, shit, really?" He seems impressed. "You got them? Wow."

I point at his bare chest and roll my wrist telling him to get dressed.

"Let me just explain," he says, heading for the bathroom.

"Give me her phone. Lyric's."

"It's right on my desk."

I snap it up. A door opens and light flows down the hall before it's flicked off.

"Mikey?" a woman's voice comes from the bathroom.

"Coming," Mike calls to her then whispers to me, "Stay here."

I wave him away and open Lyric's emails. Search for Neville. Find neville@powerpowder69.com. The entire first screen of messages is CCs from her lawyers. They really did not waste a single word breaking him, and though I admire it, I don't have time for it. The last email is a forwarded ticket to Coachella over a year ago. He responded with *See you there, babe.*

Babe.

He's an unworthy moron and that one word burns my gut more than any four letters ever have.

I hear Mike and the woman whispering. She giggles. I know I burst in on him unexpectedly, but I don't want to spend an hour listening to him excusing himself from a one-night stand.

Next email from Neville. No *babe*. Logistics of dinner. The entirety of the relationship seems to span a month, but I check each one.

I tell myself I'm looking for clues and threats, but that's not one hundred percent truth.

Every email I read that lacks affection or commitment

slices off another layer of tension to the seeds of relief at my core. She didn't love him. I'm not even convinced she liked him.

It shouldn't matter.

Oh, but it fucking does.

"Find anything?" Mike says to me a minute later, wearing a shirt and sweatpants this time. He plops himself into his chair and wrestles on his socks.

Did I?

Lyric was in a one-month relationship with a man who called her *babe*. They went to Coachella, some restaurants, and arranged some social media promotions. Then her lawyers blew him up, scraped him off the pavement, put him in an envelope, and mailed him back to his mother.

"No," I say. "Nothing actionable."

"Hello there." A woman with curly blond hair stands at the bedroom door wearing a man's bathrobe.

"I... babe." Mike—second sock half-drooping off the end of his foot like a cooked noodle— seems caught out. He's never been serious enough about a woman to bring her around for an introduction, now this one is out here introducing herself. "Come on."

"You didn't give me the key." She holds her hand out for it. "I'll go get breakf—"

"Yeah!" His agreement is designed to interrupt. Whatever she was going to say, he didn't want her to say it in front of me.

She looks at him warmly then turns to me, hand out. "Hi, I'm Donna."

I shake with her. "Nice to meet you, Donna. I'm—"

"This is Anton," Mike says, exasperated. "My brother."

"Oh, tourniquet brother!" She smiles, making a connection that I wish to God she hadn't.

"Yeah. Jeez. Um… okay!" Socks on, Mike stands. "We should go."

"I have work, so I may be gone when you get back." She tucks his left sleeve inside out so it lays flat against his scar.

How self-involved am I to not realize I'm interrupting something that's more important than PEG logs?

"I'll go myself." I stand. "It's fine. Donna, glad to meet you." Did I already say that? Shit. I feel like a caged rat being handed a broken hair tie.

I'm out the door into the cool night air when I hear Mike.

"Hey!" He's chasing me down the stairwell. "What is wrong with you?"

"Go inside before you ruin your socks."

"Wait a minute and I'll come with you."

"Stay with Donna."

"She's fine. Look, I told her the story about my arm. It's like a story you tell someone when… you know. Come on."

"Put it on a billboard if you want. It's your story to tell."

"I wasn't trying to make you look bad." He pats his pockets the way he does when he's looking for his cigarettes, but they're not there.

"It's fine. You can't tell it without making me look bad."

"Which is why I don't tell anyone unless… what I'm saying is, I know how you are about what happened, and you shouldn't be."

"I said it's fine. I'm not mad."

But I am mad, just not at him. Not at Donna. I'm free-floating mad for reasons. Just reasons.

"You did your best," Mike says.

"Gold star for me."

"Why are you like this?"

"Like what?"

"This!" He holds out his palm, presenting me. I'm *this*. "My fucking God, it's like you're the one who lost the arm."

"It's not!" I shout. "I'm the one who walked away whole. I know you forgave me for fucking up, but that makes it worse. If you won't remember what I did, then I have to remind myself constantly or I'll fuck up again. What do I walk away whole from then?"

He raises his arm then drops it. "Man, you're such a... forget it."

He starts to walk back upstairs to Donna, who'll tuck in his sleeve and probably help him with his socks if I'm not standing there watching.

"I'm sorry I interrupted, but I need you," I say. He stops. "I need you because..." This is what I'm mad about. Yes, my fuckup and guilt and tourniquets and limbs—but also... "When I think about this guy... what he wrote... how he wants to hurt her..." I step up to him. "I can't control everything she does for much longer. She only needs to be exposed once. For one minute. If it's the wrong minute... I'll walk away whole again, but I'll be too broken to do anything."

"Okay, you cannot be the only one guarding her, ever. Okay? Because your head is fucked. We cannot lose the Crowne account."

"We won't."

"Are we ever going to have a real office? Because we told each other we wanted to be something and if you changed your mind, you need to tell me.""

"Yeah. But I'm not thinking straight. You have to come."

"Oh, you need me all right. I'm the talent of this operation."

Panic is replaced with relief. I do need him to keep me in control. I have failed him, and I'd fail without him.

"Put some fucking shoes on."

The Meta offices are as crowded at nine thirty as they are at lunchtime. Tanya's there, fresh as a daisy. Security never sleeps.

She leads us into a small, windowless room with two keyboards at a table with two smaller monitors each. They face a wall that's a monitor—corner to corner.

"You're all set to go. Logs are already up." She closes the door, leaving us alone.

Throwing myself into the chair, I pull up the PEG logs from the same time as Neville's emails. Mike works backward from the most recent. Lyric's phone sits between us for reference.

This takes hours.

I match IPs with the Instagram direct messages. At first, I find the ones I know Neville sent, scanning through more *babes* until I get to… *Why'd you have to go and do that?*

She didn't reply. Good for her.

But after? New account. Same IP. Same device ID.

Worn out cunt.

And after? Same device ID.

You're just a shallow, unfuckable bitch.

What if someone cut your tits off and rubbed salt in them. I'd laugh when you cried. If you begged I'd piss on you to wash the salt off.

"We got him." I tap the screen. "It's over."

"Walk me through it."

"This is the last one where this device ID and this IP are together. After that, he got smart but not that smart. So check out the PEGs. This is the same device ID on a jpg." I scroll to the dick pic.

"Man." He cringes. "I do not want to see that shit."

"He wised up and cloaked his IP, but same phone."

"So we call the cops."

"Fuck that. They won't do anything until she's hurt. We're going to Castaic."

CHAPTER 38

ANTON

ONE CRACK in the bowl is all it takes to get the water to flow out. With the PEG logs, the crack in Neville's secret widens to a half-mile area. After that, it takes us twenty minutes to geolocate him from public information.

His friends have him in videos drinking beer at bars and watching the games from a trailer parked in his parents' yard. The backgrounds made him easy to geolocate. Google maps shows the placement of the trailer on the far end of a two-acre property.

"How far do you want to go?" Mike asks when we make the second spin around the house.

"I don't know."

"You don't know, or you don't want to say?"

"Yes."

He leans forward and points toward a spot on the back fence. "There."

I pull over, put the car into park, and start to get out when Mike stops me.

"I don't want to lose this client."

"We won't." I'm promising something I'm not sure I can deliver. After the tourniquet, I took an inventory of things I don't know, and how to lose the Crowne account wasn't on it. How to neutralize a threat wasn't either. That, I know how to do.

We come in over the back fence. The trailer may have been new when he moved into it, but Neville's not much for maintenance.

There's workout equipment in front. Free weights, mostly. A few other torture devices on uneven ground. Empty beer bottles set up on a sawhorse. Mike's feet crunch on broken glass. I shift a shredded Miller Lite can with my foot. Target practice.

"He's armed," Mike whispers.

I nod. So are we, but I leave the gun in its holster.

We sneak around the side. TV light shines through the back window. It's after three in the morning. He's probably asleep, but I'm not taking any chances.

Mike gently pushes down the door handle. Not locked. Someone feels safe in his little yard. Good.

My brother swings open the door and we rush into the cramped space. Neville's standing at the open refrigerator, in a dirty white T-shirt and nothing else, balls hanging down like a half empty sack of driveway rocks.

That little dick touched her. That's the only thought that enters my head. And she touched it, then she was betrayed. He should have done nothing but worship her.

He shouts some meaningless vowel and throws the gallon of milk in his hand at Mike. I have him face down on his grimy linoleum floor with my knee pressed between his shoulder blades before he can make another sound.

"I don't have anything!" Neville says.

"Hush." I put my hand on the side of his head and lean on it. He's not going to be easy to keep down. He's been using the workout equipment, that's for sure. "Keep still and we won't slit your throat."

He knots his brow, concerned that was even on the table.

Mike sits at the computer. Two screens. Porn on one. A chat room on the other. Neville makes sounds behind my palm, and though there's not an articulate word among them, I know what he's asking.

"All the good shit's in my parents' house," he says, spit flying. He tries to get his hands under him to push up, but I dig the angle of my knee into the flat of his back.

"We're not here for that."

I glance at Mike, who is lighting a cigarette as a blue bar creeps across the bottom of a dialog box. Neville grunts, trying to throw me off. I punch him in the side of the head, then shake out my hand. He's got a hard skull.

"What are you here for?" Neville asks.

The blue bar fills and the dialog box blips away.

"I came here to borrow a cup of milk or rip your dick off, and you just spilled all the milk."

The fear in his eyes is satisfying, but it's nothing compared to the constant fear he's put in Lyric's.

"Would you look at this," Mike says from the computer setup. "A whole file of screenshots. Is that… Lyric?"

"Is it?" I ask, looking at Neville because I know the answer.

"It's like an altar, but in a folder."

Neville wiggles, and I barely manage to hold him down. Rage is making me stronger, but it won't be long before fear does the same to him.

"So, now what choice do I have? You think you're smart?

You think you can make her scared? That get you off, you little bitch? You worthless bag of garbage? You shitstain."

"I don't know what you're talking about!" This time, he gets me off him.

I find myself thrown under a fold-out table. Metal clicks against metal as a drawer opens. I can't see shit from under here, so I get out my gun.

Too late. Mike already has his Glock pressed against Neville's temple, cigarette dangling from his lips. Neville's hands are up, and his gaze is fixed on the open drawer in front of him.

I get out and look inside. There's a Colt 45 mixed in with the kitchen utensils. I take it and slide it into my waistband.

Neville coughs. Covers his mouth. Mike almost shoots him.

"There's no smoking in here, dude."

"You should put up a sign," Mike says, inhaling and exhaling without removing the cigarette from his lips.

I push Neville into the desk chair. He lands with his legs spread and his balls flattened against the black pleather. For a moment, I consider him. His face. His hair. His body. The cheek swelling where I hit it. The muddy eyes triangulating from my brother, to me, to the gun, back to Mike, who's holstered his gun to flick his ashes into the sink.

He touched her with those hands. Kissed her with that mouth. I have no control over the images that flash in my head. They are my experiences but from his point of view.

"What happened to your fucking arm?" Neville asks Mike.

"I was pulling a dollar out of a lion's mouth."

"Where's your phone?" I ask.

"Kitchen counter."

I grab it and point the screen to him. Facial recognition opens it right up. I hand it over to Mike.

"If you're ordering pizza," Neville says, "I'm lactose intolerant."

I can't tell if he's fucking with us or he's this stupidly sincere. There's one way to find out.

"This is your only warning. Stay away from Lyric Crowne."

"I haven't gone near her in months. Even once, when we were at the same—"

"Shut up!" I bark. "We know everything. We know about the cameras, and the texts… and she loved that car, you sick fuck."

"Jesus, man," Mike says, scrolling through the phone. "How many pictures of your dick do you have to take before it looks good?"

"What the fuck happened to the car?"

"Which one of these did you send Lyric?" I ask, and he shrugs a little… just enough to admit he sent at least one.

"Is this like a glamor shot or something?" Mike holds up the phone and I'm assaulted with a dick pic.

"Find the texts he sent her. The one about raping her."

I want to hit Neville repeatedly for putting that phrase in my mouth. There's a metal knife block at the sink.

"What? No. I messaged her a reminder of what she gave up."

"Your dick?" I pull out a knife.

"Yeah! And tough shit. If she doesn't like it, she can delete it. But I bet she still has it. She's a fucking bitch, but I never said I'd rape her."

I lay the knife on the counter. Between fucking with us or

being stupidly sincere, he's definitely the latter. I don't need Mike to find the texts. This is our guy.

"You did." I pull off another, skinnier knife.

"It's not rape if she wants it."

I dump all the knives in the sink and throw the block at him.

———

Near dawn. In the car. Driving home with bloody knuckles. Mike is next to me, scrolling through Neville's phone.

"The texts aren't here," he says.

"Deleted."

"Maybe." He puts down the phone. Neville's computer rig rattles in the back. "What now?"

"We tell Ted Crowne that we got him. Lyric is free."

"And we stole evidence. Roughed the guy up. Made it impossible to prosecute in an American court?"

"She can go home. That's what's important."

———

We have Neville Bennett's computer but not his bitterness. He's going to keep that and carry it around, unleashing it on someone, somewhere, some time. If Lyric hears from him again, I won't hesitate to do what the law won't.

When I get back to the house, I intend to wash my hands and go to bed, but my blood is half adrenaline and a quarter testosterone. The soap makes my knuckles sting, and I keep thinking about that little man and his ball sac dragging on the seat of his chair.

The sight enraged me, and the memory of it nags at me.

It's not jealousy that Lyric chose to get near that sac—though I'm not delusional enough to deny that the thought of him touching her makes me want to rip off his head. It's the ugliness and weakness of this man who held power over her.

We're all ugly and weak. Every man is vulnerable.

Neville and I share soft flesh that rips when hot metal hits it, and when the shrapnel cools, we will scar the same. Our bones can be broken with the same impact. Plaque covers our teeth and fugitive hair grows all over our bodies.

Lyric is safe, and though she's beautiful, she is just as weak and vulnerable.

One sack of bone protects another from a third.

The power pulsing through my veins runs its course, leaving me in the bathroom, leaning into the mirror to see every pore and wrinkle.

What vanity, to convince myself I could keep her safe.

Her lights are off. There will be no sleep for me, but I can hold her in my arms and tell myself I'm satisfied. The job is done. I'm free to turn my back on her again. It's all lies.

Before I think too hard about it, I slip downstairs, out the kitchen door, across the yard. I put in the code for the back gate, then the house, locking the door behind me.

She's a low lump on the bed, curled on her side, facing the window. I kick off my shoes and get into bed with her, curving my feeble, pathetic body around the shape of hers.

"Hey," she whispers, half asleep. "You okay?"

"You're safe." I put my arm around her waist and nuzzle her hair, taking in the scent of her under the dying sage of her shampoo. "You're safe now."

LYRIC

MY HEAD RISES AND FALLS, and one ear is filled with the *thupthupthup*. I don't remember Anton coming into the room, but I remember how his heart beat under me. It's his chest I'm resting on.

After everything that happened between us, I should be uncomfortable and angry. I'm supposed to be bitter and resentful, but I'm not.

"You're safe now," he says.

Teasing wakefulness, I fall asleep again, then wake just enough to feel unfamiliar contentment.

My lungs expand, breathing in the energy to wake my brain.

"What time is it?" I ask without opening my eyes.

"Early." He strokes my hair away, pulling the strands out of my eyelashes. Lips brush my forehead. "Late."

"Damn." I turn my head and open my eyes to meet his.

I remember him being this close. The brush of his eyebrows, the thicker spot of beard on the left side of his chin. I touch the outer corner of his eye, counting the lines.

There are more now. How many more did he get in the years since I saw him? Did he get that much older when I didn't?

"You're safe." He lays his hands on either side of my face, stroking with his thumbs. "He's not going to bother you anymore."

"Who?"

He seems to consider telling me before deciding against it. "It doesn't matter. You can go home."

He pulls me to him and kisses me, preventing another question. I accept his mouth and tongue, rolling on top of him. He's solid under me, holding my head near his. My surrender is so complete, there's not a bone in my body willing or able to resist. In this drowsy, lazy moment, I let myself want him without reservation.

Our kiss goes from comforting to urgent. Our hands move from safety to resolve, yanking clothes to the side, pushing toward skin. Straddling my legs on either side of him, I feel his erection against me. He pushes me down by the hips, and the kiss pauses while a cracking sound escapes his throat.

"Anton," I whisper.

"Lyric."

"Yes." My reply isn't just consent. It's permission to be who we are. No games. No pretending.

He understands, locking his arms around me and rolling us over, kissing me before taking off my underwear, pushing up my T-shirt to kiss my chest, lingering on the hard apex while taking down his pants. I use my feet to help him get them down, wrapping my hand around his cock, running my thumb along the drop at its tip.

He wedges his hips where my legs meet, running his lips

down my cheek and throat. I'm so wet, the length of him slides along the length of me.

Speaking against my skin, he says, "Hold on."

After he gets the condom on, I wrap my legs around him. With a simple shift, his head rests where I'm open. With an urgency I haven't let myself feel in so long I push forward, and he's where he belongs.

"Jesus. Fuck." He mutters a prayer and obscenity, all in one.

"Anton." I take his face in my hands.

"Lyric." He goes slowly, embracing every moment.

"Thank you."

"Lyric, Lyric, finally."

When I wake up, he's not there, but there's a note folded on the breakfast nook. I stare at it. My hands shake. I inhale only because I force myself to.

I don't want to look at it. If it's four lines, I'm going to break into a million and a half pieces. Who's going to pick me up then? Where am I going to run?

He said I was safe. I'm not supposed to be afraid anymore. That was the deal.

But a deeper, harder, more tangible terror closes its fist over me. Somewhere, at some point, in some moment I forgot to guard myself against, I opened myself to him. I have feelings.

Shit.

Laying my hand over the note as if I want to push it deep into the wood, I slide it off.

Open it.

. . .

> *Buttons—*
> *I left you some Zivchik in the fridge. You should try it.*
> *—A*

My laugh is so loud and lasts so long that I must sound insane. I go to the fridge and take out a bottle of soda, laughing again. I only stop to drink it, then start again.

I am exactly what I seem—utterly insane to love him again.

Flipping the page, I see another note.

> *PS: We took care of your problem. You are safe now.*

CHAPTER 40

ANTON

G ETTING AROUND THE C ROWNES' Bel-Air house without a map was easier the second time around. I got right to Ted's office without a single wrong turn and delivered the news, expecting he'd tell me we should have called the cops.

He didn't.

"How do you know what you did won't make it worse?"

"I don't. But we have his equipment, and we planted an AirTag in his shaving bag. He's on a plane over the Pacific Ocean right now."

Ted nods.

This is my cue to tell him I've been sleeping with his daughter.

Is there any comfortable time to tell a woman's father that?

"Mr. Crowne, about our contract."

Is there any comfortable time to tell a client you've slept with the principal multiple times since you were hired?

"Yes." He snaps his fingers and walks over to his desk, opening the top drawer. "Speaking of that. Logan worked up an offer and scope of work." He hands me a folder. "It's bigger, if you can staff up in the right time frame."

"I—" He's telling me something and I need to change tracks before I sound like an idiot. "That shouldn't be a problem." I open the folder and flip through the pages, skimming the parameters of the job.

"What you found here opened up a real can of worms. We need a team with fresh eyes."

Fresh eyes in India, Qatar, Dubai. Mexico is the closest country.

"This is all overseas." Not all. Alaska's on the list. That seems like splitting hairs.

"We can help you manage the visas and authorizations."

I close the folder. I need time. I need space. I need to know if I'm with this man's daughter, and it's not fully up to me. "I'll run this by Mike."

"Good."

We shake on it.

CHAPTER 41

LYRIC

My house is back and I'm back in my house.

They cleaned it up. Butterbomb's been sent to the paint shop on Santa Monica Blvd. The equipment is gone from the dining room table, but little signs of the disruption remain.

Every edge and angle doesn't need to line up. I'm plenty neurotic, but I'm not a neat freak or ever-so-orderly. At least, I didn't think I was until I start noticing things. My framed poster for The Lobster is a little crooked, leaving a right triangle of bright white next to it. The coffee maker is unplugged and the top screw on the switchplate isn't in all the way. The edges of square shade on the bedroom overhead light aren't parallel to the walls.

The house is safe, and clean, and ready for me to live in again—but this is how I'd shoot a room where everything's wrong.

I touch surfaces, straighten what's crooked, make crooked what's too aligned. With my foot, I rub indents of ladders and stepstools from the rugs and look up from that spot to see what above was changed.

Everything's changed. I can't get my arms around it all.

First things first. Get the bags out of the car and unpack.

The Mini Cooper is parked in the middle of the driveway, leaving no space for another car, and I think, that's where a person puts their car when they're not expecting anyone.

My first impulse after I get my stuff out and slap the back closed is to call a friend to chase away the alone-ness.

But how would the position of the car change if a person was expecting someone? And how could you tell a character's intent by where they parked? If I left space, am I inviting trouble? Sending a message?

Danger. A stalker. She's alone. She cannot be protected.

She leaves space? Act two break. She has to deal with him.

This isn't a mystery. We know who he is. He's impossibly charming and treacherous. No one believes her.

Act one break, no. Stop. This movie has been made a hundred times.

Oak leaves skitter over a parked car. Passage of time.

This movie has been made a hundred times, but not by me.

Handprints on the hood. A seat all the way forward after the tall man put it back.

A gas gauge.

Jesus. The whole thing is ready to write itself. It's just me in a chair, typing.

I don't make movies anymore. I'm not in this stupid business. No scripts. No meetings. No waiting for the phone to ring or disappointment when it does.

By the time I consider sitting at my laptop, the entire thing has blossomed in my brain, and the desire to bang it out, type it out, nail it down, whatever, is just because I have to.

Leaving my packed bags sitting in the driveway like good little sentinels, I run inside and open my laptop on the dining room table. Just the broad strokes. Some dialog. A transition that tells the story. The phone rings. I shut off notifications. Add one more thing before I stop to pee. One more. Drink water. Then the fourth sequence rolls like a story that I have no control over and it's get it down now or lose it forever.

It's hours before I get hungry. I wish Anton was here. He'd bring me a sandwich. He'd put my hair in a tie and rub my neck. But I don't have him. That's just what it is.

That's when the second-guessing starts.

Do I put in a part for Liang? Will he be bummed if I don't? Or if it's so obvious that I've done it that it bums him out anyway?

Is it too close to what just happened to me? Is that bad? Or good?

Exciting enough? Original enough? Commercial enough?

"Fuck." I close the laptop. "I hate this."

I check my phone. Some check-in texts. Gossip in the chat. Photos of costumes for the masque. I squeal and heart, tip-tap, switch to a Liang text. I kind of miss Instagram, but not that much.

What I miss is Anton. I miss him wanting to know where I am, caring if I'm all right. I miss his eyes constantly on me. I need to reach for him across whatever space separates us. I type him a text.

—hey—

My finger freezes mid-tap, leaving the message unsent.

Once I send it, I'm going to have to deal with this script and the questions that made me text in the first place.

Is there a part for Liang?

What does the market want?

How do I finance it?

Is it original enough?

Or I could just walk away. Trash it. Forget it.

It's original enough.

Is it though?

Yeah. It's plenty original, because I'm out of the business and it doesn't matter. I don't have to finance it or think about how it's going to be reviewed. It's pure amusement because it's not like I have anything better to do without my socials. No one's ever going to judge it. It isn't even words on paper because it's not getting printed out for a crew.

I have to think. Anton's job is over. I'm not his responsibility anymore.

And I should just type a few pages and see how I like this thing.

I leave the text unsent. As soon as I put the phone down, it buzzes. Voicemail from Kevin. I listen.

"Hey, Lyric. Just wanted to update you on the whole account thing we're taking care of for you over at Meta. I have some good news. Can you give me a call back?"

The last time I saw Kevin was at the Meta campus, where he waved goodbye as Anton and I got in the car and kissed because Anton had stood up for me, asking for things I didn't understand.

I didn't want to feel anything, but we did fuck, and more times than there's an oops-cuse for.

And late last night, we had a really nice fuck and then he was gone.

I tap the phone screen with my fingernail, but not to

open, or watch, or read anything. The whole day went by and he hasn't called me, but I haven't given him a single word to go on either. Was this how it was in New York? Did we talk during the day?

We didn't.

I remember because when he bailed on me, I didn't notice until the next morning. He wasn't in bed. He kept startup hours, but he never worked through the night. Not at the office, at least.

The first thing I thought was that he'd found someone who wasn't a shitty filmmaker, but as gratifyingly painful as it had been to impale myself on that explanation, I knew it wasn't true.

Then the note.

Fuck.

This is fine.

I blamed myself when he left. If I'd been better, he would have stayed. If all the help he'd given me when I was making *Standard Deviation* had paid off. If I'd been more of an auteur, more marketable, more shocking, better with people, he would have stayed. Had he needed my help? Had I been so wrapped up in my career I'd forgotten to rub his neck with camphor? Had I brought him sandwiches when he worked late? Had I encouraged him the way he'd encouraged me?

No. No. Yes. Yes. Whatever. Now is now.

I type a few options into a text to him, delete all of them except the original —*hey*— before sending, and decide middle school has been over too long for me to act like this. If I can't figure out how I feel, I don't need to text him.

Now that the danger is gone, what am I to him? What is he to me?

I don't know what we are. I want to know. I need to know, and the first person to ask is myself. I start writing the unoriginal, genre script which may or may not have a part for Liang, just because I can.

Then, when I least expect it, Anton texts.

—hey—

CHAPTER 42

ANTON

I SHOULD GO to Mike first. This contract is lucrative, long term, and exactly what we've been hoping for. I don't let myself be happy about it until I'm in the car, and I think, we've done it. We built something, Mike and I. He's set and settled. We both are. The travel will be disruptive, but we did it.

I want to share this with Lyric more than anyone. She saw me working at a business that wasn't my own and I always wanted to bring her purpose instead of the grind. Mike's answer will be what it will be. He wants what he wants. I need to tell her. I need her reaction.

Avoiding the distraction of my mother's love, I go around the back. A fist grips my heart when her car isn't there, and I have to remind myself that it's fine. She can go where she wants now. She'll be okay.

But she's more than out of the house.

She's gone.

Nothing in the closets. Nothing in the drawers. The

counters are wiped, and the sheets are gone. It's as if she was never here.

No. There's one less bottle in the fridge. I text her.

—hey—

Three letters. She deserves more, but she responds immediately in kind.

—hey—

—how was the zivchik?—

As I type another text asking where she is and if she's all right, another comes.

—not bad!—
—ratta-tatting, talk later?—

I didn't realize I was pacing like an expectant father until I stop in my tracks. She's typing like a machine gun.

"Good for you," I say to an empty kitchen, giving her last text an approving reaction. "Good for you, buttons."

She won't talk to me now and I can't delay telling Mike what's happening.

Mike's laughter reaches the back house as I'm locking the door. He's by the pool with Mom. Great. Saved me the trip.

When I get past the back gate onto the patio of the front house, I see Mike and my mother at the table with icy glasses and cans arrayed like a suburb of cylindrical buildings. The surprise is a third person.

I only met Donna once. It was late and I wasn't

completely myself. So I stand there, staring at her as if she's going to turn into some other individual whose presence can be more easily explained.

Mom waves me over. No time to figure it out before I go over there.

"Hello." I kiss Mom on the cheek and punch Mike on the arm.

"You remember Donna?" he says.

Donna smiles wide, pleased as hell to be here. I wonder if she knows she did something impossible.

"Yes." I give her a nod, then turn to Mike. "I need to talk to you."

"Okay." He holds his arm to the side, palm up, letting me know I'm free to talk to him right here. I can't tell if he's being purposefully obtuse or if he got that way when my back was turned.

"It's business."

"Can I take a day off?" Mike asks. "We just finished a job."

I press my thumbs into the corners of my eyes. Yes, he can take a day off after a spectacular success. But I cannot.

He gets the hint, standing so he can go to Donna's chair and kiss her. "Can I leave you here for a minute?"

"Sure." She kisses him back and smiles.

Jesus Christ. He's asking her permission to talk to me. I pace into the house, leaving the sliding glass door open for him. The sitting room chairs are all empty, but I stand anyway. When Mike comes in, I slide the door closed behind him.

"This Donna." I say it as if she's an anonymous non-person, and it takes his split-second reaction to show me I'm out of line. I should have seen that, but I feel fucked in the head. I just haven't realized it until now.

"That's her name."

"Right. Sorry." I glance at the back, where Donna's trying to clean up and Mom is trying to stop her. "She seems great."

"She is."

"You brought her to meet us so…"

"Yeah?" He's suspicious and he should be.

"Is this your first serious relationship? In your life, has this ever happened before?"

"Not like this. No."

"So you wouldn't be interested in working three continents over say… two years?"

"What?"

Finally, Donna's convinced to sit down, but I can feel Mike wanting to get back out there before Mom says something he has to explain.

"We got a new proposal from Crowne Industries. It'll take us all over. I can't do it alone, the way it's structured, and I understand if you don't want to start flying all over the world with Donna here."

I must be completely transparent, because he laughs so hard he erupts into a coughing fit. I slap his back until he waves me off.

"I think you really should quit," I say.

"You and Donna both." He clears his throat and takes me by the shoulder. "But let's lay it all out on the table, okay? I have to see the scope of work first. Then I gotta review it with her, because I'm not living without that woman. She's everything."

"Right, so—"

"And you," he interrupts, shaking my shoulder, "need to cope with Lyric Crowne before you decide what you want for yourself. You need to not act like a fucking dick."

"What's that supposed to mean?"

"You need to *talk* this time. No little poems on the kitchen table. No disappearing."

"I thought you were on my side on that."

"I was. But now?" He waves toward the table outside, where the love of his life is drinking apple soda with our mother. "I see it different." He pokes my chest hard enough to hurt. "You need to catch up."

Mom and Donna are on their way inside with pitchers and glasses. Looks like Mom lost this one. Mike punches my arm one last time and joins them to help.

A minute ago, I wanted to tell Lyric about the contract so she could be happy for me. It was easy to forget that I left her behind once.

It's all different now. We're not a couple. We have no commitment to each other.

But I suddenly dread telling her. Her reaction isn't going to be what I thought. Or maybe it will be. The infinite unknowns are too painful. This is why I left that stupid note I thought explained everything.

She's working. Ratta-tat. Great excuse to text instead of call.

—do you have time to talk?—

—give me an hour?—

I tap back an agreement that sounds casual and assured, then delete it in favor of a single letter *—y—*, but before I send it, an additional message comes in.

—the masque thing is tonight—

She doesn't ask if I'm going with her—just if I'm going. I don't have to escort her. She's safe now. She doesn't need a babysitter. She's free to come and go as she pleases without a nasty ogre tying her down. So, no.

Why do I feel like I'm walking on the ledge above a fifty-foot drop?

—you should go—

Three dots roll where her answer would show up, then they disappear, then pop up again, as if she's deleting questions and reactions as fast as she's typing them. I could answer the obvious ones first.

—It was Neville. He won't be bothering you again—

But as much as that's the point, it's not the point.

—you don't need me any more—

Finally, an answer comes through.

—all bets are off?—

—yes—

—are you coming with me tonight then?--
—we won't tell Dante. You can still come as my hot bodyguard—
Right. I'm not invited. Not really.

—Do you want me to come?—

I don't know what I want her to say. Dress-up isn't my thing. So, I don't want to go. But I want to go with her. I want to be with her every minute of every day. I want to be her shadow.

First, I have to tell her that everything is different. She has to rest assured that I'm not taking off again.

Her text is three letters.

—duh—

—what does that mean?—

—Dante said he already put you on the list as security and Larry's been so mean and scary since I kicked him out—

This woman.

—ok Brenda. I'll protect you, but I'll expect something in return—

—Larry has all the money—

Of course he does. Larry doesn't even exist and he's starting to really piss me off.

—We will discuss tonight. Get back to work—

CHAPTER 43

LYRIC

LIANG and I Uber over to Echo Park. The driver has two phones mounted on the dash. Google and Waze compete to get there faster, if anything about the speed we're traveling is fast.

Liang touches up his lipstick with his silver-sequined cowboy hat and mask pushed back. His contouring is perfect, and his fake lashes are blackest black without a single bit of stray powder. He's not trying to look like a woman—but the most beautiful buckaroo in the world. He gets pretty close.

"Are you nervous?" I ask as he smushes his lips together. "About meeting the Starlight guy?"

"José?" He snaps his handheld mirror closed. "Nope. Not with these lips."

"They look like ten coats of wet shellac." I slide my gold cowboy hat forward. The leather eye mask slips into place and the long fringe at the bottom of the mask falls over the rest of my face and sweep over my breasts. I unzip the front of my gold vest another inch.

That's for Anton.

"So," Liang says, reading my mind. "Your man's coming?"

"He's not—" I stop myself. Even the first two words of denial are absurd. "Yes."

"Why do you sound like you're talking yourself into bungee jumping?"

I've barely articulated how I feel to myself, and I'm not sure I can talk it through out loud. "Have you ever been afraid to want something?"

"Uh, yeah."

"There's a thing I've been trying not to want and I'm not doing a good job at it."

"You're calling Anton-your-ex a *thing*?"

"Well, that makes it easier, and I know you have a problem with him—between him leaving and the shovel incident..."

"Pretend I don't."

We crawl along Alvarado. The supermarket parking lot is lit up like an operating room. The hills behind tilt upward with dark, wild brush.

"Fine." I chase away the doubts that keep me from being honest with myself. "Now that Neville's gone and my phone isn't radioactive with like, 'I'm gonna rape you' texts, I don't know... something broke. A wall or a dam." I take a deep breath. I sound like an idiot who memorized a dictionary of clichés. "I thought I'd be relieved... and I am... but it's not this joyful, running-through-wheat-fields feeling. It's more like the fear was taking up all this space and I thought when it was gone, it would be gone. And it is. The loud, 'I'm going to die' fear boxed up all its shit and left. But there's some stuff left under the couch or..." I throw up my hands in frustration. "I don't know what I'm trying to say."

"Are we still talking about Anton?"

"Yes. I think. Pretty sure."

"I thought you guys were meant for each other. I thought you were going to make it for real, but he left." Liang shrugs. "You handled it great. A week of crying. Then you packed up and started over. I wanted to be like you so bad. Complete control." He gives my emotional regulation a chef's kiss.

"For your consideration, best actress in a leading role…" I make a drumroll on my thighs. "Lyric Crowne."

It only takes ten seconds of laughter to clear the path of my thoughts until I knock into what I'm trying to avoid. Anton. My mind is an empty white screen with a crow's feather in the center. Wearing black from head to toe. Slightly curved. Perfectly made. Anton cannot be ignored, nor can the void of the screen if he walks off it.

"I'm so scared, Liang. I'm scared to tell him how I feel, and I'm scared of him and me staying in this nowhere while I keep feeling more things, and I'm scared he'll leave me a note and take off."

I look at Liang staring out his window.

"You were so laser-beamed on your movie that all he did was revolve around you. I didn't want what happened to *Standard Deviation*, but I figured you guys would break up for sure if it succeeded. When it kind of bombed…" He stops himself with a cringe. "Sorry."

"It did. It bombed. My fault, not yours."

"Whatever. When it bombed, I thought you'd wake the fuck up and revolve around him a little, but then it all happened really fast and boom, he was gone."

"Poof," I whisper.

"I swear it broke my heart too, but I couldn't say anything because you were a wreck. Lipstick and mascara everywhere, then you were getting boxes from the liquor store for the both of us and I was like… okay. Let's do this."

A little laugh escapes me. I grab his hand. "I'm so sorry it's always about me. But thank you."

"Yeah, well, I like it here. So just keep your lashes on and we'll be fine."

The driver turns onto Glendale, where residential buildings coexist with semi-industrial warehouses, and pulls up to one of them. Club Amea. A big, cinderblock box with a purple neon sign by the door that's small enough to fit in a tote. Total scene. The space inside the cast-iron fence is packed. Anton won't be in this crowd. He's on the list for the back entrance. Security.

I wish he was in the front. This is a lot of people and though Liang helps me out of the car so my gold seven-inch platforms don't buckle under me, I want Anton next to me.

We get right in, because obviously.

Down a long, black hallway bathed in dots of purple light, Liang's silver-and-Swarovski look is amazing.

The ballroom's hopping. Not with a dance floor. That's not the understated ambient lounge music scene we've got here. There's this buzz of energy. It zaps the skin. It's alive, and suddenly, I'm awake even though I didn't realize I was sleeping. I wasn't even officially tired, but now I can sense that something's going to happen. Something bigger than any one person. Even bigger than me.

We get to the bar.

"Me first." I flick Liang my card between two fingers. "Something with bourbon."

"I love when you get butch." He takes the card and orders for both of us, leaning forward so his crystals click against the bar.

I put my back to it, leaning on my elbows to look relaxed while I desperately scan the room for Anton. I catch sight of Colleen in her red mask and fringe. She went the honky-tonk route with the outfit. It's a choice. Could be Jake next to her in the full cowboy with worn-out Levi's and a vintage Stetson with a studded black leather mask.

"Have you talked to the Department of Defense?" A man's voice comes from my right. Like me, he's got his elbows on the bar, but with his back to the crowd. Do I know him? Black hat, mask, fringe, shirt, neck scarf. He's a walking color-suck, and his name is Anton Markov.

"Did I ask to be defended?"

"Yes." Under his mask, his eyes scan the length of my legs to the hem of my leather skirt. "But you don't need it. You've weaponized that outfit."

"Ratta-tat," I say.

I feel naked. I didn't even notice my drink had arrived. I look away before his intensity breaks me. Jake waves me over, but I'm not interested in anyone but Anton right now.

"So you're writing?" he asks into my ear, fringe brushing the edge of the lobe.

"Yeah. Jumped right back in."

"That's good. Very, very good."

"Yeah?"

"Yeah, I'm happy."

"Me too." I'm about to kiss him through our fringed masks when I feel something cold on my shoulder. It's Liang, touching me with the cold glass of bourbon-something. "Thanks," I say.

Anton's moved his attention away from me to my friend.

"Liang," Anton says, taking off his hat so he can look him in the eye. "I owe you an apology."

"For?" He doesn't sound ready to accept what he's owed, but Anton goes ahead anyway.

"For…" Anton searches for the word. "Coming at you like that. I wasn't thinking. But I shouldn't have. I was being a dick."

"You were."

"I'm sorry. Truly."

Liang shifts his weight from one foot to the other. He's not going to accept, and he doesn't have to. "I'll think about it. Only because you thought you were protecting her from that asshole."

"Okay," Anton says, putting his hat back on.

"Okay," Liang replies from behind his mask.

I sip the short bourbon-and-whatever, somehow getting the little straw through the fringe.

In the pause, two people approach us.

"Liang?" the man asks.

"Yes? Oh! José! From Starlight, right?"

I fade back, making myself invisible.

"That went well," I say to Anton while Liang chats up his potential employer.

"I'm not so sure."

"Why not?"

"We should talk."

His tone is so solemn I'm gripped with a new kind of fear. It washes away all inner pretense that I can just love him without being hurt by him. He's going to tell me that he left the first time because he didn't love me and doesn't now that he doesn't have to protect me.

I'm being irrational.

I can't help it. All my self-control was fake. I'm just a woman on Thompson Street with a note.

He feels something, right?

What if he doesn't?

I straighten my arm and knock over a glass. Six people snap up five phones before they get wet.

"I have to go to the bathroom," I say. I don't know why I'm being this way.

"I'll go with you."

"No!" I hold up my hands. "Just… let me go. It's fine."

I back up and turn, pushing through the crowd.

The bathrooms are across the room and around a corner, down a hall, far away from him, where I need to be.

I do my business and stand in front of the mirror, face covered by the mask. Maybe I don't have to look at him. I'll let him talk and he won't see my reactions. I'll let him correct his past mistake by telling me verbally instead of with a note.

I push the hat back to expose my face.

No. Make him look. I don't have to be ashamed of my own hurt. If he exposed his face to apologize to Liang, I can show him mine to hear the worst. I put the mask back on to melt back into the crowd and head for the bar, where I saw Anton last.

I'm still in the hall when the fire alarm goes off.

CHAPTER 44

ANTON

WHEN LYRIC ASKS me to stay back and turns away, I decide to let her go, but the farther away she is, the harder she pulls me toward her. She disappears into the crowd. My heart blocks my throat.

It's fine. We got him. I can't panic every time she's out of my sight.

"Hey," a masked woman says. It's Kelly. From dinner. She's holding hands with a man whose mask reveals enough of his face to make clear I don't know him.

"Hi."

"Anton, this is Leo."

He reaches for a handshake. "They call me Insidious."

"Yes, I—" I stop myself before I tell him he was on Lyric's list. He's here, and she's not. It was Neville anyway. "Good to meet you."

Kelly tells Insidious how much she likes his gaming stream, half-facing me as if I'd be interested, which I'm not really. When my phone vibrates in my pocket, I'm grateful for the excuse to turn away.

It's Mike. I put my phone to one ear and press the other one closed to block out the noise.

"Anton."

"Mike, listen, I'm out."

That doesn't stop him. He's shouting with urgency, as if he needs me to hear every word when I only hear every third or fourth phrase.

"… rig was… looked everywhere… clean…"

"What?"

"… nothing and unless… but not even…"

"I can't hear you."

"… dick but not… wrong."

"Can you just text me?"

I hang up the phone. I turn back to Kelly and Insidious, but they're gone. Good. All I want to do is wait for Lyric to get back. She's going to need a fresh drink, so I push to the bar to get her one. Dante Crowne is behind it, talking to a manager. I nod to him. He nods back but keeps talking.

Mike's text comes in.

**—Neville's rig was clean.
No malware. Zero. Nothing to
indicate he pulled this off—**

My entire body crackles with alarm.

—Are you sure?—

**—It wasn't him. I'm not sorry we
fucked him up, but it wasn't his hack—**

Shit.
Lyric.
Where's Lyric?
And where's Insidious?
That's when the fire alarm goes off.

CHAPTER 45

LYRIC

As soon as the alarm starts, I back down the hall, and good thing, because there's a rush of people coming toward me. I would have been run right over, but now I'm swept up in the crowd like a leaf in a river. It's chaos. Masks off, hats on the floor. It's hard to not trip over them.

Anton.

Where is he?

He's probably outside already, waiting for me. He's probably panicking that I'm on fire. But now there's this crowd trying to get out a narrow doorway and I can barely move my arms to get the phone to text him.

Someone grabs my arm and says my name.

"Jake!"

"This way."

He pulls me hard. I come out from between two guys in sleeveless plaid flannel and stand next to him by the wall.

"I saw a clear way out," he says, pointing against traffic. "This way."

Jake takes me by the wrist and pulls me through, hugging

the wall. I don't see any smoke, but I hope he's not taking us into the fire.

"Where?" I shout.

"This way!" He grips me so hard it hurts. I can't get away.

"But—"

I'm yanked through a doorway into an empty hall that ends in a set of stairs people are coming up.

"No exit," one of them shouts, banging into me.

My platform shoe comes out from under me, and I twist my ankle, jerking Jake back. He pulls me up.

"Let go!" I say.

"Here!" He won't release me. Instead, he pushes into the door that's been abandoned by everyone who's tried it, waving his phone over the electronic lock. It snaps open.

"How did you do that?"

He just rushes through. I limp out behind him, swearing to myself that I'll never wear anything but sneakers ever again. We're in a five-car underground parking lot. I recognize Dante's Rivian pickup.

Jake shuts the door. The screaming alarm is cut down to a faraway cry.

"How do we get out of—?"

Jake swings me around and I'm immediately off-balance again, thrown against the wall with the wind knocked out of me.

I've never seen him like this. His eyes are bugging out and his mouth is set in a snarl. He puts his hand over the bottom of my face. There's a cloth in it.

"Breathe!" He's scary as fuck, so I don't. My lungs are empty, but I hold it. "You never fucking do anything anyone asks you to do!"

I kick and twist, then drop into dead weight, forcing him

to hold me up and keep me pinned at the same time. Swinging wildly, my fist lands hard on his face. He takes the cloth away and I suck in air so hard my breath rattles.

"You stuck-up bitch!"

"It was you!"

He comes for me again. I shift. Teeter on my twisted ankle. He's between the door and me.

"Your brother the hacker," I realize.

"All you had to do was say yes."

"Get out of the way." Putting any weight on my left ankle releases a screaming pain that buckles me to the knee.

"One time!"

I look around for another way out. The ramp up to the street ends in a gate, and I'm not sure I'll make it there hopping on seven-inch platforms.

"Your mother sold me that house."

"I sat through Neville." He steps toward me.

I squeal on the left ankle, trying to move back while he approaches cautiously with the rag.

"She had the key."

"I was patient. Then the Gigachad shows up."

"You went in and put all that stuff in my light switches."

"And it's like everything I did to prove to you I was a good guy..."

My shoulders hit something. I reach back. It's a concrete pillar with an electrical box attached. I slide sideways to avoid him. Fail. He spins me around. It's not a box bolted to the pillar. It's a fire extinguisher.

"... none of it mattered."

"I'm sorry," I grunt. He pulls me back as I grab the fire extinguisher.

"I was never going to hurt you"—he pulls me, but I hold

the two-foot-high red cylinder as if my life depends on it—
"but then you…"

My hands slip away as the extinguisher comes loose. He falls back, letting go of me. I scramble forward, limping around the excruciating pain in my ankle.

The door we came through clacks.

"Hey!"

It's Anton. I'd know that voice anywhere.

Jake turns onto his side and starts to stand. I pick up the fire extinguisher and throw it at him, but I'm not standing right. Without leverage, the throw has no power. It bounces off his shoulder, knocking him halfway down, and rolls away.

Anton dives for it. So does Jake. They wrestle for it, then suddenly Jake lets go and the inertia and weight throw Anton back, toward me. He lands on the concrete with a thud.

"Fuck you!" I say. I lift the fire extinguisher and swing it wildly at Jake. Mid-swing—when it's too late to change my mind—I'm sure he's going to grab it and bash in Anton's skull.

But I hit my target on the side of the head. Jake, my friend for going on three years, drops like a bag of laundry. The fire extinguisher falls from my hands when they cover my mouth.

The fire alarm is still going. Jake doesn't move.

"Lyric!" Anton shouts impatiently, as if it's not the first time he's had to. "Let's go."

With the overhead lights behind him, Anton's face is in the shadow, so my brain assumes half his face is black because of some trick of the lighting.

He tugs me toward the door. The light changes. He is face is half blood.

"Anton. Your face."

"It's fine."

"You're bleeding."

"I'll carry you if I have to."

"Okay, okay. Just…" I lean on him and hop to the exit on one foot.

I get three clops in before he wraps his arm around my waist and, holding me hip to hip, carries me through the door. The fire alarm is still going so loudly we can't hear each other talk. I can't walk. Anton has so much blood flowing from his forehead to his eye, he can't see. We go through another doorway. I lean on the bar to let him through, pushing it so hard that when we're both on the other side, it bounces shut.

CHAPTER 46

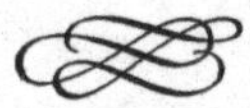

LYRIC

A VENDING machine casts the only light on the small room. Round table in the center with four chairs. There's a wall of lockers. A washer-dryer. Posters describing worker's comp laws in 12pt type. We're in the staff lounge. Not the way out. Anton turns. Signals me to do the same.

The alarm stops.

"Thank God," I say. A second later, the door locks with an invisible *clack*. At least that's what it sounds like. I push the bar and yep. "Locked."

"Fuck." Anton drops into a plastic chair. I try again. Nope. "Forget it. The alarm unlocks everything and when it goes off... fuck."

"I got it."

I text Dante.

> *—hey so long story. There's a concussed*
> *dude in the underground garage and*
> *Anton and I are locked in the breakroom—*

Hopping around on one seven-inch platform, I find light switches above the countertops, and the room is bathed in cold, unforgiving light.

"Holy crap!" I cry, rushing to Anton, forgetting about my foot and nearly spraining my other ankle. His face is bathed in bright red and the wound over his eyebrow is still gushing.

"I'm fine," he says. "We need to wrap that ankle."

"You're bleeding literally to death." I take a handful of napkins from a pile and cover the bleeding. "Hold that down I think?"

"Head wounds just bleed a lot." He holds the napkins against the bleeding with one hand and, taking me by the wrist with the other, pulls me toward a chair. "It's nothing. Sit down."

"Do you feel all right? Dizzy? Um, what are the rest of the symptoms?"

"I don't have a concussion." He stands. I sit.

"You got hit in the head with a fire extinguisher."

"I got a hard graze from the metal handle. Please. Sit down and get those shoes off."

With his free hand, Anton opens the huge first aid box on the wall. It has everything.

"Get tape. And the gauze. All of it. And something to clean the wound with."

A text comes in from Dante.

—LAFD will retrieve the "concussed dude"
and I'll get to you after I deal
w/ KTLA and the 800 people in the front lot—

Apparently, the entire first aid kit is designed to come off the wall, because Anton pulls it away, leaving a plastic mount behind. He slides it on the table and sits next to me. The napkins drop off his head like recycled paper butterflies.

"Give me your foot." He plucks a packet and ace bandage from the assortment.

"I want to take care of your head." I find the gauze, tape, spray disinfectant.

He sighs and takes me by the left calf, draping my leg over his lap. The weight of the shoe bends my ankle down. It hurts, but it's not like it's going to get much worse.

"My head's fine." He unbuckles my shoe.

"Ow, fucker!"

"Stay still."

"*Ow ow ow ow ow.*" A stabbing pain engulfs my entire foot and—finding that too small for its ambitions—runs up to my knee.

"Almost off."

"It was fine until you started to—*ow ow ow yee!*"

The shoe falls to the floor. I realize how hard I'm gripping the edge of the table and how clenched straight my body is. He gently slides off my stocking, which makes me so tense I can barely focus on the tiny antiseptic spray directions.

"Can you wiggle your toes?"

Still tense, I wiggle them.

"Bend the ankle?"

I bend it, then jolt with pain.

"Is it broken?" I take out the entire stack of gauze pads and rip one open.

"How the fuck should I know?" He twists the flat packet, making a cracking noise. "I'm not a medic, and I'm a shitty security guy." He lays the packet on my ankle. It's cold. "Couldn't see Jake coming. Didn't even cross my mind."

"Mine either. Come here." I lean forward with the spray and gauze ready, cupping my hand to protect his eye. "The doctors on TV always says this is gonna sting." I spray it without waiting for confirmation.

"Fuck!"

"Sorry."

"You are not."

He's right. I'm not. I spray him again. It doesn't seem to hurt him as much. I put the bandage over the cut, pressing to make it stick.

"What did you want to talk about?" I rip open another gauze packet. "From before I went to the bathroom and all this happened?"

Maybe he'll say what I've been too chickenshit to reveal.

"Not now." He puts his other hand on the cold pack, pressing down harder.

"When?" Now that the gauze is out, I can't apply it without the tape. I need three hands. "What else are we doing that's so important?"

"First aid."

I put down the gauze and find the tape. While I reach for the little scissors, he goes for the ace bandage, and our fingers brush against each other. He stops and takes my hand, looks me in the eye, and says… nothing. He lets go, gets the ace bandage, and looks at my foot as he wraps it.

His face is still covered in blood. Tape won't stick. There's so much to do. I find the antiseptic wipes and open one.

"Mike and I had this plan. When we found that susceptibility in the Crowne Industries network, we decided this was our way in." He sucks in a breath when I get close to the open wound.

"Sorry. Almost done."

"It was huge. Your family company had been so deeply infiltrated we could scale a whole business off fixing it before it was deployed. I'd deal with whatever conflicts our past relationship created as they came up, but I'd be transparent. Except that you never told them much."

"That was my prerogative." I toss the bloody wipe and tape the bandage to his head while he wraps my ankle.

"Sure, I get it. And it shouldn't have mattered. But Logan gave the hardware infiltration to his internals and your father put us on family… then there was the hack… *Jake's* hack. And you needed security, so you and I just picked up where we left off."

"I wouldn't say that."

"Wouldn't you, Mrs. Longbottom?"

He pauses long enough for me to ask a question or defend myself against the accusation that I led him back to where we were. But I can't decide what to say. All I know is the ballooning dread in my chest.

"Since I left New York, a lot has happened. It changed me. How could I come back here, after all that, and feel for you again? It made no sense. It wasn't logical. You meant nothing to me. I changed. You changed. And then, you sat at dinner and ignored me. All I wanted was for you to see me. I would have stood on the table and sung the 'Star-Spangled Banner' for a second of your attention."

"I would've given you a thousand dollars to see that." I'm smiling and maybe half-joking, but I'm misreading him. He stays serious and focused.

"We need to keep your father as a client."

"You can, right?"

"We got an offer from Crowne Industries."

"Really?" This sounds like good news to me, but he swallows hard, eyes on my foot as if he just ran over my cat.

"I have it in my hand, and all I can think is, will I be where she can see me? Will I still have a moment of her attention?"

"You will," I say on an exhale of relief. "I want something with you. I was meaning to tell you; I was just afraid it wasn't the same for you. I want us. You and me. Like we were, but better."

He wraps the last of the bandage and smooths it down. Shifts it. Smooths it again.

"Did you see clips for this?" he asks.

"What?"

"Clips? The little—"

"No." I shake the buzzing out of my head. "I mean no, I just told you I want to try again. Do it better this time. And no, I didn't see the clips."

He fishes around the container for them. Keeps fishing.

"Anton." I snap my fingers in front of his face. "You have my complete attention."

"Crowne has their domestic security covered. The contract is overseas. All over, but not here."

"Oh. Wow. That's big."

"It's everything we ever wanted." He unpacks the little compartments, looking for the clips. "But I'll be gone at least fifty weeks a year, and if you're writing again, you need to be here in LA forty-eight of them."

"Yeah. That complicates things. Or makes it all really simple."

He pauses with a tourniquet in his hands, then tosses it. Just another thing that's not what he needs, when he needs it.

"What do you want?" I ask.

"I can stay if you want."

"Here we go again."

"Where 'here' are we going?"

"You didn't actually change. You're still note-guy."

"I'm telling you. I'm talking to you." He tosses things away more violently. A dropper of eyewash rolls onto the floor.

"You're treating me like a duty. 'I'll stay if you want,' like now I'm the one responsible for your misery?"

"What misery?" The compartments are empty. He grabs the roll of tape.

"The misery of you staying here, with me, instead of turning the Markov Group into a 'world-class security firm' like you said."

"I never said I'd be miserable." He wraps the tape around the bandage to hold it down.

"Hey. Siri. Define. Subtext."

"You are impossible. I spent two years serving you hand and foot because I loved you. And when I ask you to marry me—"

"We're doing this again?" I ask.

"You shut me out!"

"You walked!"

"You keep saying I left you, but that's not true. You left me when the first bad review came in and you never came back." He rips the tape with his teeth. "You were too closed off to see the good reviews and too closed off to see me, right there, trying to pull you out of it."

"That's too tight."

"No, it's not."

"My toes are going to turn blue."

"Lyric. Tell the truth. You don't trust me. You never trusted me to take care of you."

"Maybe I don't need a nurse."

"So, that's it then? Because when you're hurting, I'm going to take care of you. I'm going to feed you, and fuck you, and destroy anyone who tries to hurt you. This is who I am. If who I am, in my bones, is going to shut you down, then you don't want me, and you never did."

The door opens with a bang. Dante stands there, taking stock of the situation with a cop and a fireman behind him.

"Thank God," I say.

"You're welcome," he replies. "What the hell happened with the fire extinguisher?"

CHAPTER 47

LYRIC

THE ROOFTOP GREENHOUSE on top of The Point Hotel is packed, loud, and bright. Plants hang from the glass ceiling and Koreatown stretches below us. The soundtrack is a whooshing ambient under a recording of birds chirping and calling. I like it here, with or without posting about it.

"So the cops took our statements. And it turned out Jake had it all on his home computer, which his brother built and left in the garage when he went to go work for the FBI."

Kelly drops her fork. "I'm sorry, but this is making me totally sick."

"His mother, the realtor? She says she didn't know he went into the house she sold me and rewired stuff."

"I still can't with this." Liang's next to me wearing a black mesh tee with sunglasses dangling from the neck. His brunch has been reduced to streaks of yellow yolk and piles of uneaten salad.

"Okay, enough." Kelly picks up her phone. "We're going to just do something fun right now. Come on my side. Let's show them what a happy Lyric looks like."

Kelly holds out her phone. My face is next to hers on the screen, smiling with hot pink lipstick and perfectly black-lined eyes. I look pretty damn good, but I'm not sure what a happy Lyric is supposed to look like. It isn't this.

"Excellent," she says after she takes the shot, lowering her arm to manage the caption and hashtags. "I'll tag you. They'll know you're fine. I'll say the great Lyric Crowne's taking a mental health break."

"Well, just so you know." I look from one to the other. "They did kind of sort that out for me."

Wide eyes. Open mouths that melt into smiles. Liang claps.

"What?" Kelly finally says.

"You're back?" Liang scrolls and taps, looking for my account.

"Did your muscle take care of it?" Kelly asks.

My muscle is Anton. Obviously.

"No clue. Not my circus, not my clowns." I push away my plate. "But yeah."

Liang finds my account then holds it up to show me what I already know. "It's the same."

"I didn't post anything yet. I've been busy."

"With that man you just avoided talking about?" Kelly tilts her head and pushes her pucker to one side of her face.

"Kind of." I drink my coffee and watch Kelly over the rim.

"Good," she says with a sharp nod. "Worth it. I hope he keeps you so busy you never post again."

"And…" I can't believe what's going to come out of my mouth, but I'm too excited to keep it on the back of my tongue. "I started writing again."

Kelly stares blankly. I never told her making movies ever

meant anything to me. But Liang looks up from his phone, perfect brows knotted in the middle.

"I'm sorry, what?" He places his phone on the table gently, as if he's afraid he's going to break it.

"There's nothing in there for you so far," I say quickly. "But I can get you on screen in the next draft."

He grins and shoves my shoulder. "Stop."

"No, I mean it. I won't abandon you."

"You are so sweet." He doesn't seem upset or disappointed at all. "I'd love to be in whatever you do... if I have time." He scrunches his shoulders and face into an apology.

"Oof," Kelly starts, as if Liang backhanded an insult.

But he didn't. I know when he's messing with me and when he's being sincere. And right now, trying to hide a smile, he has something to tell me.

"Spit it out," I demand.

He sits up straight and lays his hands on the table. "I can't say yet."

"Your nails aren't polished," I say. "And the other day, between the phone call and coming over, your face was naked. You had a literal beard."

Liang covers his mouth with his hand. Kelly hasn't put it together.

"You weren't at class," I say. "You were auditioning. And those were the sides. You weren't sure if you did it right."

"Yes!" Liang squeaks, then says, "Do you know how few roles there are for nonbinary people?"

"Spill it!" I cry.

"I can't."

"You signed an NDA?"

He nods, two fists in front of his mouth.

"Keep it generic. Come on!"

"TV series," he squeaks.

"Holy shit!" I'm so excited I grab his arm and squeeze, fully nonverbal for a good four seconds. "You didn't have acting class that day."

"No!" he squeaks.

"Is it done? Did you sign?"

"They're drawing up the contract." He's so excited he can barely get out the words.

"And no makeup because the character is...?" I'm leading him into finishing my sentence, but he doesn't bite.

I let go of his arm and he stops covering his mouth, gaining his composure. "So, on a *different subject...*" He glances at each of us. It's not a different subject, but he's skirting his NDA. Good man. "True story. My father was in the military, and when I have my face on, it's a problem for him."

We let out a collective *aaah*. Laing's father was indeed in the military before they moved here, and he truly can't understand his son's desire to be beautiful, but what Liang means is that he got a part in a show about the military, or war, or whatever. What matters is that it's his show now.

"Netflix?" Kelly asks. "Hulu? Network? Which?"

"Nope." He draws two fingers across his closed lips.

"Oh my God," I say, looking at my plate. "You did it." I'm so overwhelmed I grab his hand and repeat myself. "You did it."

"Thank Goddess I came to LA, right?" He squeezes my hand, making eye contact.

"Thank Goddess." When I raise my arms to hug him, they feel lighter than they have in years.

"So," Kelly says, "I'm really happy for you, Liang, but

Lyric, spill it. What happened after you gave police statements?"

"I went home."

"What happened with Anton, you idiot?"

I exhale a long, vocal sigh. "Do I have to? When I was done, he was already on his way home. We texted but... he has things he's doing, and I don't fit... we have commitments and..." I shrug. "We just don't fit. It's fine."

Liang makes an elongated *mm* of doubt. "Is it?"

Lying and pretending it's all fine doesn't cut it anymore.

"No, but it's life. Win some, lose some. I lost this round, but I just want him to be happy."

I hang my hat on that, making it my single focal point.

One of us is happy.

CHAPTER 48

ANTON

"It's everything!" Mike swings his arm over the breadth of the office on Rue la Bruyère.

The windows look out onto a day so gray, it could almost be mistaken for London. The cobbled street is bordered by eighteenth-century limestone buildings with interiors of cracking plaster and questionable wiring.

"It has an apartment attached," Donna offers.

"It's a room with a hot plate," I say.

"It's temporary," Mike says. "Come on."

"If it's just you?" Donna adds unhelpfully.

I like her enough. She's good to my brother. But she's a little too eager to decide how much space a person living alone needs, as opposed to a couple.

I didn't ask to be in a threesome, but Mike wants to be near Donna, and Donna loves Mike as much as she loves to travel. I'm happy for them. Really. My life is a penumbra between scheduled phone calls with Lyric. They last as long as they last. We decide nothing because there's no acceptable choice. We just drift into each other's orbit, then away.

"This shithole isn't the Markov Group," I say, walking out before they can try to convince me otherwise.

"Anton!" Mike chases me across the street, coat flying. He gets in front of me. I look back. Donna's not following. "Look, she feels really bad. She didn't mean it like that."

"I'm not upset with her."

"Then what is it?"

"We're choosing international headquarters." I count off the requirements on my fingers. "We have to speak the language. It has to be central and well-connected. It has to start small with room to scale, but we're wasting time looking at offices without enough floorspace or bandwidth."

He laughs at me as if I'm Jerry Lewis and he's already French.

"I'm wrong?"

"No," he says, still laughing. "You're absolutely right. We're in the wrong part of town." He takes a deep breath and stops laughing.

"Then what's funny?"

"You, pretending you actually want to be here at all, and if we just found the exact right spot, you'd be happy."

"I'm not here to be happy."

I want to walk down the block where there's a pizza place that has a menu item called a "fuck pie." I want to eat a few slices of fuck, made by people who think that's funny. But Donna's in the vestibule of the limestone office building, waiting at a respectful distance. Mike's not going to follow without her.

"Ah. Okay. Sure. You're here to plant a flag," he says.

"Yes. I want to do what we came to do. And if Paris isn't right, we go back to London, or try Brussels."

"Hi." Donna's hands are jammed deep in her pockets. "I'm sorry, Anton. I feel like a real wrench in the works."

"You're fine. This is your move too."

"But I was thinking."

Donna does a lot of thinking. I'm not sure if she's a genius or a busybody.

"Yes?"

"You guys said you wanted headquarters in Europe so you could both move around Asia and Africa easier."

I expect her to suggest Morocco or Algeria, where they speak French, and I guess she could be making a jackpot suggestion. But the thought of looking at another continent is exhausting. I just want to be home.

And where is that?

"Go on," Mike says.

"And I think what I'm stuck on, I guess, is the 'both of you' part? Not to, like, assume… but it's been like two weeks and… well, what I've noticed is that you…" She's talking about me. "You um… hate everywhere?"

She looks at Mike. He shrugs. Turns to me.

I shrug. "What?"

"You kinda do," Mike says.

This is great. Someone should either shoot me or buy me a slice of fuck pie, and I don't see any guns.

"I'm going to get something to eat," I say, heading for the pizza joint.

I don't want a fuck pie. I open the world clock on my phone. I do hate everywhere. I've never been to Brussels, but I hate it. And every other French-speaking country, topped only by English-speaking countries and territories.

"Hey," Mike says softly. "Dude."

"Do you see this?" I hold up my phone. He doesn't

understand what I'm showing him. "It's five in the fucking morning."

"No, it's—"

"In Los Ángeles, it's five in the god damn morning, and I can't call home at two in the fucked afternoon. What am I supposed to do? Live here where it's all wrong?"

"Call home?"

"I. Can't. Call. Her. Now." With my palm out, I present him with my phone as if he's never seen one before. "I'm living a different existence."

"Yes." He nods slowly.

"I want lunch. She's still sleeping. When I eat breakfast, she's done with dinner. Our bodies are not in the same reality. Are you hearing me? Every day, I want to experience what she's experiencing, and I can't because the sun's in the wrong place."

"This is why you hate everything."

"It's just…" I stare at the phone. The minute flips. "I'm trying not to be a sap. I'm trying to stay focused on the business we promised each other. But the line holding me down… it's been cut and I'm drifting away. Do you see?"

Again, I show him the world clock as if he needs to just look at it to understand.

He doesn't. He can't as long as his eyes stay on me.

"I see." He puts his hand on my shoulder. "I see what you see." He pulls me forward and hugs me.

CHAPTER 49

LYRIC

I TYPE out the last scene I'm going to do tonight. The stalker picks up the phone at a party when the heroine calls a mutual friend. That's how he gets her number. Though he was at a vintage store and not a party, that's how Jake got mine.

Little things like that keep clicking into place. This script may go nowhere, but it's cathartic.

I close my laptop and stretch my fingers. It's late, and what I spent the last few hours cramping my hands over... it's something.

Two pretty clean acts, and a third that's not going to be a problem. UNTITLED STALKER THRILLER definitely wants to be *something*. But what? And whose?

I can make this movie. Maybe with studio financing if I start pounding the pavement. Maybe with Crowne cashflow —my unclaimed One Big Thing.

I held the family gift in reserve as if somewhere deep in my gut, I knew *Standard Deviation* wouldn't work.

Sell it.

Just see if you can sell it. Get it off your desk, or not.

Go to him.

And what if that's a mistake? What if Anton is my *Standard Deviation*? Just a series of expensive life lessons that will wound and scar until I stop making the same mistakes?

It's threeish in the morning. Noonish in Paris.

"Yes!" I snap up my phone and call him. His name pops up.

I don't know what I'm going to tell him. Something honest. I want him, but I don't know how to have him. I'm going to ask him if he's a mistake. If he's an experience I'm supposed to file away.

What if I'm filing the wrong experience? What if I wasn't supposed to learn to avoid abandonment? What if I was supposed to learn to trust the people who love me?

His number rings, and rings, and rings...

Anton. Am I supposed to feel this way? Or am I supposed to learn not to feel this way?

...and rings and...

I hit the red button.

He can't tell me anyway. He doesn't have the answer any more than I do.

Mom gets up early these days, so I figure showing up at seven o'clock won't be that big a deal. Waiting four hours was the best I could do under the circumstances. The Bel-Air house is dark and as eerie as an empty church. The sky is turning ultramarine over the canyon. The goldfinches compete with the last of the crickets. I could stand on their patio all day, but the sun's going to rise, and the leaf blowers and cars will start their intrusive humming. It'll get hot, even for October.

"Lyric," Mom says, coming out onto the patio with me, "you're coming around early. Do you want some coffee?"

"I'm good." I put my arm around her. "You're not really shaky. Is it the medication?"

"Mornings are always easy."

"Why don't I know that?"

"I don't know. Look at you though." She takes my hands and looks me up and down. "Did you change something?"

"No."

"Hair maybe?"

"Not really. I didn't brush it."

"Hm."

"You asked me this the last time you saw me. Are you okay?"

"You didn't have your face in your phone last time I saw you. This time the change is… different."

"Well, I should ask—"

"I need to ask—"

We stop at the same time and laugh. Mom sits on the edge of a patio chair with her hands folded between her knees. She is silent, waiting for me to start.

"So, um…" I sit in the chair next to her. "I don't actually know what to do." I wait for a reaction, get none, and continue. "So, Anton, you remember him?"

She nods. I can't read it.

"He's working for Logan and Dad, out in Europe, and I really… I feel so many things about him but mostly just like this emptiness? Or, no. More like this big space inside myself that's squeezed flat like a plastic bag. But a huge plastic bag.

Like once I put stuff in it, it'll be so much stuff, but Anton is the only stuff that'll fit."

Still, no reaction, just attention.

"But he's out there doing what he wants to do, and I'm here, where I want to be, and where I can take another shot at a movie, because the last one… I didn't mean to be cagey about it all this time, but it kind of sucked," I say.

"Did it?"

"Yeah, and I felt like that meant I sucked, so I didn't tell you."

She laughs. "Did you think I'd agree with that assessment?"

"Well, if you didn't think I sucked, that would make you wrong. Right? And if you did think I sucked, that would hurt my feelings. You see the conundrum. I was trying to keep everything at neutral."

"And so you want to stay here and try again, but Anton is there. And if you stay here, you could lose him and still suck?"

"Right."

"And you don't know what to do?"

"I want to know. I have to know."

"You want to know what?"

"When you saw Anton and I together, did you get the tingle?"

"Oh. Lyric. Honey." Mom tilts her head and blinks quickly with a little flutter, and I know what that means.

"You didn't."

"You can't build your life around that."

"Shit."

There's the answer I came for, right in my mother's nervous system. No tingle. No true love. Anton is just a life experience I'm supposed to file away. He's stories I'm supposed to tell to the children I have with another person once I commit to staying here without him.

"Okay!" I stand. "Is Dad up?"

"I'm up," he says from the doorway with a reading tablet in one hand. He kisses my cheek.

"How long were you standing there?"

"Not too long." He leans on the railing with the rising sun behind him. "You wanted to talk to me or just say hello?"

"Well. So." I clear my throat of unexpected gunk. "There's the matter of the One Big Thing?"

"Ah, the last OTB. Great. Let's get that off my desk."

"I want to shoot a trailer to take around." I sniff. A ton of snot gathers in the back of my throat and my eyes sting. "Or they'll just buy it and give it to, like, Scott Ridley or something? Which..." My breath stutters. "So that's the plan and... I'll get you a budget if you need it... or I could make a trailer on my own dime and if you think it's worth the investment..."

I break down into sobs, crouching as if I want to melt into the Italian tiles.

"Hey," Dad crouches with me. "Is this because your mother didn't—"

"Tingle!" I spit out the word and a lump of snot at the same time.

"Doreen," Dad says flatly.

"Why would I lie?" Mom asks.

"I don't expect you to *lie*, but you could explain the entire point."

"What?" I ask, blind with tears. "There's a point? Is it that he was my security so we weren't supposed to... you know?"

Dad takes out a linen hankie, shakes it, and passes it to

me. I wipe away what feels like an entire raw egg white off my face.

"The point," he says. "is if you're disappointed that this person *isn't* your one true love, they probably are. If you're relieved—"

"Then they're not?"

"Probably not."

I sit with my back to the railing, knees bent, and blow my nose. "Jesus, it's like an omelette."

Down below, where the driveway curves up the hill and around the house, there's a clatter and hum of an opening gate.

Dad cranes his neck to see. "Ah, I have to go."

"Why?"

"I have a meeting." He kisses my forehead, stands, and walks into the house.

I scoff, wiping my nose before I sniff. "It's Sunday."

"He's committed, your father."

"Yeah." I look over the canyon, balling up the hankie. "What do you think, Mom? About me trying to make another movie? Is that dumb? You never saw the last one but..."

I stop because Mom's shaking, and it's not the Parkinson's. She's laughing.

"What?" I ask.

"We saw it, Lyric."

"How?"

Mothers aren't supposed to roll their eyes at their daughters, so when my mother tightens her mouth and does the quickest eyeroll in history, I can clearly see her at my age. "Your father's friend at Darwin Media—"

"Ben Newitch?"

"He sent us a DVD. He said it showed promise but might not 'be for everyone.' Exact words."

"Kiss of death," I say.

There's another clattering sound from halfway up the hill. The garage door. I lean back to see Mom and Dad's valet, Gerrick, coming out and dashing out of sight.

"So." I'm afraid to ask the rest, but I have to now, even through the cringe. "What did you think?" I immediately chicken out. "No. Wait. Forget it. Don't tell me."

"It was…"

"Ugh, Mom." I hold up my hands, desperate for her to stop.

She stands and comes to me, letting me hope for a minute that my brutally honest mother could find it in her heart to keep her opinions to herself.

"It was not for everyone." She holds my hands tightly. "It was for me."

"You don't have to say that." If she tries to turn this into some kind of speech about how she's my audience, I'm going to literally puke.

"I am aware." She squeezes my hands so hard it hurts, then loosens without letting go. "It had your vigor. Your energy. It was your voice. The daughter I love so much was inside every shot. The sixth-grade girl writing bizarre monologues and acting them out on video… the woman who always wants everything to be even… who was so kind to her friends… she was also kind and fair to her characters." She lets my hands drop and leans on the railing next to me. "I would have known it was you even if your name wasn't on it. I could feel your presence right there in the room and I got to hold my daughter from thousands of miles away."

"That's funny." I laugh to myself even though I am not

amused. "I always thought it failed because it was too much me." I turn toward the canyon, elbows on the railing. "It's like I don't even know what I'm doing."

A car comes around the second switch up the hill and turns into the garage. It takes me a second to place it.

"It's a white Range Rover," I say to myself.

Mom stands next to me, watching. "If you say."

There are thousands of those all over Los Angeles.

Right?

What are the odds? Especially with him somewhere in Europe this week... what's the likelihood it's the same car without the dusting of brittle fall leaves on the hood?

I was always good at math, but not good enough to calculate the odds in my head or patient enough to get out a pen when confirmation is four minutes away on foot.

"I'll be right back."

I break into a run. Inside, around a corner, unable to stop when I hear voices around the next turn. One is Dad. The other... I catch a scent of burned bread and fucking a millisecond before I smack right into Anton.

CHAPTER 50

LYRIC

HIS HANDS HOLD MY BICEPS. They're the only reason I don't fall backward.

"You're here," he says in harmony with me, because I say it at the exact same time.

"Hey," I start, but get lost in the depth of his stare and the strength of his hands. "What are—"

"I came—" He interrupts himself to not interrupt me. He takes his hands away. "Go."

"No, you."

"You. Please."

Dad moves somewhere out of my peripheral vision.

"You're here." I said that already, and it's obvious, but my brain's hissing and popping with scrubbing bubbles that clean out any thought that's not the sight or sound of Anton. "I didn't..."

My mouth is open but the rest of the sentence pops into a splash of soap midair.

"It's too..." He stops himself, nervous, looking over my shoulder, probably for my father, but I can't check to see if he's there when Anton is right in front of me in three dimensions. "I didn't expect you to be here."

"Oh." The joy is sucked out of me. I wasn't expected. Does he regret coming? Was he going to slip in and out of town without calling? "Oh." I step back before tearing my eyes away from him. "That's fine. I can—"

"It's fine—"

"Yes. I can just… um…" I'm confused. Everything with him seemed fine on the phone, but he missed a couple of calls, and I can't deal. "I should go, I guess." I go around him, head down because I can't look at him.

"Wait," Anton says, reaching into his pocket. "I have something for you."

His hand comes out with a folded piece of paper. I've seen that paper before, but without the man attached to it.

What was it I learned?

Something about trusting the people who love me?

He pinches open the paper. His hands are shaking. Maybe he's hungry or something, but I don't think so. He seems nervous. Too nervous. Stooping a little, focused so hard on that little slip of paper.

"No." I snap the note away from him. "You love me, you dipshit fuckhead. You came back for some whatever meeting with my father, but you were going to call me… no, you weren't. You were going to come right over to my house and crawl into bed with me. Because you love me and you can't live without me and this note isn't a note. It's a receipt for that shirt which"—I notice his black button-front shirt for the first time—"isn't a fucking turtleneck."

"Lyric," he says softly.

"Look!" I unfold it. It's four fucking lines in black ink. "See?" I hold it up, convincing myself it isn't what it is.

"I can't go on like this."

I'd like to congratulate him on the full sentence, but the reality of the note is weighing on me, and it's killing me to see him stand here and choke like an actor with stage fright.

"Is that what this says?" I ask.

"No. Give it to me and—" He reaches for it, but I snap it away.

"I tried to call you."

"I was on a plane."

"Before I read this, I want to tell you what I was going to say." I pull in a deep breath and take in the sight of him in this moment of potential, when the story of who we are together is unwritten. He's so beautiful it hurts. I can barely speak, but I have to. "I want you to know, Anton, that I was going to tell you I'm having a hard time being without you. So I want to come to wherever you land… to be with you, after I make this movie, if I make it… but let's assume I do. I was going to ask you to wait for me and tell you that no matter what you said, or actually, no matter what you wrote here." I hold up the note. "I know you love me. I trust you. Okay?"

"Okay."

"So." I open the note. "Four lines from Anton Markov."

"Can you not? Your parents are going to hear it."

I can, and I will, parents or not. They love me and so does he, even if he's breaking up with me.

"'Dear Lyric. I'm sorry.'" I look up. "For fuck's sake. Please say it's not the same note."

He shrugs and clears his throat.

"Fuck." I read again. "'This is unbearable.' You can say that again." A quick glance at him reveals a tiny upturn of a smile.

"'I am weak without you.' We're on a roll here. Okay. 'I am useless under a different sun than you.' Wait."

That's not the same. He changed that line. I read it again, to myself this time, to make sure I got it right.

"It wasn't finished," he says.

"Wow." I fold it and let my hand drop. "I feel kind of… ah… so…?" I read it again. "What does it mean?"

"Besides that I'm not much of a poet?"

"No, really, you're not, but…"

His smile breaks wide, and it takes every drop of my discipline not to kiss him.

"It means I'm coming home. To you."

"No, you don't have to."

"I will. I told Mike."

"You can't crush Mike's dreams!"

"What? Are you—?" He opens his mouth, slaps it shut as if it can't hold the enormity of his bafflement. "My God, buttons, I'm standing here, both feet on the ground, tired but fully in my faculties, telling you that I love you. I want to be with you. I'd rather reroute my entire life than wake up one more morning without you, and you're standing there, Lyric Crowne… *my* Lyric Crowne, in her parents' whatever-room, telling me to make sure my life revolves around *Mike*?"

"But…" I look around. My parents are out on the patio, on the other side of an open wall. "You can't just drop everything to rub my neck and bring me sandwiches."

"Yes, I can."

"You cannot. I won't allow it." My shout echoes off the walls. "I won't."

He crosses his arms. "Try and stop me."

I am so frustrated, I don't even know what I'm fighting for. Maybe the visions I had last night of waiting for a couple of years, staring at the sky in longing as we went about our business on opposite sides of the world. Maybe I'm fighting for him to keep his own path intact, or maybe I'm terrified of being responsible for what he gives up in my name.

"Dad!"

"What?" My father strolls in at his own pace.

I point at Anton as if I'm accusing him of murder. "He's working for you? Him?"

Dad's eyes go from me, to Anton, and back again. "Not if he's bothering you."

"He's supposed to have an office somewhere..." I wave my hands. "Far? That's the deal?"

"What's this about?" Again with the looking between Anton and me.

"He wants to do the job from *here*." I say it as if it's the most laughable proposition ever proposed.

"I love her," Anton says with a shrug, arms still crossed.

"In Los Angeles!" I continue with the same assumed hilarity.

"She has to be here. I want to be with her."

"Does she want to be with you?" Dad asks flatly, like Walter fucking Cronkite.

"Right now?" Anton looks my way, studying the length of me, then back at my father. "I'm not so sure."

"Of course I want to be with you. I love you. I miss you. Every minute. Ever since you've been gone, I've had this pain." I touch the place in the back of my neck where my tension always settles. "Right here."

"I have something for that." Anton raises an eyebrow.

He wants to put my hair back into a tie and rub camphor on the back of my neck as much as I want him to do it.

There's nothing wrong with that. There's nothing to be afraid of.

But I knew that already. I'm not afraid. Liang found his way. Anton will find his. I'll find mine.

"You can make your own choices," I say.

"I know that."

"And yes, I love you."

"I also know that."

I put my fingertips over his mouth. "Can you shush?"

"Hm." He smiles. His lips are so soft I almost forget what I wanted to say.

"What's going on?" Mom says from somewhere behind me.

"I have no clue," Dad replies.

"You're not staying to protect me?" I take away my fingers for the answer.

"No." He cups my jaw with one hand, letting his thumb brush my cheek. A wedge of the rising sun slices the room, catching the cut of his cheek and glinting on the edge of his iris. "You'd be fine without me. I mean, I'll still have to destroy anyone who... I don't know... hurts you."

"Right," I say, locked in his gaze, turning my face into the crackle of his touch.

"Steps on your toe."

"Of course."

"Says 'no' to you."

"Fair, fair." I'm down to a whisper. There's nothing outside our bubble. Only the sunlight pierces it.

"So, if I stay?"

"Stay with me."

"Okay, so. Mr. Crowne." Anton looks over my shoulder. I forgot my parents were there and snap out of the cocoon he and I created. "If you can accommodate a change of plans, the Markov Group has to relocate their main office."

"Well…" Dad holds out his hands like a guy who has no control over the situation—which he's never been in his life. "We'll have to figure it out."

"We'll figure it out." I say like a woman who believes it, turning to Anton and taking his hand. "We will. You're staying and we'll—"

"Who wants breakfast?" Mom asks. "Yes, everyone." She claps her hands before she gets an answer, then takes Dad by the arm. "Come help me whip something up."

She pulls him away to one of the kitchens. He walks a little more slowly for her. Neither of them looks back.

When Anton and I are alone, I throw my arms around his shoulders and kiss his face. He holds me up until the sun rises above the doorway.

"You still have that ring?" I say into his neck. He drops me to the floor.

"Do you want it?"

"Not really." I take his hand and pull him out to the patio, walking backward to see the sunlight on his face. "Just asking."

"I have it somewhere."

"If you come across it sometime, it was really nice." We step outside and walk to the railing to look over the canyon. I feel at peace, content, and for the first time in a long time, like everything in my life is aligned. "I guess what I'm saying is, I know you're staying."

He tucks a strand of hair behind my ear. "You know what I do have though?"

"What?"

He takes me by the shoulders and sits me down, then steps behind me.

"Something I picked up in Paris." He tugs my hair to the top of my head and with a few moves, ties it away from the back of my neck.

"A new Hermès hair tie?"

"*Oui*." I try to touch it, but he slaps my hand away. "They only had a gold buckle though. And..." I hear a metallic scrape. He's unscrewing a container. "Something for this spot back here."

I feel the pressure of his cold, slick fingers in the place where I keep my tension. He gently slides them up and down. Then my nostrils sting right up to the sinuses.

"Oh, God, I can smell it."

"It's okay?"

"I love it. I love it more than I ever loved anything in my life, ever."

I'm so relieved I'm almost in tears. He says nothing while his hands move, soothing away my tension and fear, rubbing away my rough edges, scaring away my fear, and leaving only wholeness behind.

He wants to be here for me, and I want nothing more than his love.

EPILOGUE ONE

LYRIC

SIX MONTHS LATER

BENE GRAZIE ISN'T the hottest restaurant in town, but it's the one Anton chose for its logistical advantage, as it's between LAX and my agent's office on Wilshire and Maple.

I pick a booth. If I'm going to spend an entire meal acting like a lovestruck teenager—and if our short history of reunions is any guide, that's exactly what's going to happen—I don't want to do it with three-hundred-sixty degrees of ears and eyes around.

The tablecloths are white and draped like untucked hospital corners. The lamps are post-industrial iron with five filament bulbs each, and the walls are some mid-tone, low-profile, non-color you're not supposed to think about while you're eating.

Which is good, because I'm not thinking about the décor at all. I just had the most hideous meeting in the history of meetings.

So when Anton walks in ten minutes late, I'm so busy obsessing over how to fix what I found out at the meeting was broken, that I don't see him until his face is right in mine and all I can smell is his baked bread scent and the fresh toothpaste on his breath. He gives me a kiss, and when I try to turn away, he holds my face to his until our tongues touch and we've both completely committed to the kiss. I love him for demanding my attention. He deserves it and I love giving it.

"You're embarrassing me," I whisper, then kiss him again, holding him close. "I like it."

"I haven't even started." After one last peck, he drops his bag at the end of the booth and sits across from me. "What's all this?" He waves at the ripped-out notebook pages covering the table, connected by flowchart lines.

"I had that meeting."

"How'd it go?"

"Lawrence Friedburn, king-above-all-others, has decided that I actually wrote a four-episode TV show—take it or leave it—if, and only if, I patch up the glaring plot hole his intern spotted, and, yes"—I pick up all the pages, stacking them in order so I can reproduce the flowchart—"I hope they're paying her." I tap the pile into a neat stack. "How was your flight?"

He's more handsome every time I see him, especially after an absence. Two weeks this time. That's as long as it's ever been without him. It's hard, but he's thriving, and he always comes home to me.

"Fine. Are you discouraged?" He picks up the menus sitting on the edge of the table and passes me one.

"By Lawrence?"

"I know you were excited about that meeting."

"Fuck him for being right. It's a plot hole and it's also better for TV."

"Fuck him." Anton opens his menu. "What do you recommend?"

"It's halfway decent French nouvelle for a restaurant with an Italian name." I look at him over the top of the menu to find he's looking right back at me. He's here, with me, and though I don't feel unsafe generally, when he's near, I feel invincible. "The lobster bisque is pretty good for me right now."

"I've been on sloppy beans for two weeks." He snaps his menu closed and puts it to the side without breaking his gaze.

If we were in a comic book, he'd have wavy lines of intensity coming out of his eyes and I'd have hearts popping out of me. If it was a dirty comic, there'd be little gremlins poking between my thighs. This isn't either. It's real life, and I can't look away.

"I missed you." I lay my menu on top of his then take his hand. "And I have something to tell you."

"Me too." He runs his thumb along the heel of my hand. It tingles so hard I shudder.

"You first."

"I don't—"

"Hey, my name is Danny and I'll be taking your order." The waiter is a vicious little interrupter, but Anton doesn't let my gaze waver. "Tonight's fish special—"

"Two lobster bisque," Anton interrupts.

"Great." Danny picks up the menus. He could be growing a new head out of a zit on his chin and I'd be oblivious. "Anything else?"

"No." Anton leans forward, tugging me closer. Danny

slides the menus off the table and steps out of the frame of my peripheral vision.

"You should say something nicer to Danny, like 'no, thank you' or at least smile at the guy."

"You're lucky I can even form words sitting across from you."

"Stop it." I pull my hand away, smiling.

"After two weeks, I'm going mad."

"Mad? Are you trying to sound fancy?"

"Come here." He wags his fingers to get my hand back, and of course I do it. "I brought you something."

"You did?" I bite my lip. He usually brings me candy specific to wherever he's traveled and feeds it to me in bed.

"But then you called Lawrence Fried-whatever the king-above-all-others."

"I did." I don't know where Anton's going with this, but I'm intrigued.

"He's not king."

"No?"

"No. He's not mad enough. I am the mad king, and you're my loyal subject. Not his."

"Yes, Your Highness."

"Correct." He kisses my hand. "If you want what I brought you, here's how it's going to be. I'm not going away from my kingdom for this long ever again."

"But, Your Highness, how will you… um… do the foreign relations things…"

"Open your legs."

"Oh dear," I say with feigned innocence.

"Obey." His voice is lower, so I have to pay that much more attention to hear it. "Let me see how good you are. Look at your king when you spread your legs."

If the center seam of my pants was always rubbing right up against me, I haven't noticed until this moment. But it is, and the hot little gremlins between my legs have reproduced a few generations. I put my hands on the leather cushion and lean back, eye to eye with him as I uncross my legs.

He shakes his head as if disappointed.

"I can make your life very difficult if you don't spread your legs like you mean it." Under the table, he uses his foot to shove my knees farther apart. At some point, he slipped out of his shoe. "Better. Now…" He lays his foot between my legs and pushes it forward.

I gasp, looking around the room.

"Eyes on me," he says, and how can I disobey? This restaurant is full of people in their thirties who have their phones glass-down in the table in case the babysitter calls. They wouldn't approve. They'd think I was a filthy whore and a poor subject of the king. "What have you been doing without me?"

I'm supposed to tell him all the ways I thought about him when he was sleeping on the other side of the world. All the times I pleasured myself. But I'm feeling playful.

"I had the kitchen painted."

"I told you that you didn't have to do that." He moves his foot back and forth. He's toying with me, and knowing that doesn't help. I like being toyed with. A little. By him.

"But I want it to look nice for you… um… sire? When you move in."

"I told you not to go to the trouble and you directly disobeyed. What should I do with you?"

Anton increases the pressure, watching my long, aroused exhale, then glancing to the side.

The server arrives with a bowl in each hand.

"Two bisques." He lays them in front of us and takes a big wooden phallus from his apron. "Black pepper?"

"No." Anton tries to wave him away for both of us, but I like pepper.

"Please," I say, pointing at my soup. The server spins the crackling grinder two times. "A lot please."

Anton watches me, using the ridges and edges of his foot to find my hardest, wettest self. It's torment to not groan or close my eyes.

When my soup has a dusting of black flakes, I thank Danny, who leaves with a little nod.

"Now," Anton says, "about your punishment."

"I'll do whatever filthy thing you say." My whispered tone has no disgust in it. It's filthy in the way hot things are. That's exactly what makes all of it send shivers of liquid electricity down my spine. I'm sure the bottom's going to drop right out of me.

He knows it too. He sees right under my clothes. I'm powerless here, and I like it too damn much.

"Yes, you will."

"You are a terrible king." I clutch for pearls that aren't there.

The pathetic half-compliment leaves lips that want too badly to please him. I hate the neediness, but I can't breathe without the promise that he'll fulfill it.

"Eat."

I'm hungry, so I lean forward to do it. He watches me like a guy studying for a test, and I watch him like a girl trying not to give him the satisfaction of taking a class in seduction. Business. Manners. Open legs straddling a man's foot.

Anton eats his soup and makes circles against me. He doesn't spill a drop doing it either. The entire spoonful ends up in his mouth while his foot does more than a foot was designed to do. My shoulders are hunched, my lungs empty with the power of the gasp they just released.

"Spread wider."

The command alone is enough to send another rush of fluid between my legs. Obeying it makes every vein and bone vibrate. I'm not sure when or how I agreed to this arrangement, but my body's put the kibosh on refusing it.

"You can't make me come in front of the entire court," I say.

"Finish your soup."

I take a spoonful, because again, I'm hungry, but I'm also ravenous to please him.

"Push forward. Move enough to feel it." He eats, watching while I keep my gyrations as subtle as possible.

Under his watchful gaze and stiffened foot, I eat my soup.

When it's almost done, he says, "What color?"

"What color, what?"

He pushes between my legs, eyes closed as if praying for patience. "The kitchen."

"Zivchik green." A bolt of unexpected pleasure forces a groan out of me. "I mean yellow."

The king has to know I'm lying. Soda bottles and kitchens don't share a palette.

"Look at me, peasant." He leans back, allowing his leg to go straighter, pushing harder into me. I open my eyes, realizing I'd closed them. "Are you lying?"

His foot goes still, and he smiles.

"Are you not pleased? Doesn't my king enjoy apple soda?" I ask, touching the imaginary decolletage under my T-shirt.

"Hands on the table."

I do it, but the inability to control the ache is keeping me from recalling the name of a single color on the spectrum. "… but… why did you stop moving?"

"Hump harder if you need to, or I'll send you to the dungeon."

"We're going to get kicked out of here."

"Show me how you get yourself off."

I want to show him. More than that, I want to display my pleasure for him. Hands still on the table, I lean back and rotate my hips against his foot.

Anton inspects my nails, then turns my hands over, pulling open the creases.

"What are you…?" I close my eyes again and rub myself on him.

"You have paint under your nail, and it's not Zivchik yellow."

I make eye contact, pulling attention away from the growing threat of overwhelming climax for a second. "The painters missed a spot and it was easier…"

"What color is this?"

"Butterbomb."

He moves his foot back and forth, and I explode on it, humping and jerking as little as possible, clutching the tablecloth in my fists as I bite back any sound from my throat.

God, I missed him.

EPILOGUE TWO

ANTON

I MISSED HER, and too much. Maintaining HQ for the Markov Group in Los Angeles still came with travel until we were set up.

We're set up. We have to be. I'm done with being away from her at all. Moving into her house isn't going to solve it either. There's going to be a real life with her, or nothing.

And yet, I'm nervous.

She loves me. She's committed to me. To us, together.

Still, I asked her once before and she broke my heart. I've been carrying around my proposal for two weeks out of a fear I told myself didn't exist any longer. The stakes seem higher now. If she won't have me, I'll stay for as long as she'll have me, but the old wound will reopen.

"Do you like it?" She flips on the kitchen light. "Supposedly yellow stimulates your appetite, so… ta-da!"

"Butterbomb." The kitchen isn't exactly the same color as her car. It's a little lighter and brighter. "Why am I hungry all of a sudden?"

"Because you had soup with a side of foot-sex for dinner."

She opens the fridge and leans into it. Coming up behind her, I look at the shelves. "How about a sandwich? I have turkey. No. *We* have turkey and gouda."

"I told you I brought you something," I say, reaching into my jacket pocket. The velvet box is there—on my person, where it's been since I found it two weeks ago, right before I left. As long as it stays there, I have nothing to worry about.

"The public orgasm wiped my memory clean." She grabs the paper packages and stands, gasping when she finds me closer than she expected. I take away the sandwich stuff and put it on the counter, reaching behind her to close the refrigerator. "What is it?"

Does she look concerned because I'm concerned?

"I was packing up to move... and..." I clear my throat, fondling the box. "I came across something you might be interested in."

"Really?" She leans on the counter. "So it's not candy?"

"I just... I want to give it to you, but it comes with a promise." I lift the box from my pocket, a soft black cube with rounded edges, and open it to reveal the diamond ring I got for her a millennia ago—back when I was obligated to do the right thing. This is different.

"Oh, hey!" She reaches for it, but I pull it back. "Don't be a tease."

"Lyric. I'm not giving you a ring."

"No? What the fuck then?"

"I'm giving you my heart. I'm giving you my life. I don't want you to accept this ring unless you're going to marry me."

"Duh."

"Duh?"

"When I brought it up on my parents' patio, did you think I was asking about a piece of jewelry?"

She's looking at me as if I'm an idiot, and the damn truth is, I am worse than an idiot.

"I did."

"You fucking dork," she laughs.

"I am." I take out the ring and pick up her left hand, holding the ring at the tip. I'm smiling at my absolute darkness so hard I'm barely staying on the sane side of laughter. "It never occurred to me that the woman would ask."

"Duh," she whispers. "You are King Duh."

"And you," I say, pushing the ring onto her finger, "are the queen of this kingdom."

She holds up her hand to view the diamond. "This is a nice piece of jewelry." She brings down her hand then puts her arms around my waist. "The guy it comes with is kinda all right too."

"Good. Because I wouldn't let you marry a man who wasn't 'kinda all right.'"

"Always looking out for me."

"Always. Now let's talk about painting that bedroom."

I pick her up and throw her over my shoulder. She squeals the entire way up the stairs, laughing when I throw her onto the bed.

I am home, with her, in the kingdom we will create together.

THANK YOU FOR READING

If you missed any of the four other Crowne books, you can get them right here!

<u>Iron Crowne</u> ~ Enemies to Lovers

<u>Crowne of Lies</u> ~ Marriage of Convenience

<u>Crowne Rules</u> ~ Forced Close Proximity

Fake Crowne ~ Fake Relationship

Read all the Crownes and want to dig into more contemporary romance? Fear not. I won't leave you hanging...

Star-Crossed | Hardball | Bombshell | Bodyguard | Only Ever You | Lead Me Back

If you're a mood reader who also gets the urge for some kinky, dark stuff, keep scrolling for my BDSM and Mafia titles.

AFTERWORD

There are two more Crowne books. Maybe you're counting and saying, no, there's one. But if you were paying attention, there's two.

However, I cannot guarantee they'll be written any time soon.

I don't have stories for either right now, but that's not the reason. I do love them dearly—Ted and Doreen and their whole clan. Billionaires who pay their taxes. Who wouldn't want to bring more fantasies like this into the world?

It's more that I'm one person and I can't write super fast. I've tried. It's just not physically possible for me to do all the jobs I need to do and crank out six books a year any more.

Right now, the mafia is calling me, and it's an especially different kind of mafia that comes from a deeper, darker place than I've ever been. I can't ignore it, nor can I ignore the readers who crave it.

So, I have to alternate between dark and light(er). I'm told this is terrible for business. I should pick dark or contemporary and just stay consistent. I know that's the right way to build a brand, but I can't do it. My brain train doesn't run on a single track and the conductor's drunk most of the time.

I'm sorry. The train will come around to the Crownes again or I could get hit by a runaway caboose, in which case my daughter's probably going to be in charge when she's 21.

If you want the whens and wheres of what drops, or if you want to know when the mafia stuff goes live, choose your method of contact below. I show up on all the social media platforms with varying degrees of regularity, but I ALWAYS get my newsletters out twice a month, and there's usually a freebie or three in there.

CD REISS NEWSLETTER
FACEBOOK GROUP
FACEBOOK PAGE
TWITTER
TIKTOK
INSTAGRAM

I ALSO WRITE DARK SHIT

THE SUBMISSION SERIES

The *USA Today* bestselling *Submission Series*

Monica insists she's not submissive. Jonathan Drazen is going to prove otherwise, but he might fall in love doing it.

One Night With Him

MAFIA BRIDE

When he forced me to marry him, I cried for love I'd never know. When he locked me away, I cried for the freedom I lost forever.

Every other tear I've shed is for my soul, because I'm falling for the devil himself.

Mafia Bride Trilogy

THE GAMES DUET

Adam Steinbeck will give his wife a divorce on one condition. She join him in a remote cabin for 30 days, submitting to his sexual dominance.

Marriage Games — Separation Games

<hr>

GIRL ON THE EDGE

Two married, military doctors come home to find they're rougher,
edgier, sexier than they ever were.

Girl on the Edge

There's more, but I'm trying to not overwhelm you.

ACKNOWLEDGMENTS AND WARNINGS

WHERE I ACKNOWLEDGE MY FAILURES

Ozzy Dots didn't survive the pandemic, but it was the best vintage store in Los Angeles. Fight me.

I have a spreadsheet that jibes the whole family and their important dates. Would you know it if you started sketching it all out on the back of an envelope? You would not. Please do not do math w/r/t Dante and Mandy's children and whether or not they should exist at this point, nor the placement of Lyric on this or that coast during Byron's wedding, Dante's time in Cambria with Mandy, or even Colton and Skye's presence at the Shooting Star Showcase. Logan works. Do that one. Otherwise…just let it flow, man. Let it flow and let it go. That's the way of happiness. Thank you.